# BRICK SHAKESPEARE

# BRICK SHAKESPEARE

## THE COMEDIES—A MIDSUMMER NIGHT'S DREAM, THE TEMPEST, MUCH ADO ABOUT NOTHING, AND THE TAMING OF THE SHREW

AS TOLD AND ILLUSTRATED BY
JOHN MCCANN, MONICA SWEENEY,
AND BECKY THOMAS

Skyhorse Publishing

Copyright © 2013 by Hollan Publishing, Inc.

Skyhorse Publishing books may be purchased in bulk at special discounts for sales promotion, corporate gifts, fundraising, or educational purposes. Special editions can also be created to specifications. For details, contact the Special Sales Department, Skyhorse Publishing, 307 West 36th Street, 11th Floor, New York, NY 10018 or info@skyhorsepublishing.com.

Skyhorse and Skyhorse Publishing are registered trademarks of Skyhorse Publishing, Inc.®, a Delaware corporation.

www.skyhorsepublishing.com

10 9 8 7 6 5 4 3 2 1

Library of Congress Cataloging-in-Publication Data is available on file.

ISBN: 978-1-62873-733-2

Printed in China

Editor: Kelsie Besaw

Designer: Brian Peterson

Production manager: Abigail Gehring

# ACKNOWLEDGMENTS

This second installment of *Brick Shakespeare* would not be possible without our fantastic editor, Kelsie Besaw, whose effort and attention to detail really made this book great. To Tony Lyons, Bill Wolfsthal, and Linda Biagi, for giving us the opportunity to produce such a creative project, and to everyone at Skyhorse for making it all happen. Our special thanks go to Allan Penn, for all of the extra effort with our photography, and to Holly Schmidt for the continued encouragement and support.

John would like to give a big thank you to his parents, Cathy and Ed, and to the Clemmers. Becky would like to thank her brother, Michael, for always sharing his toys with her. And Monica would like to thank her Grandma, for always giving her a place for LEGOland.

William Shakespeare wrote or collaborated on thirty-eight plays during his lifetime, and among them were seventeen comedies. During the Elizabethan era when Shakespeare lived and wrote, the term "comedy" did not mean that a play was funny, but that it had a lighter tone and a happy ending, usually involving a marriage or two. But that does not mean Shakespeare's comedies are not funny! Shakespeare was a master of wit and wordplay, which is why his skill is still charming audiences to this day.

While many of Shakespeare's tragedies explore dark themes like death, betrayal, murder, and revenge, his comedies focus on themes like courtship and marriage, using them to look closer at social pressures, relationships, and human behavior of the time period. The lighter tone is deceptive, as Shakespeare did not hesitate to use his comedies to turn a critical eye (and pen) to the follies of the time.

*Brick Shakespeare: The Comedies* presents four of the Bard's most famous and clever comic works in LEGO form, each of which has been carefully abridged. The fun brick scenes depict Shakespeare's plays just as they were originally written (perhaps with more plastic than he had imagined), with helpful narrative in between to explain what we did not include. Whether you are just being introduced to Shakespeare or are a seasoned devotee, we hope you enjoy this creative and constructive new take on Shakespeare's comedies!

# CONTENTS

# A Midsummer Night's Dream

# INTRODUCTION

*A Midsummer Night's Dream* is a magical, whimsical comedy that, while written around 1590, remains a fan favorite on the stage! The play explores themes of love and marriage and ends, as all good Elizabethan comedies should, with a wedding celebration. It also addresses ideas of reality and perception: the title itself refers to the characters' strange experiences that they encounter during the play, which seem dreamlike and unreal when they awaken the next morning.

The action of the play centers around three main groups: the young lovers, the laborers-turned-actors, and the fairies, all of whom find themselves deep in the forest surrounding Athens. The forest itself stands apart from the civilized world of Athens, and the young lovers and the actors seek out this space in hopes of escaping the "real world" where parents and authority figures try to control their paths.

Nonetheless, the forest has its own set of authority figures: the king and queen of the fairies, Oberon and Titania. King Oberon attempts to bring order to his domain by neatly pairing off the young lovers, as Puck later says, "Jack shall have Jill;/Nought shall go ill" (III.ii.508–9). Oberon uses magic to manipulate the young lovers and make his targets fall madly in love with the next person they see, a plan with unexpected but hilarious consequences. The forest setting highlights the strange and mysterious things that happen there, where affections are distorted, and voices and strange noises whisper through the trees. In the woods, everything gets turned around before it is finally set right.

This comedy is one of the most loved of Shakespeare's plays because it includes all the best aspects of the genre: a magical setting, young lovers thwarted by social pressures, and a hilariously acerbic catfight for good measure. Much of the draw of this play, in Shakespeare's time and our own, is the dynamic theatricality of the production. There are slapstick humor and special effects, magical transformations and creatures, all of which delight audiences, even when played out on the page rather than the stage.

**THESEUS, Duke of Athens**

**EGEUS, Father to Hermia**

**LYSANDER, in love with Hermia**

**DEMETRIUS, in love with Hermia**

**PHILOSTRATE, Master of the Revels to Theseus**

**QUINCE, the Carpenter**

**SNUG, the Joiner**

**BOTTOM, the Weaver**

**FLUTE, the Bellows-mender**

**SNOUT, the Tinker**

**STARVELING, the Tailor**

**HIPPOLYTA, Queen of the Amazons, betrothed to Theseus**

**HERMIA, daughter to Egeus, in love with Lysander**

**HELENA, in love with Demetrius**

**OBERON, King of the Fairies**

**TITANIA, Queen of the Fairies**

**PUCK, or ROBIN GOODFELLOW, a Fairy**

**PEASBLOSSOM, Fairy**

**COBWEB, Fairy**

**MOTH, Fairy**

**MUSTARDSEED, Fairy**

**PYRAMUS**

**THISBE**

**WALL**

**MOONSHINE**

## Not Pictured:

Characters in the Interlude performed by the Clowns

Other Fairies attending their King and Queen
Attendants on Theseus and Hippolyta

# ACT I. Scene I (1–225).

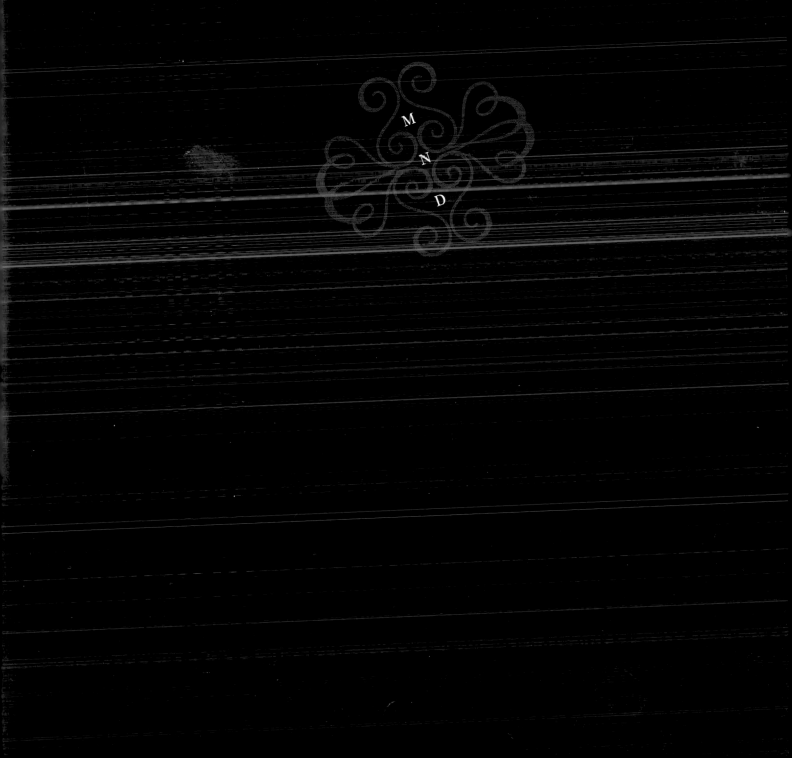

**THESEUS**
Now, fair Hippolyta, our nuptial hour
Draws on apace; four happy days bring in
Another moon: but, O, methinks, how slow
This old moon wanes! she lingers my desires,
Like to a step-dame or a dowager
Long withering out a young man's revenue.

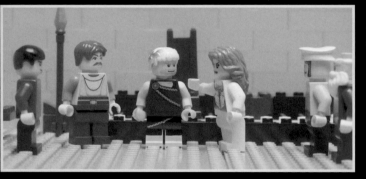

**HIPPOLYTA**
Four days will quickly steep themselves in night;
Four nights will quickly dream away the time;
And then the moon, like to a silver bow
New-bent in heaven, shall behold the night
Of our solemnities.

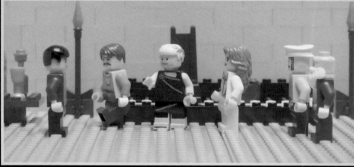

**THESEUS**
Go, Philostrate,
Stir up the Athenian youth to merriments;
Awake the pert and nimble spirit of mirth;
Turn melancholy forth to funerals;
The pale companion is not for our pomp.

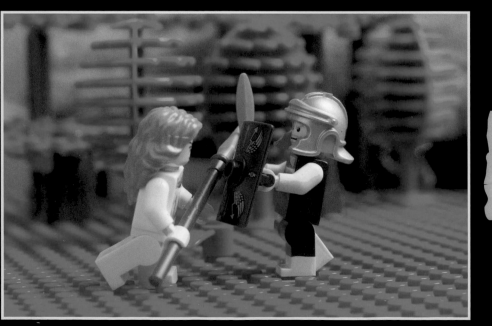

**THESEUS (cont.)**
Hippolyta, I woo'd thee with my sword,
And won thy love, doing thee injuries;
But I will wed thee in another key,
With pomp, with triumph and with revelling.

**EGEUS**
Happy be Theseus, our renowned duke!
**THESEUS**
Thanks, good Egeus: what's the news with thee?

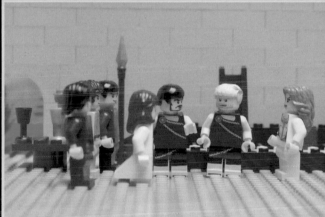

**EGEUS**
Full of vexation come I, with complaint
Against my child, my daughter Hermia.
Stand forth, Demetrius. My noble lord,
This man hath my consent to marry her.
Stand forth, Lysander: and my gracious duke,
This man hath bewitch'd the bosom of my child;
Thou, thou, Lysander, thou hast given her rhymes,
And interchanged love-tokens with my child:
Thou hast by moonlight at her window sung,
With feigning voice verses of feigning love,
And stolen the impression of her fantasy
With bracelets of thy hair, rings, gawds, conceits,
Knacks, trifles, nosegays, sweetmeats, messengers
Of strong prevailment in unharden'd youth:
With cunning hast thou filch'd my daughter's heart,
Turn'd her obedience, which is due to me,
To stubborn harshness: and, my gracious duke,
Be it so she; will not here before your grace
Consent to marry with Demetrius,
I beg the ancient privilege of Athens,
As she is mine, I may dispose of her:
Which shall be either to this gentleman
Or to her death, according to our law
Immediately provided in that case.

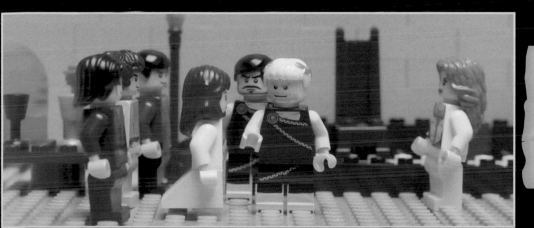

**THESEUS**
What say you, Hermia? be advised fair maid:
To you your father should be as a god;
One that composed your beauties, yea, and one
To whom you are but as a form in wax
By him imprinted and within his power
To leave the figure or disfigure it.

THESEUS (cont.)
Demetrius is a worthy gentleman.

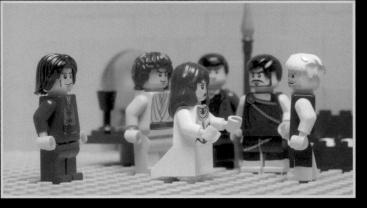

HERMIA
So is Lysander.
THESEUS
In himself he is;
But in this kind, wanting your father's voice,
The other must be held the worthier.
HERMIA
I would my father look'd but with my eyes.
THESEUS
Rather your eyes must with his judgment look.
HERMIA
I do entreat your grace to pardon me.
I know not by what power I am made bold,
Nor how it may concern my modesty,
In such a presence here to plead my thoughts;
But I beseech your grace that I may know
The worst that may befall me in this case,
If I refuse to wed Demetrius.

THESEUS
Either to die the death or to abjure
For ever the society of men.
Therefore, fair Hermia, question your desires;
Know of your youth, examine well your blood,
Whether, if you yield not to your father's choice,
You can endure the livery of a nun,
For aye to be in shady cloister mew'd,
To live a barren sister all your life,
Chanting faint hymns to the cold fruitless moon.
Thrice-blessed they that master so their blood,
To undergo such maiden pilgrimage;
But earthlier happy is the rose distill'd,
Than that which withering on the virgin thorn
Grows, lives, and dies in single blessedness.

HERMIA
So will I grow, so live, so die, my lord,
Ere I will my virgin patent up
Unto his lordship, whose unwished yoke
My soul consents not to give sovereignty.

**THESEUS**
Take time to pause; and, by the next new moon—
The sealing-day betwixt my love and me,
For everlasting bond of fellowship—
Upon that day either prepare to die
For disobedience to your father's will,
Or else to wed Demetrius, as he would;
Or on Diana's altar to protest
For aye austerity and single life.

**DEMETRIUS**
Relent, sweet Hermia:

**DEMETRIUS (cont.)**
and, Lysander, yield
Thy crazed title to my certain right.
**LYSANDER**
You have her father's love, Demetrius;
Let me have Hermia's: do you marry him.

**EGEUS**
Scornful Lysander! true, he hath my love,
And what is mine my love shall render him.
And she is mine, and all my right of her
I do estate unto Demetrius.
**LYSANDER**
I am, my lord, as well derived as he,
As well possess'd; my love is more than his;
My fortunes every way as fairly rank'd,
If not with vantage, as Demetrius';
And, which is more than all these boasts can be,
I am beloved of beauteous Hermia:
Why should not I then prosecute my right?
Demetrius, I'll avouch it to his head,
Made love to Nedar's daughter, Helena,
And won her soul; and she, sweet lady, dotes,
Devoutly dotes, dotes in idolatry,
Upon this spotted and inconstant man.

**THESEUS**
I must confess that I have heard so much,
And with Demetrius thought to have spoke thereof;
But, being over-full of self-affairs,
My mind did lose it. But, Demetrius, come;
And come, Egeus; you shall go with me,
I have some private schooling for you both.
For you, fair Hermia, look you arm yourself
To fit your fancies to your father's will;
Or else the law of Athens yields you up—
Which by no means we may extenuate—
To death, or to a vow of single life.
Come, my Hippolyta: what cheer, my love?
Demetrius and Egeus, go along:
I must employ you in some business
Against our nuptial and confer with you
Of something nearly that concerns yourselves.
**EGEUS**
With duty and desire we follow you.

**LYSANDER**
How now, my love! why is your cheek so pale?
How chance the roses there do fade so fast?
**HERMIA**
Belike for want of rain, which I could well
Beteem them from the tempest of my eyes.
**LYSANDER**
Ay me! for aught that I could ever read,
Could ever hear by tale or history,
The course of true love never did run smooth;
But, either it was different in blood,—

**HERMIA**
O cross! too high to be enthrall'd to low.
**LYSANDER**
Or else misgraff'd in respect of years,—
**HERMIA**
O spite! too old to be engaged to young.
**LYSANDER**
Or else it stood upon the choice of friends,—
**HERMIA**
O hell! to choose love by another's eyes.

**LYSANDER**
Or, if there were a sympathy in choice,
War, death, or sickness did lay siege to it,
Making it momentary as a sound,
Swift as a shadow, short as any dream;
Brief as the lightning in the collied night,
That, in a spleen, unfolds both heaven and earth,
And ere a man hath power to say "Behold!"
The jaws of darkness do devour it up:
So quick bright things come to confusion.

**HERMIA**
If then true lovers have been ever cross'd,
It stands as an edict in destiny:
Then let us teach our trial patience,
Because it is a customary cross,
As due to love as thoughts and dreams and sighs,
Wishes and tears, poor fancy's followers.
**LYSANDER**
A good persuasion: therefore, hear me, Hermia.
I have a widow aunt, a dowager
Of great revenue, and she hath no child:
From Athens is her house remote seven leagues;
And she respects me as her only son.
There, gentle Hermia, may I marry thee;
And to that place the sharp Athenian law
Cannot pursue us. If thou lovest me then,
Steal forth thy father's house to-morrow night;

**LYSANDER (cont.)**
And in the wood, a league without the town,
Where I did meet thee once with Helena,
To do observance to a morn of May,
There will I stay for thee.

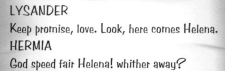

**LYSANDER**
Keep promise, love. Look, here comes Helena.
**HERMIA**
God speed fair Helena! whither away?

**HELENA**
Call you me fair? that fair again unsay.
Demetrius loves your fair: O happy fair!
Your eyes are lode-stars; and your tongue's sweet air
More tuneable than lark to shepherd's ear,
When wheat is green, when hawthorn buds appear.
Sickness is catching: O, were favour so,
Yours would I catch, fair Hermia, ere I go;
My ear should catch your voice, my eye your eye,
My tongue should catch your tongue's sweet melody.
Were the world mine, Demetrius being bated,
The rest I'd give to be to you translated.
O, teach me how you look, and with what art
You sway the motion of Demetrius' heart.

**HERMIA**

I frown upon him, yet he loves me still.

**HELENA**

O that your frowns would teach my smiles such skill!

**HERMIA**

I give him curses, yet he gives me love.

**HELENA**

O that my prayers could such affection move!

**HERMIA**

The more I hate, the more he follows me.

**HELENA**

The more I love, the more he hateth me.

**HERMIA**

His folly, Helena, is no fault of mine.

**HELENA**

None, but your beauty: would that fault were mine!

**HERMIA**

Take comfort: he no more shall see my face;
Lysander and myself will fly this place.
Before the time I did Lysander see,
Seem'd Athens as a paradise to me:
O, then, what graces in my love do dwell,
That he hath turn'd a heaven unto hell!

**LYSANDER**

Helen, to you our minds we will unfold:
To-morrow night, when Phoebe doth behold
Her silver visage in the watery glass,
Decking with liquid pearl the bladed grass,
A time that lovers' flights doth still conceal,
Through Athens' gates have we devised to steal.

**HERMIA**

And in the wood, where often you and I
Upon faint primrose-beds were wont to lie,
Emptying our bosoms of their counsel sweet,
There my Lysander and myself shall meet;
And thence from Athens turn away our eyes,
To seek new friends and stranger companies.
Farewell, sweet playfellow: pray thou for us;
And good luck grant thee thy Demetrius!
Keep word, Lysander: we must starve our sight
From lovers' food till morrow deep midnight.

# ACT I. Scene II (1–97).

*M*
*N*
*D*

*H*ermia and Lysander prepare for their escape, but Helena has a secret plan of her own. She decides to tell Demetrius about the lovers' flight, in hopes that he will be so grateful he will turn his affections her way. She sets off to find him and share her news. Meanwhile, a group of workmen are practicing a play to present to Theseus at his wedding to Hippolyta.

QUINCE
Is all our company here?
BOTTOM
You were best to call them generally, man by man, according to the scrip.
QUINCE
Here is the scroll of every man's name, which is thought fit, through all Athens, to play in our interlude before the duke and the duchess, on his wedding-day at night.
BOTTOM
First, good Peter Quince, say what the play treats on, then read the names of the actors, and so grow to a point.

QUINCE
Marry, our play is, The most lamentable comedy, and most cruel death of Pyramus and Thisby.
BOTTOM
A very good piece of work, I assure you, and a merry. Now, good Peter Quince, call forth your actors by the scroll. Masters, spread yourselves.
QUINCE
Answer as I call you. Nick Bottom, the weaver.
BOTTOM
Ready. Name what part I am for, and proceed.
QUINCE
You, Nick Bottom, are set down for Pyramus.
BOTTOM
What is Pyramus? a lover, or a tyrant?
QUINCE
A lover, that kills himself most gallant for love.

BOTTOM
That will ask some tears in the true performing of it: if I do it, let the audience look to their eyes; I will move storms, I will condole in some measure. To the rest: yet my chief humour is for a tyrant: I could play Ercles rarely, or a part to tear a cat in, to make all split.

**BOTTOM (cont.)**
The raging rocks
And shivering shocks
Shall break the locks
Of prison gates;

And Phibbus' car
Shall shine from far
And make and mar
The foolish Fates.

This was lofty! Now name the rest of the players. This is Ercles' vein, a tyrant's vein; a lover is more condoling.

**QUINCE**
Francis Flute, the bellows-mender.
**FLUTE**
Here, Peter Quince.
**QUINCE**
Flute, you must take Thisby on you.
**FLUTE**
What is Thisby? a wandering knight?
**QUINCE**
It is the lady that Pyramus must love.
**FLUTE**
Nay, faith, let me not play a woman; I have a beard coming.
**QUINCE**
That's all one: you shall play it in a mask, and you may speak as small as you will.

**BOTTOM**
An I may hide my face, let me play Thisby too, I'll speak in a monstrous little voice. "Thisne, Thisne;" "Ah, Pyramus, lover dear! thy Thisby dear, and lady dear!"

**QUINCE**
No, no; you must play Pyramus: and, Flute, you Thisby.
**BOTTOM**
Well, proceed.

QUINCE

Robin Starveling, the tailor.

STARVELING

Here, Peter Quince.

QUINCE

Robin Starveling, you must play Thisby's mother.

Tom Snout, the tinker.

SNOUT

Here, Peter Quince.

QUINCE

You, Pyramus' father: myself, Thisby's father:

Snug, the joiner; you, the lion's part: and, I

hope, here is a play fitted.

SNUG

Have you the lion's part written? pray you, if it

be, give it me, for I am slow of study.

QUINCE

You may do it extempore, for it is nothing but roaring.

BOTTOM

Let me play the lion too: I will roar, that I will

do any man's heart good to hear me; I will roar,

that I will make the duke say "Let him roar again,

let him roar again."

QUINCE

An you should do it too terribly, you would fright

the duchess and the ladies, that they would shriek;

and that were enough to hang us all.

ALL

That would hang us, every mother's son.

BOTTOM

I grant you, friends, if that you should fright the

ladies out of their wits, they would have no more

discretion but to hang us: but I will aggravate my

voice so that I will roar you as gently as any

sucking dove; I will roar you an 'twere any

nightingale.

QUINCE

You can play no part but Pyramus; for Pyramus is a sweet-faced man; a proper man, as one shall see in a summer's day; a most lovely gentleman-like man: therefore you must needs play Pyramus.

BOTTOM

Well, I will undertake it. What beard were I best to play it in?

QUINCE

Why, what you will.

BOTTOM

I will discharge it in either your straw-colour beard, your orange tawny beard, your purple-in-grain beard, or your French-crown-colour beard, your perfect yellow.

QUINCE

Some of your French crowns have no hair at all, and then you will play bare-faced. But, masters, here are your parts: and I am to entreat you, request you and desire you, to con them by to-morrow night; and meet me in the palace wood, a mile without the town, by moonlight; there will we rehearse, for if we meet in the city, we shall be dogged with company, and our devices known. In the meantime I will draw a bill of properties, such as our play wants. I pray you, fail me not.

BOTTOM

We will meet; and there we may rehearse most obscenely and courageously. Take pains; be perfect: adieu.

QUINCE

At the duke's oak we meet.

BOTTOM

Enough; hold or cut bow-strings.

# ACT II. Scene I (60–145).

**OBERON**

Ill met by moonlight, proud Titania.

**TITANIA**

What, jealous Oberon! Fairies, skip hence:
I have forsworn his bed and company.

**OBERON**

Tarry, rash wanton: am not I thy lord?

**TITANIA**

Then I must be thy lady: but I know
When thou hast stolen away from fairy land,
And in the shape of Corin sat all day,
Playing on pipes of corn and versing love
To amorous Phillida. Why art thou here,
Come from the farthest Steppe of India?
But that, forsooth, the bouncing Amazon,
Your buskin'd mistress and your warrior love,
To Theseus must be wedded, and you come
To give their bed joy and prosperity.

**OBERON**

How canst thou thus for shame, Titania,
Glance at my credit with Hippolyta,
Knowing I know thy love to Theseus?
Didst thou not lead him through the glimmering night
From Perigenia, whom he ravished?
And make him with fair Ægle break his faith,
With Ariadne and Antiopa?

**TITANIA**

These are the forgeries of jealousy:
And never, since the middle summer's spring,
Met we on hill, in dale, forest or mead,
By paved fountain or by rushy brook,
Or in the beached margent of the sea,
To dance our ringlets to the whistling wind,
But with thy brawls thou hast disturb'd our sport.
Therefore the winds, piping to us in vain,
As in revenge, have suck'd up from the sea
Contagious fogs; which falling in the land
Have every pelting river made so proud
That they have overborne their continents:

**TITANIA** (cont.)
The ox hath therefore stretch'd his yoke in vain,
The ploughman lost his sweat, and the green corn
Hath rotted ere his youth attain'd a beard;
The fold stands empty in the drowned field,

**TITANIA** (cont.)
And crows are fatted with the murrion flock;
The nine men's morris is fill'd up with mud,
And the quaint mazes in the wanton green
For lack of tread are undistinguishable:
The human mortals want their winter here;
No night is now with hymn or carol blest:
Therefore the moon, the governess of floods,
Pale in her anger, washes all the air,
That rheumatic diseases do abound:

**TITANIA** (cont.)
And through this distemperature we see
The seasons alter: hoary-headed frosts
Far in the fresh lap of the crimson rose,
And on old Hiems' thin and icy crown
An odorous chaplet of sweet summer buds
Is, as in mockery, set: the spring, the summer,
The childing autumn, angry winter, change
Their wonted liveries, and the mazed world,
By their increase, now knows not which is which:
And this same progeny of evils comes
From our debate, from our dissension;
We are their parents and original.

**OBERON**

Do you amend it then; it lies in you:
Why should Titania cross her Oberon?
I do but beg a little changeling boy,
To be my henchman.

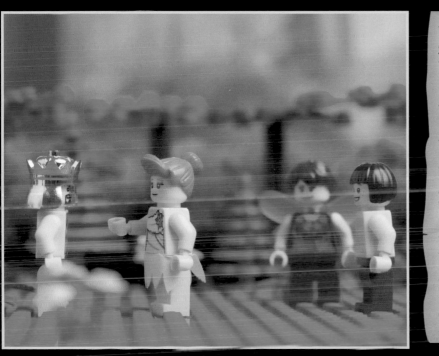

**TITANIA**

Set your heart at rest:
The fairy land buys not the child of me.
His mother was a votaress of my order:
And, in the spiced Indian air, by night,
Full often hath she gossip'd by my side,
And sat with me on Neptune's yellow sands,
Marking the embarked traders on the flood,
When we have laugh'd to see the sails conceive
And grow big-bellied with the wanton wind;
Which she, with pretty and with swimming gait
Following,—her womb then rich with my young squire,—
Would imitate, and sail upon the land,
To fetch me trifles, and return again,
As from a voyage, rich with merchandise.
But she, being mortal, of that boy did die;
And for her sake do I rear up her boy,
And for her sake I will not part with him.

**OBERON**

Give me that boy, and I will go with thee.

**TITANIA**

Not for thy fairy kingdom. Fairies, away!
We shall chide downright, if I longer stay.

**OBERON**

How long within this wood intend you stay?

**TITANIA**

Perchance till after Theseus' wedding-day.
If you will patiently dance in our round
And see our moonlight revels, go with us;
If not, shun me, and I will spare your haunts.

29

# ACT II. Scene I (189–245).

Angry at Titania's rebellion, Oberon decides to get even. He sends Robin Goodfellow to fetch him a special flower to make "man or woman madly dote/Upon the next live creature that it sees" (II.i.172–73). He plans to use the flower to make Titania fall in love with something absurd, thereby making her forget her changeling child and give him up to Oberon. As he waits for Robin to return, Demetrius and Helena interrupt him. Demetrius has come into the forest to find Hermia and Lysander, and Helena follows him doggedly. Oberon watches them, invisible.

**DEMETRIUS**
I love thee not, therefore pursue me not.
Where is Lysander and fair Hermia?
The one I'll slay, the other slayeth me.
Thou told'st me they were stolen unto this wood;
And here am I, and wode within this wood,
Because I cannot meet my Hermia.
Hence, get thee gone, and follow me no more.

**HELENA**
You draw me, you hard-hearted adamant;
But yet you draw not iron, for my heart
Is true as steel: leave you your power to draw,
And I shall have no power to follow you.

**DEMETRIUS**
Do I entice you? do I speak you fair?
Or, rather, do I not in plainest truth
Tell you, I do not, nor I cannot love you?

**DEMETRIUS**
Tempt not too much the hatred of my spirit;
For I am sick when I do look on thee.
**HELENA**
And I am sick when I look not on you.

**HELENA**
And even for that do I love you the more.
I am your spaniel; and, Demetrius,
The more you beat me, I will fawn on you:
Use me but as your spaniel, spurn me, strike me,
Neglect me, lose me; only give me leave,
Unworthy as I am, to follow you.
What worser place can I beg in your love,—
And yet a place of high respect with me,—
Than to be used as you use your dog?

**DEMETRIUS**
You do impeach your modesty too much,
To leave the city and commit yourself
Into the hands of one that loves you not;
To trust the opportunity of night
And the ill counsel of a desert place
With the rich worth of your virginity.

**HELENA**
Your virtue is my privilege: for that
It is not night when I do see your face,
Therefore I think I am not in the night;
Nor doth this wood lack worlds of company,
For you in my respect are all the world:
Then how can it be said I am alone,
When all the world is here to look on me?

**DEMETRIUS**
I'll run from thee and hide me in the brakes,
And leave thee to the mercy of wild beasts.

### HELENA
The wildest hath not such a heart as you.
Run when you will, the story shall be changed:
Apollo flies, and Daphne holds the chase;
The dove pursues the griffin; the mild hind
Makes speed to catch the tiger; bootless speed,
When cowardice pursues and valour flies.

### DEMETRIUS
I will not stay thy questions; let me go:
Or, if thou follow me, do not believe
But I shall do thee mischief in the wood.

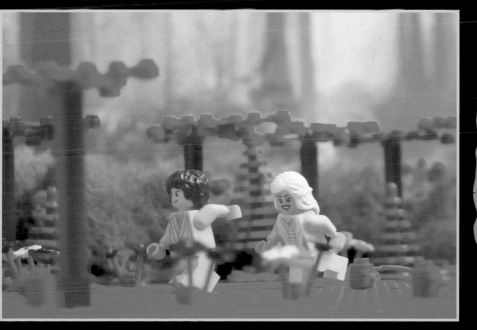

### HELENA
Ay, in the temple, in the town, the field,
You do me mischief. Fie, Demetrius!
Your wrongs do set a scandal on my sex:
We cannot fight for love, as men may do;
We should be wood and were not made to woo.
I'll follow thee and make a heaven of hell,
To die upon the hand I love so well.

M N D

*O* beron, touched by Helena's unrequited love, decides to expand his love-flower plot. When Robin Goodfellow returns with the magic flower, Oberon says that he will bewitch Titania himself and instructs Robin, "A sweet Athenian lady is in love/with a disdainful youth. Anoint his eyes,/but do it when the next thing he espies/may be the lady. Thou shalt know the man/by the Athenian garments he hath on" (II.i.263–66). Robin dutifully sets off to do so, and Oberon leaves to find Titania.

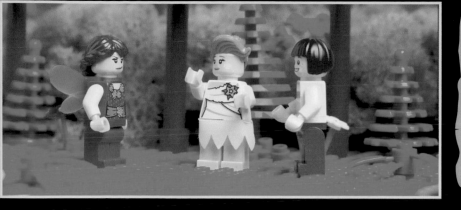

## TITANIA
Come, now a roundel and a fairy song;
Then, for the third part of a minute, hence;
Some to kill cankers in the musk-rose buds,
Some war with rere-mice for their leathern wings,
To make my small elves coats, and some keep back
The clamorous owl that nightly hoots and wonders
At our quaint spirits. Sing me now asleep;
Then to your offices and let me rest.

## FAIRIES
You spotted snakes with double tongue,
Thorny hedgehogs, be not seen;
Newts and blind-worms, do no wrong,
Come not near our fairy queen.
Philomel, with melody
Sing in our sweet lullaby;
Lulla, lulla, lullaby, lulla, lulla, lullaby:
Never harm,
Nor spell nor charm,
Come our lovely lady nigh;
So, good night, with lullaby.
Weaving spiders, come not here;
Hence, you long-legg'd spinners, hence!
Beetles black, approach not near;
Worm nor snail, do no offence.
Philomel, with melody
Sing in our sweet lullaby;
Lulla, lulla, lullaby, lulla, lulla, lullaby:
Never harm,
Nor spell nor charm,
Come our lovely lady nigh;
So, good night, with lullaby.

## OBERON
What thou seest when thou dost wake,
Do it for thy true-love take,
Love and languish for his sake:
Be it ounce, or cat, or bear,
Pard, or boar with bristled hair,
In thy eye that shall appear
When thou wakest, it is thy dear:
Wake when some vile thing is near.

Fairy
Hence, away! now all is well:
One aloof stand sentinel.

**LYSANDER**

Fair love, you faint with wandering in the wood;
And to speak troth, I have forgot our way:
We'll rest us, Hermia, if you think it good,
And tarry for the comfort of the day.

**HERMIA**

Be it so, Lysander: find you out a bed;
For I upon this bank will rest my head.

**LYSANDER**

One turf shall serve as pillow for us both;
One heart, one bed, two bosoms and one troth.

**HERMIA**

Nay, good Lysander; for my sake, my dear,
Lie further off yet, do not lie so near.

**LYSANDER**

O, take the sense, sweet, of my innocence!
Love takes the meaning in love's conference.
I mean, that my heart unto yours is knit
So that but one heart we can make of it;
Two bosoms interchained with an oath;
So then two bosoms and a single troth.
Then by your side no bed-room me deny;
For lying so, Hermia, I do not lie.

**HERMIA**

Lysander riddles very prettily:
Now much beshrew my manners and my pride,
If Hermia meant to say Lysander lied.
But, gentle friend, for love and courtesy
Lie further off; in human modesty,
Such separation as may well be said
Becomes a virtuous bachelor and a maid,
So far be distant; and, good night, sweet friend:
Thy love ne'er alter till thy sweet life end!

**LYSANDER**

Amen, amen, to that fair prayer, say I;
And then end life when I end loyalty!
Here is my bed: sleep give thee all his rest!

**HERMIA**

With half that wish the wisher's eyes be press'd!

**PUCK**

Through the forest have I gone.
But Athenian found I none,
On whose eyes I might approve
This flower's force in stirring love.
Night and silence—Who is here?
Weeds of Athens he doth wear:
This is he, my master said,
Despised the Athenian maid;
And here the maiden, sleeping sound,
On the dank and dirty ground.
Pretty soul! she durst not lie
Near this lack-love, this kill-courtesy.

**PUCK (cont.)**

Churl, upon thy eyes I throw
All the power this charm doth owe.
When thou wakest, let love forbid
Sleep his seat on thy eyelid:
So awake when I am gone;
For I must now to Oberon.

**HELENA**
Stay, though thou kill me, sweet Demetrius.
**DEMETRIUS**
I charge thee, hence, and do not haunt me thus.

**HELENA**
O, wilt thou darkling leave me? do not so.
**DEMETRIUS**
Stay, on thy peril: I alone will go.

**HELENA**
O, I am out of breath in this fond chase!
The more my prayer, the lesser is my grace.
Happy is Hermia, wheresoe'er she lies;
For she hath blessed and attractive eyes.
How came her eyes so bright? Not with salt tears:
If so, my eyes are oftener wash'd than hers.
No, no, I am as ugly as a bear;
For beasts that meet me run away for fear:
Therefore no marvel though Demetrius
Do, as a monster fly my presence thus.
What wicked and dissembling glass of mine
Made me compare with Hermia's sphery eyne?

HELENA (cont.)
But who is here? Lysander! on the ground!
Dead? or asleep? I see no blood, no wound.
Lysander if you live, good sir, awake.
LYSANDER
And run through fire I will for thy sweet sake.
Transparent Helena! Nature shows art,
That through thy bosom makes me see thy heart.
Where is Demetrius? O, how fit a word
Is that vile name to perish on my sword!

HELENA
Do not say so, Lysander; say not so
What though he love your Hermia? Lord, what though?
Yet Hermia still loves you: then be content.

LYSANDER
Content with Hermia! No; I do repent
The tedious minutes I with her have spent.
Not Hermia but Helena I love:
Who will not change a raven for a dove?
The will of man is by his reason sway'd;
And reason says you are the worthier maid.
Things growing are not ripe until their season;
So I, being young, till now ripe not to reason;
And touching now the point of human skill,
Reason becomes the marshal to my will
And leads me to your eyes, where I o'erlook
Love's stories written in love's richest book.

**HELENA**

Wherefore was I to this keen mockery born?
When at your hands did I deserve this scorn?
Is't not enough, is't not enough, young man,
That I did never, no, nor never can,
Deserve a sweet look from Demetrius' eye,
But you must flout my insufficiency?
Good troth, you do me wrong, good sooth, you do,
In such disdainful manner me to woo.
But fare you well: perforce I must confess
I thought you lord of more true gentleness.
O, that a lady, of one man refused.
Should of another therefore be abused!

**LYSANDER**

She sees not Hermia. Hermia, sleep thou there:
And never mayst thou come Lysander near!
For as a surfeit of the sweetest things
The deepest loathing to the stomach brings,
Or as tie heresies that men do leave
Are hated most of those they did deceive,
So thou, my surfeit and my heresy,
Of all be hated, but the most of me!
And, all my powers, address your love and might
To honour Helen and to be her knight!

**HERMIA**

Help me, Lysander, help me! do thy best
To pluck this crawling serpent from my breast!
Ay me, for pity! what a dream was here!
Lysander, look how I do quake with fear:
Methought a serpent eat my heart away,
And you sat smiling at his cruel pray.
Lysander! what, removed? Lysander! lord!
What, out of hearing? gone? no sound, no word?
Alack, where are you speak, an if you hear;
Speak, of all loves! I swoon almost with fear.
No? then I well perceive you all not nigh
Either death or you I'll find immediately.

*T*he workmen have moved their play rehearsal space to the woods, so that they would not be disturbed by the bustle of town. Puck finds them, remarks that they are practicing close to where Titania sleeps, and watches the men bumble about theatrically for some moments. He decides to liven up the play with a bit of magical mischief.

PUCK

What hempen home-spuns have we swaggering here,
So near the cradle of the fairy queen?
What, a play toward! I'll be an auditor;
An actor too, perhaps, if I see cause.

QUINCE
Speak, Pyramus. Thisby, stand forth.
BOTTOM
Thisby, the flowers of odious savours sweet,
QUINCE
Odours, odours.
BOTTOM
—odours savours sweet:
So hath thy breath, my dearest Thisby dear.
But hark, a voice! stay thou but here awhile,
And by and by I will to thee appear.

PUCK
A stranger Pyramus than e'er played here.

**FLUTE**
Must I speak now?

**QUINCE**
Ay, marry, must you; for you must understand he goes but to see a noise that he heard, and is to come again.

**FLUTE**
Most radiant Pyramus, most lily-white of hue,
Of colour like the red rose on triumphant brier,
Most brisky juvenal and eke most lovely Jew,
As true as truest horse that yet would never tire,
I'll meet thee, Pyramus, at Ninny's tomb.

**QUINCE**
"Ninus' tomb," man: why, you must not speak that yet; that you answer to Pyramus: you speak all your part at once, cues and all Pyramus enter: your cue is past; it is, "never tire."

**FLUTE**
O,—As true as truest horse, that yet would never tire.

**BOTTOM**
If I were fair, Thisby, I were only thine.

**QUINCE**
O monstrous! O strange! we are haunted. Pray, masters! fly, masters! Help!

42

**PUCK**
I'll follow you, I'll lead you about a round,
Through bog, through bush, through brake, through brier:
Sometime a horse I'll be, sometime a hound,
A hog, a headless bear, sometime a fire;
And neigh, and bark, and grunt, and roar, and burn,
Like horse, hound, hog, bear, fire, at every turn.

**BOTTOM**
Why do they run away? this is a knavery of them to make me afeard.

**SNOUT**
O Bottom, thou art changed! what do I see on thee?

**BOTTOM**
What do you see? you see an asshead of your own, do you?

**QUINCE**
Bless thee, Bottom! bless thee! thou art translated.

**BOTTOM**

I see their knavery: this is to make an ass of me;
to fright me, if they could. But I will not stir
from this place, do what they can: I will walk up
and down here, and I will sing, that they shall hear
I am not afraid.

> The ousel cock so black of hue,
> With orange-tawny bill,
> The throstle with his note so true,
> The wren with little quill,—

**BOTTOM**
The finch, the sparrow and the lark,
The plain-song cuckoo gray,
Whose note full many a man doth mark,
And dares not answer nay;—
for, indeed, who would set his wit to so foolish
a bird? who would give a bird the lie, though he cry
"cuckoo" never so?

**TITANIA**
I pray thee, gentle mortal, sing again:
Mine ear is much enamour'd of thy note;
So is mine eye enthralled to thy shape;
And thy fair virtue's force perforce doth move me
On the first view to say, to swear, I love thee.

**BOTTOM**

Methinks, mistress, you should have little reason for that: and yet, to say the truth, reason and love keep little company together now-a-days; the more the pity that some honest neighbours will not make them friends. Nay, I can gleek upon occasion.

**TITANIA**
Thou art as wise as thou art beautiful.
**BOTTOM**
Not so, neither: but if I had wit enough to get out of this wood, I have enough to serve mine own turn.
**TITANIA**
Out of this wood do not desire to go:
Thou shalt remain here, whether thou wilt or no.
I am a spirit of no common rate;
The summer still doth tend upon my state;
And I do love thee: therefore, go with me;
I'll give thee fairies to attend on thee,
And they shall fetch thee jewels from the deep,
And sing while thou on pressed flowers dost sleep;
And I will purge thy mortal grossness so
That thou shalt like an airy spirit go.
Peaseblossom! Cobweb! Moth! and Mustardseed!

| PEASEBLOSSOM | MOTH |
|---|---|
| Ready. | And I. |
| COBWEB | MUSTARDSEED |
| And I. | And I. |

ALL
Where shall we go?

TITANIA

Be kind and courteous to this gentleman;
Hop in his walks and gambol in his eyes;
Feed him with apricocks and dewberries,
With purple grapes, green figs, and mulberries;
The honey-bags steal from the humble-bees,
And for night-tapers crop their waxen thighs
And light them at the fiery glow-worm's eyes,
To have my love to bed and to arise;
And pluck the wings from painted butterflies
To fan the moonbeams from his sleeping eyes:
Nod to him, elves, and do him courtesies.

# ACT III. Scene II (110–343).

M
N
D

**O**beron discovers that Puck has bewitched the wrong Athenian youth, saying that because of his mistake he has "some true love turned, and not a false turned true" (III.ii.91). Finding Demetrius asleep, Oberon uses the magic flower on him as Puck hurries off to lead the other Athenian lovers to the spot. When Puck arrives, the two watch what happens.

**PUCK**
Captain of our fairy band,
Helena is here at hand;
And the youth, mistook by me,
Pleading for a lover's fee.
Shall we their fond pageant see?
Lord, what fools these mortals be!

**OBERON**
Stand aside: the noise they make
Will cause Demetrius to awake.
**PUCK**
Then will two at once woo one;
That must needs be sport alone;
And those things do best please me
That befall preposterously.

**LYSANDER**
Why should you think that I should woo in scorn?
Scorn and derision never come in tears:
Look, when I vow, I weep; and vows so born,
In their nativity all truth appears.
How can these things in me seem scorn to you,
Bearing the badge of faith, to prove them true?

**HELENA**
You do advance your cunning more and more.
When truth kills truth, O devilish-holy fray!
These vows are Hermia's: will you give her o'er?
Weigh oath with oath, and you will nothing weigh:
Your vows to her and me, put in two scales,
Will even weigh, and both as light as tales.

**LYSANDER**
I had no judgment when to her I swore.
**HELENA**
Nor none, in my mind, now you give her o'er.
**LYSANDER**
Demetrius loves her, and he loves not you.

**DEMETRIUS**
O Helena, goddess, nymph, perfect, divine!
To what, my love, shall I compare thine eyne?
Crystal is muddy. O, how ripe in show
Thy lips, those kissing cherries, tempting grow!
That pure congealed white, high Taurus snow,
Fann'd with the eastern wind, turns to a crow
When thou hold'st up thy hand: O, let me kiss
This princess of pure white, this seal of bliss!

**HELENA**
O spite! O hell! I see you all are bent
To set against me for your merriment:
If you were civil and knew courtesy,
You would not do me thus much injury.
Can you not hate me, as I know you do,
But you must join in souls to mock me too?
If you were men, as men you are in show,
You would not use a gentle lady so;
To vow, and swear, and superpraise my parts,
When I am sure you hate me with your hearts.
You both are rivals, and love Hermia;
And now both rivals, to mock Helena:
A trim exploit, a manly enterprise,
To conjure tears up in a poor maid's eyes
With your derision! none of noble sort
Would so offend a virgin, and extort
A poor soul's patience, all to make you sport.

**LYSANDER**
You are unkind, Demetrius; be not so;
For you love Hermia; this you know I know:
And here, with all good will, with all my heart,
In Hermia's love I yield you up my part;
And yours of Helena to me bequeath,
Whom I do love and will do till my death.
**HELENA**
Never did mockers waste more idle breath.

**DEMETRIUS**
Lysander, keep thy Hermia; I will none:
If e'er I loved her, all that love is gone.
My heart to her but as guest-wise sojourn'd,
And now to Helen is it home return'd,
There to remain.
**LYSANDER**
Helen, it is not so.

**DEMETRIUS**
Disparage not the faith thou dost not know,
Lest, to thy peril, thou aby it dear.
Look, where thy love comes; yonder is thy dear.

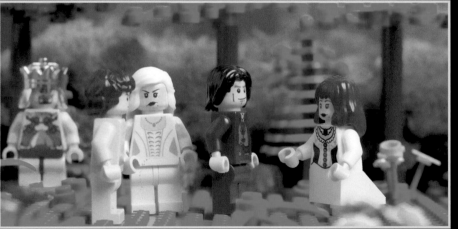

**HERMIA**
Dark night, that from the eye his function takes,
The ear more quick of apprehension makes;
Wherein it doth impair the seeing sense,
It pays the hearing double recompense.
Thou art not by mine eye, Lysander, found;
Mine ear, I thank it, brought me to thy sound
But why unkindly didst thou leave me so?

**LYSANDER**
Why should he stay, whom love doth press to go?
**HERMIA**
What love could press Lysander from my side?

**LYSANDER**

Lysander's love, that would not let him bide,
Fair Helena, who more engilds the night
Than all yon fiery oes and eyes of light.
Why seek'st thou me? could not this make thee know,
The hate I bear thee made me leave thee so?

**HERMIA**

You speak not as you think: it cannot be.

**HELENA**

Lo, she is one of this confederacy!
Now I perceive they have conjoin'd all three
To fashion this false sport, in spite of me.
Injurious Hermia! most ungrateful maid!
Have you conspired, have you with these contrived
To bait me with this foul derision?

**HELENA (cont.)**

Is all the counsel that we two have shared,
The sisters' vows, the hours that we have spent,
When we have chid the hasty-footed time
For parting us,—O, is it all forgot?
All school-days' friendship, childhood innocence?
We, Hermia, like two artificial gods,
Have with our needles created both one flower,
Both on one sampler, sitting on one cushion,
Both warbling of one song, both in one key,
As if our hands, our sides, voices and minds,
Had been incorporate.

**HELENA (cont.)**

So we grow together,
Like to a double cherry, seeming parted,
But yet an union in partition;
Two lovely berries moulded on one stem;
So, with two seeming bodies, but one heart;
Two of the first, like coats in heraldry,
Due but to one and crowned with one crest.
And will you rent our ancient love asunder,
To join with men in scorning your poor friend?
It is not friendly, 'tis not maidenly:
Our sex, as well as I, may chide you for it,
Though I alone do feel the injury.

**HERMIA**

I am amazed at your passionate words.
I scorn you not: it seems that you scorn me.

**HELENA**

Have you not set Lysander, as in scorn,
To follow me and praise my eyes and face?
And made your other love, Demetrius,
Who even but now did spurn me with his foot,
To call me goddess, nymph, divine and rare,
Precious, celestial? Wherefore speaks he this
To her he hates? and wherefore doth Lysander
Deny your love, so rich within his soul,
And tender me, forsooth, affection,
But by your setting on, by your consent?
What thought I be not so in grace as you,
So hung upon with love, so fortunate,
But miserable most, to love unloved?
This you should pity rather than despise.

**HERMIA**
I understand not what you mean by this.

**HELENA**
Ay, do, persever, counterfeit sad looks,
Make mouths upon me when I turn my back;
Wink each at other; hold the sweet jest up:
This sport, well carried, shall be chronicled.
If you have any pity, grace, or manners,
You would not make me such an argument.
But fare ye well: 'tis partly my own fault;
Which death or absence soon shall remedy.

LYSANDER
Stay, gentle Helena; hear my excuse:
My love, my life, my soul, fair Helena!
HELENA
O excellent!
HERMIA
Sweet, do not scorn her so.

DEMETRIUS
If she cannot entreat, I can compel.
LYSANDER
Thou canst compel no more than she entreat:
Thy threats have no more strength than her weak prayers.
Helen, I love thee; by my life, I do:
I swear by that which I will lose for thee,
To prove him false that says I love thee not.
DEMETRIUS
I say I love thee more than he can do.

LYSANDER
If thou say so, withdraw, and prove it too.
DEMETRIUS
Quick, come!
HERMIA
Lysander, whereto tends all this?

LYSANDER
Away, you Ethiope!
DEMETRIUS
No, no; he will
Seem to break loose; take on as you would follow,
But yet come not: you are a tame man, go!

LYSANDER
Hang off, thou cat, thou burr! vile thing, let loose,
Or I will shake thee from me like a serpent!
HERMIA
Why are you grown so rude? what change is this?
Sweet love,—

LYSANDER
Thy love! out, tawny Tartar, out!
Out, loathed medicine! hated potion, hence!
HERMIA
Do you not jest?

HELENA
Yes, sooth; and so do you.

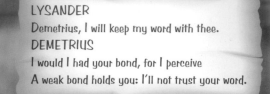

**LYSANDER**
Demetrius, I will keep my word with thee.
**DEMETRIUS**
I would I had your bond, for I perceive
A weak bond holds you: I'll not trust your word.

**LYSANDER**
What, should I hurt her, strike her, kill her dead?
Although I hate her, I'll not harm her so.

**HERMIA**
What, can you do me greater harm than hate?
Hate me! wherefore? O me! what news, my love!
Am not I Hermia? are not you Lysander?
I am as fair now as I was erewhile.
Since night you loved me; yet since night you left me:
Why, then you left me—O, the gods forbid!—
In earnest, shall I say?

**LYSANDER**
Ay, by my life;
And never did desire to see thee more.
Therefore be out of hope, of question, of doubt;
Be certain, nothing truer; 'tis no jest
That I do hate thee and love Helena.

**HERMIA**
O me! you juggler! you canker-blossom!
You thief of love! what, have you come by night
And stolen my love's heart from him?

**HELENA**
Fine, i'faith!
Have you no modesty, no maiden shame,
No touch of bashfulness? What, will you tear
Impatient answers from my gentle tongue?
Fie, fie! you counterfeit, you puppet, you!

**HERMIA**
Puppet? why so? ay, that way goes the game.
Now I perceive that she hath made compare
Between our statures; she hath urged her height;
And with her personage, her tall personage,
Her height, forsooth, she hath prevail'd with him.
And are you grown so high in his esteem;
Because I am so dwarfish and so low?
How low am I, thou painted maypole? speak;
How low am I? I am not yet so low
But that my nails can reach unto thine eyes.

**HELENA**
I pray you, though you mock me, gentlemen,
Let her not hurt me: I was never curst;
I have no gift at all in shrewishness;
I am a right maid for my cowardice:
Let her not strike me. You perhaps may think,
Because she is something lower than myself,
That I can match her.
**HERMIA**
Lower! hark, again.

**HELENA**
Good Hermia, do not be so bitter with me.
I evermore did love you, Hermia,
Did ever keep your counsels, never wrong'd you;
Save that, in love unto Demetrius,
I told him of your stealth unto this wood.
He follow'd you; for love I follow'd him;
But he hath chid me hence and threaten'd me
To strike me, spurn me, nay, to kill me too:
And now, so you will let me quiet go,
To Athens will I bear my folly back
And follow you no further: let me go:
You see how simple and how fond I am.

**HERMIA**
Why, get you gone: who is't that hinders you?

**HELENA**
A foolish heart, that I leave here behind.
**HERMIA**
What, with Lysander?

HELENA
With Demetrius.

LYSANDER
Be not afraid; she shall not harm thee, Helena.
DEMETRIUS
No, sir, she shall not, though you take her part.
HELENA
O, when she's angry, she is keen and shrewd!
She was a vixen when she went to school;
And though she be but little, she is fierce.
HERMIA
"Little" again! nothing but "low" and "little"!
Why will you suffer her to flout me thus?
Let me come to her.
LYSANDER
Get you gone, you dwarf;
You minimus, of hindering knot-grass made;
You bead, you acorn.

DEMETRIUS
You are too officious
In her behalf that scorns your services.
Let her alone: speak not of Helena;
Take not her part; for, if thou dost intend
Never so little show of love to her,
Thou shalt aby it.

LYSANDER
Now she holds me not;
Now follow, if thou darest, to try whose right,
Of thine or mine, is most in Helena.
DEMETRIUS
Follow! nay, I'll go with thee, cheek by jole.

HERMIA

You, mistress, all this coil is 'long of you:
Nay, go not back.

HELENA

I will not trust you, I,
Nor longer stay in your curst company.
Your hands than mine are quicker for a fray,
My legs are longer though, to run away.

HERMIA

I am amazed, and know not what to say.

*O*beron is not pleased with the mess Puck has made, but Puck says he was very entertained by the whole thing. The two begin the task of setting everything right. Oberon gives Puck a new magic flower that counteracts the "love" flower, then sets off to lift the spell on Titania. Puck, on Oberon's orders, leads the young lovers in a chase across the forest. He uses his magic to trick and taunt them until they are so weary they lay down on the ground to sleep. Then he creeps close to apply the magic flower to Lysander's eyes.

PUCK
On the ground
Sleep sound:
I'll apply
To your eye,
Gentle lover, remedy.

PUCK (cont.)
When thou wakest,
Thou takest
True delight
In the sight
Of thy former lady's eye:

PUCK (cont.)
And the country proverb known,
That every man should take his own,
In your waking shall be shown:
Jack shall have Jill;
Nought shall go ill;
The man shall have his mare again, and all shall be well.

# ACT IV. Scene I (75–101).

M
N
D

*O*beron finds Titania sleeping in her bower with the monstrous Bottom. He squeezes another flower into her eyes, and she wakes, free from the spell.

TITANIA
My Oberon! what visions have I seen!
Methought I was enamour'd of an ass.
OBERON
There lies your love.
TITANIA
How came these things to pass?
O, how mine eyes do loathe his visage now!

OBERON
Silence awhile. Robin, take off this head.
Titania, music call; and strike more dead
Than common sleep of all these five the sense.
TITANIA
Music, ho! music, such as charmeth sleep!

PUCK
Now, when thou wakest, with thine
own fool's eyes peep.

OBERON
Sound, music! Come, my queen, take hands with me,
And rock the ground whereon these sleepers be.
Now thou and I are new in amity,
And will to-morrow midnight solemnly
Dance in Duke Theseus' house triumphantly,
And bless it to all fair prosperity:
There shall the pairs of faithful lovers be
Wedded, with Theseus, all in jollity.

PUCK
Fairy king, attend, and mark:
I do hear the morning lark.

**OBERON**
Then, my queen, in silence sad,
Trip we after the night's shade:
We the globe can compass soon,
Swifter than the wandering moon.

**TITANIA**
Come, my lord, and in our flight
Tell me how it came this night
That I sleeping here was found
With these mortals on the ground.

*A*s Oberon and Titania depart, Theseus, Hippolyta, and Egeus arrive near the edge of the forest, intending to enjoy a hunt before Hippolyta and Theseus's wedding later that day. Instead, they find the young lovers sleeping together in a clearing.

**THESEUS**

Go, bid the huntsmen wake them with their horns.
Good morrow, friends. Saint Valentine is past:
Begin these wood-birds but to couple now?

**LYSANDER**

Pardon, my lord.

**THESEUS**

I pray you all, stand up.
I know you two are rival enemies:
How comes this gentle concord in the world,
That hatred is so far from jealousy,
To sleep by hate, and fear no enmity?

**LYSANDER**

My lord, I shall reply amazedly,
Half sleep, half waking; but as yet, I swear,
I cannot truly say how I came here;
But, as I think,—for truly would I speak,
And now do I bethink me, so it is,—
I came with Hermia hither: our intent
Was to be gone from Athens, where we might,
Without the peril of the Athenian law.

**EGEUS**

Enough, enough, my lord; you have enough:
I beg the law, the law, upon his head.
They would have stolen away; they would, Demetrius,
Thereby to have defeated you and me,
You of your wife and me of my consent,
Of my consent that she should be your wife.

**DEMETRIUS**
My lord, fair Helen told me of their stealth,
Of this their purpose hither to this wood;
And I in fury hither follow'd them,
Fair Helena in fancy following me.
But, my good lord, I wot not by what power,—
But by some power it is,—my love to Hermia,
Melted as the snow, seems to me now
As the remembrance of an idle gaud

Which in my childhood I did dote upon;
And all the faith, the virtue of my heart,
The object and the pleasure of mine eye,
Is only Helena. To her, my lord,
Was I betroth'd ere I saw Hermia:
But, like in sickness, did I loathe this food;
But, as in health, come to my natural taste,
Now I do wish it, love it, long for it,
And will for evermore be true to it.

**THESEUS**
Fair lovers, you are fortunately met:
Of this discourse we more will hear anon.
Egeus, I will overbear your will;
For in the temple by and by with us
These couples shall eternally be knit:
And, for the morning now is something worn,
Our purposed hunting shall be set aside.

**THESEUS** (cont.)
Away with us to Athens; three and three,
We'll hold a feast in great solemnity.
Come, Hippolyta.

**DEMETRIUS**
These things seem small and undistinguishable,
Like far-off mountains turn'd into clouds.
**HERMIA**
Methinks I see these things with parted eye,
When every thing seems double.

**HELENA**
So methinks:
And I have found Demetrius like a jewel,
Mine own, and not mine own.

**DEMETRIUS**
Are you sure
That we are awake? It seems to me
That yet we sleep, we dream. Do not you think
The duke was here, and bid us follow him?

**HERMIA**
Yea; and my father.
**HELENA**
And Hippolyta.

**LYSANDER**
And he did bid us follow to the temple.
**DEMETRIUS**
Why, then, we are awake: let's follow him
And by the way let us recount our dreams.

*T*he couples are wed with joy and celebration! Oberon and Titania have reconciled, and Bottom is returned to normal, although moved by the remarkable dream he had in the forest. Now that each Jack has his Jill, Theseus requests some entertainment for his lovely bride and his honored guests. Luckily Bottom and his companions are happy to oblige.

**PHILOSTRATE**
There is a brief how many sports are ripe:
Make choice of which your highness will see first.

**THESEUS**
Say, what abridgement have you for this evening?
What masque? what music? How shall we beguile
The lazy time, if not with some delight?

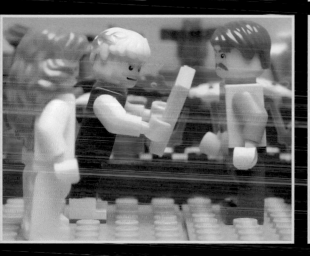

**THESEUS**
"The battle with the Centaurs, to be sung
By an Athenian eunuch to the harp."
We'll none of that: that have I told my love,
In glory of my kinsman Hercules.
"The riot of the tipsy Bacchanals,
Tearing the Thracian singer in their rage."

**THESEUS** (cont.)
That is an old device; and it was play'd
When I from Thebes came last a conqueror.
"The thrice three Muses mourning for the death
Of Learning, late deceased in beggary."
That is some satire, keen and critical,
Not sorting with a nuptial ceremony.

**THESEUS** (cont.)
"A tedious brief scene of young Pyramus
And his love Thisbe; very tragical mirth."
Merry and tragical! tedious and brief!
That is hot ice and wondrous strange snow.
How shall we find the concord of this discord?

71

PHILOSTRATE

A play there is, my lord, some ten words long,
Which is as brief as I have known a play;
But by ten words, my lord, it is too long,
Which makes it tedious; for in all the play
There is not one word apt, one player fitted:
And tragical, my noble lord, it is;
For Pyramus therein doth kill himself.
Which, when I saw rehearsed, I must confess,
Made mine eyes water; but more merry tears
The passion of loud laughter never shed.

THESEUS

What are they that do play it?

PHILOSTRATE

Hard-handed men that work in Athens here,
Which never labour'd in their minds till now,
And now have toil'd their unbreathed memories
With this same play, against your nuptial.

THESEUS
And we will hear it.

PHILOSTRATE
No, my noble lord;
It is not for you: I have heard it over,
And it is nothing, nothing in the world;
Unless you can find sport in their intents,
Extremely stretch'd and conn'd with cruel pain,
To do you service.

THESEUS
I will hear that play;
For never anything can be amiss,
When simpleness and duty tender it.
Go, bring them in: and take your places, ladies.

SNOUT [as Wall]
In this same interlude it doth befall
That I, one Snout by name, present a wall;
And such a wall, as I would have you think,
That had in it a crannied hole or chink,
Through which the lovers, Pyramus and Thisby,
Did whisper often very secretly.
This loam, this rough-cast and this stone doth show
That I am that same wall; the truth is so:
And this the cranny is, right and sinister,
Through which the fearful lovers are to whisper.

THESEUS
Would you desire lime and hair to speak better?
DEMETRIUS
It is the wittiest partition that ever I heard
discourse, my lord.
THESEUS
Pyramus draws near the wall: silence!

74

BOTTOM [as Pyramus]
O grim-look'd night! O night with hue so black!
O night, which ever art when day is not!
O night, O night! alack, alack, alack,
I fear my Thisby's promise is forgot!

BOTTOM [as Pyramus] (cont).
And thou, O wall, O sweet, O lovely wall,
That stand'st between her father's ground and mine!
Thou wall, O wall, O sweet and lovely wall,
Show me thy chink, to blink through with mine eyne!

BOTTOM [as Pyramus] (cont).
Thanks, courteous wall: Jove shield thee well for this!
But what see I? No Thisby do I see.

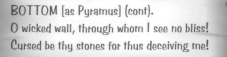

BOTTOM [as Pyramus] (cont).
O wicked wall, through whom I see no bliss!
Cursed be thy stones for thus deceiving me!

THESEUS
The wall, methinks, being sensible, should curse again.

BOTTOM
No, in truth, sir, he should not. "Deceiving me" is Thisby's cue: she is to enter now, and I am to spy her through the wall. You shall see, it will fall pat as I told you. Yonder she comes.

FLUTE [as Thisbe]
O wall, full often hast thou heard my moans,
For parting my fair Pyramus and me!

FLUTE [as Thisbe] (cont.)
My cherry lips have often kiss'd thy stones,
Thy stones with lime and hair knit up in thee.

BOTTOM [as Pyramus]
I see a voice: now will I to the chink,
To spy an I can hear my Thisby's face. Thisby!

FLUTE [as Thisbe]
My love thou art, my love I think.

BOTTOM [as Pyramus]
Think what thou wilt, I am thy lover's grace;
And, like Limander, am I trusty still.
FLUTE [as Thisbe]
And I like Helen, till the Fates me kill.

BOTTOM [as Pyramus]
Not Shafalus to Procrus was so true.
FLUTE [as Thisbe]
As Shafalus to Procrus, I to you.

BOTTOM [as Pyramus]
O kiss me through the hole of this vile wall!

FLUTE [as Thisbe]
I kiss the wall's hole, not your lips at all.

BOTTOM [as Pyramus]
Wilt thou at Ninny's tomb meet me straightway?
FLUTE [as Thisbe]
'Tide life, 'tide death, I come without delay.

SNOUT [as Wall]
Thus have I, Wall, my part discharged so;
And, being done, thus Wall away doth go.

# ACT V. Scene I (251–335).

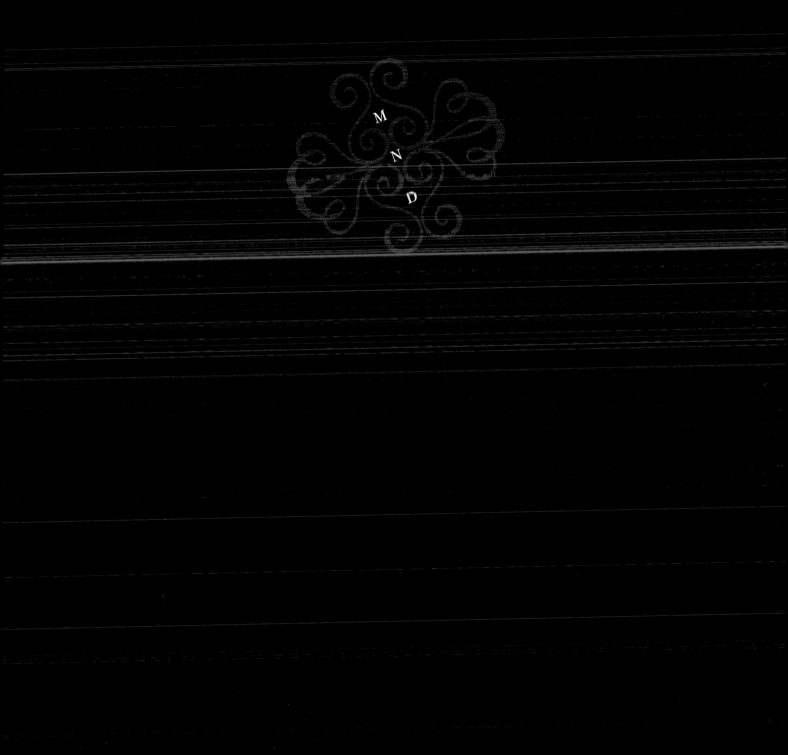

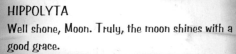

DEMETRIUS
And then came Pyramus.

BOTTOM [as Pyramus]
Sweet Moon, I thank thee for thy sunny beams;
I thank thee, Moon, for shining now so bright;
For, by thy gracious, golden, glittering gleams,
I trust to take of truest Thisby sight.

BOTTOM [as Pyramus]
But stay, O spite!
But mark, poor knight,
What dreadful dole is here!
Eyes, do you see?
How can it be?
O dainty duck! O dear!

Thy mantle good,
What, stain'd with blood!
Approach, ye Furies fell!
O Fates, come, come,
Cut thread and thrum;
Quail, crush, conclude, and quell!

THESEUS
This passion, and the death of a dear friend, would
go near to make a man look sad.

HIPPOLYTA
Beshrew my heart, but I pity the man.

BOTTOM [as Pyramus]
O wherefore, Nature, didst thou lions frame?
Since lion vile hath here deflower'd my dear:
Which is—no, no—which was the fairest dame
That lived, that loved, that liked, that look'd
with cheer.
Come, tears, confound;
Out, sword, and wound
The pap of Pyramus;
Ay, that left pap,
Where heart doth hop:

BOTTOM [as Pyramus] (cont.)
Thus die I, thus, thus, thus.
Now am I dead,
Now am I fled;
My soul is in the sky:
Tongue, lose thy light;

BOTTOM [as Pyramus] (cont.)
Moon take thy flight:

BOTTOM [as Pyramus] (cont.)
Now die, die, die, die, die.

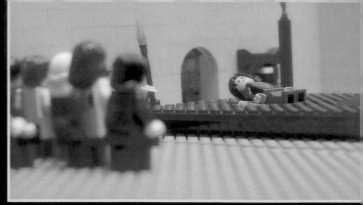

DEMETRIUS
No die, but an ace, for him; for he is but one.

LYSANDER
Less than an ace, man; for he is dead; he is nothing.

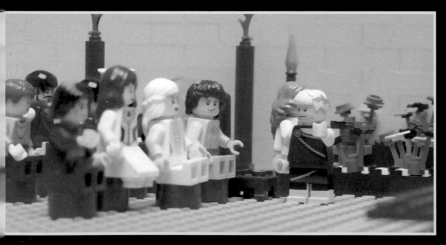

THESEUS
With the help of a surgeon he might yet recover, and prove an ass.

HIPPOLYTA
How chance Moonshine is gone before Thisbe comes back and finds her lover?

**THESEUS**
She will find him by starlight. Here she comes; and her passion ends the play.

**HIPPOLYTA**
Methinks she should not use a long one for such a Pyramus: I hope she will be brief.

**DEMETRIUS**
A mote will turn the balance, which Pyramus, which Thisbe, is the better; he for a man, God warrant us; she for a woman, God bless us.

**LYSANDER**
She hath spied him already with those sweet eyes.
**DEMETRIUS**
And thus she means, videlicet:—

**FLUTE [as Thisbe]**
Asleep, my love?
What, dead, my dove?
O Pyramus, arise!
Speak, speak. Quite dumb?
Dead, dead? A tomb
Must cover thy sweet eyes.
These my lips,
This cherry nose,
These yellow cowslip cheeks,
Are gone, are gone:
Lovers, make moan:
His eyes were green as leeks.

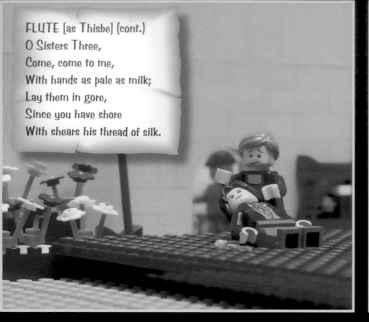

FLUTE [as Thisbe] (cont.)
O Sisters Three,
Come, come to me,
With hands as pale as milk;
Lay them in gore,
Since you have shore
With shears his thread of silk.

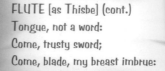

FLUTE [as Thisbe] (cont.)
Tongue, not a word:
Come, trusty sword;
Come, blade, my breast imbrue:

FLUTE [as Thisbe] (cont.)
And, farewell, friends;
Thus Thisby ends:
Adieu, adieu, adieu.

THESEUS
Moonshine and Lion are left to bury the dead.
DEMETRIUS
Ay, and Wall too.

# ACT V. Scene I (406–421).

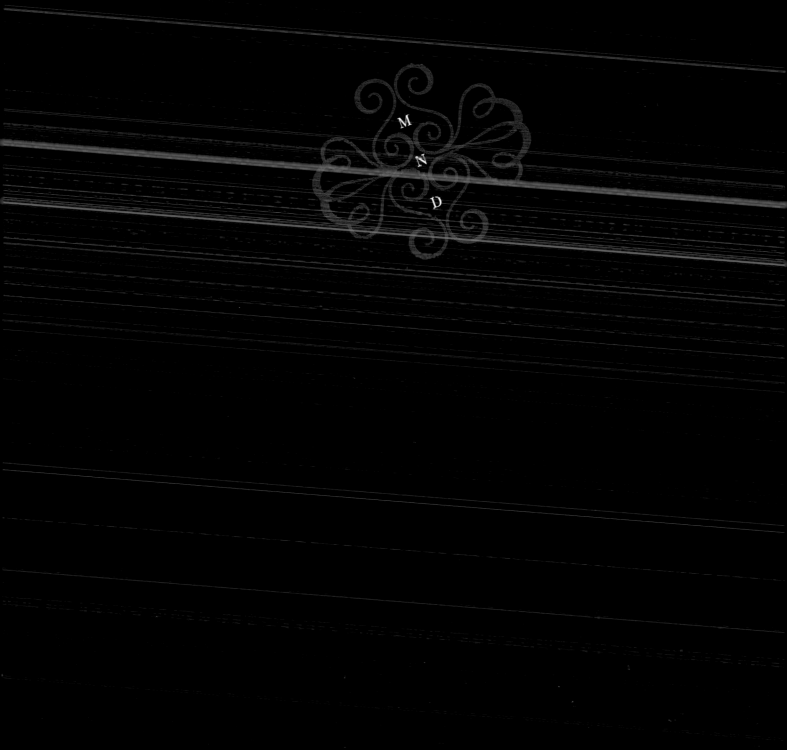

## PUCK

If we shadows have offended,
Think but this, and all is mended,
That you have but slumber'd here
While these visions did appear.
And this weak and idle theme,
No more yielding but a dream,
Gentles, do not reprehend:
if you pardon, we will mend:

And, as I am an honest Puck,
If we have unearned luck
Now to 'scape the serpent's tongue,
We will make amends ere long;
Else the Puck a liar call;
So, good night unto you all.
Give me your hands, if we be friends,
And Robin shall restore amends.

T

# INTRODUCTION

*The Tempest* was written around 1610 and is thought to be one of the last of Shakespeare's plays. The play centers on Prospero, the Duke of Milan, and his daughter Miranda, who have been stranded on a deserted island for many years, since Prospero's ambitious brother stole his position as Duke and set Prospero and Miranda adrift.

While many of Shakespeare's other plays explore the theme of magic to some extent, *The Tempest* deals with this topic directly. Magic is both the cause and the solution to the problems that arise in the play: Prospero ignored his duties as Duke of Milan, spending his days studying as his brother plotted to overthrow him. But when Prospero and baby Miranda are sent out to sea, they are able to survive because Gonzalo slips them Prospero's magic books.

As with other plays that explore magical themes, Prospero's craft is sometimes used to draw parallels to the *art* of theater. In fact, some scholars think the character Prospero represented Shakespeare himself, as the artist-magician who set the fantastical scenes of the play in motion. Prospero spends much of the play running around behind the scenes, moving his plan along with the help of his magical right-hand man. The way he uses his magic is particularly theatrical as well: he plays on his audience's perception, using strange noises to lead them where he wants them to go and intimidating them with visual displays and neat parlor tricks, like having a banquet disappear into thin air.

There are also interesting themes of colonization in *The Tempest*. The play was written during a time of busy exploration, when European sailors were visiting faraway lands, like the many islands around the Americas, and encountering people and cultures that had never been heard of before. For this reason many people have called it the "New World Play," both because they believe it is set on an island in the New World and because it deals with themes of power and colonization. Regardless of Shakespeare's original intent, many aspects of the play have resonated with people from cultures that have been colonized, and this particular reading of the play has become popular. The character of Caliban, specifically, serves to represent colonized people. Caliban had been master of the island before Prospero and Miranda arrived, and when they landed, he graciously shared all of the secrets of the island so they could survive and prosper. But at the time that the play is set, Caliban acts as Prospero's servant because he had tried to rape young Miranda.

*The Tempest* is a fascinating play, filled with existential meditations and hilarious drunken rambles, as well as insightful reflections on global politics that echo in a world many hundreds of years beyond that in which it was written.

**ALONSO, King of Naples**

**SEBASTIAN, his brother**

**PROSPERO, the right Duke of Milan**

**ANTONIO, his brother, the usurping Duke of Milan**

**FERDINAND, son to the King of Naples**

**GONZALO, an honest old Counsellor**

**ADRIAN, a Lord**

**FRANCISCO, a Lord**

**CALIBAN, a savage and deformed Slave**

**TRINCULO, a Jester**

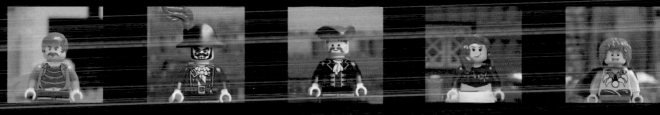

**STEPHANO, a drunken Butler**

**MASTER of a Ship**

**BOATSWAIN**

**MIRANDA, daughter to Prospero**

**ARIEL, an airy Spirit**

**Not Pictured**

**MARINERS**

**IRIS, presented by Spirits**
**CERES, presented by Spirits**

# ACT I. Scene I (1–64).

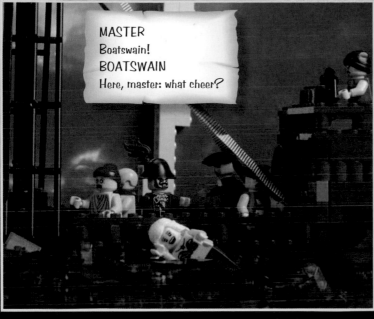

**MASTER**
Boatswain!
**BOATSWAIN**
Here, master: what cheer?

**MASTER**
Good, speak to the mariners: fall to't, yarely, or we run ourselves aground: bestir, bestir.

**BOATSWAIN**
Heigh, my hearts! cheerly, cheerly, my hearts! yare, yare! Take in the topsail. Tend to the master's whistle. Blow, till thou burst thy wind, if room enough!

**ALONSO**
Good boatswain, have care. Where's the master? Play the men!

BOATSWAIN
I pray now, keep below.
ANTONIO
Where is the master, boatswain?

BOATSWAIN
Do you not hear him? You mar our labour: keep your cabins: you do assist the storm.
GONZALO
Nay, good, be patient.

BOATSWAIN
When the sea is. Hence! What cares these roarers for the name of king? To cabin: silence! trouble us not.
GONZALO
Good, yet remember whom thou hast aboard.

BOATSWAIN
None that I more love than myself. You are a counsellor; if you can command these elements to silence, and work the peace of the present, we will not hand a rope more; use your authority: if you cannot, give thanks you have lived so long, and make yourself ready in your cabin for the mischance of the hour, if it so hap. Cheerly, good hearts! Out of our way, I say.

**GONZALO**
I have great comfort from this fellow: methinks he hath no drowning mark upon him; his complexion is perfect gallows. Stand fast, good Fate, to his hanging: make the rope of his destiny our cable, for our own doth little advantage. If he be not born to be hanged, our case is miserable.

**BOATSWAIN**
Down with the topmast! yare! lower, lower! Bring her to try with main-course.

**BOATSWAIN** (cont.)
A plague upon this howling! they are louder than the weather or our office.
Yet again! what do you here? Shall we give o'er and drown? Have you a mind to sink?

**BOATSWAIN**
Work you then.

**SEBASTIAN**
A pox o' your throat, you bawling, blasphemous, incharitable dog!

**ANTONIO**
Hang, cur! hang, you whoreson, insolent noisemaker! We are less afraid to be drowned than thou art.

**GONZALO**
I'll warrant him for drowning; though the ship were no stronger than a nutshell and as leaky as an unstanched wench.

**BOATSWAIN**
Lay her a-hold, a-hold! set her two courses off to sea again; lay her off.
**MARINERS**
All lost! to prayers, to prayers! all lost!

**BOATSWAIN**
What, must our mouths be cold?

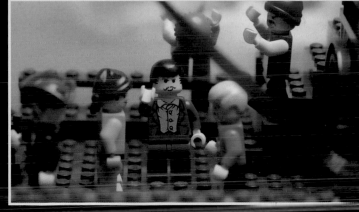

**GONZALO**
The king and prince at prayers! let's assist them,
For our case is as theirs.
**SEBASTIAN**
I'm out of patience.

**ANTONIO**
We are merely cheated of our lives by drunkards:
This wide-chapp'd rascal—would thou mightst lie drowning
The washing of ten tides!

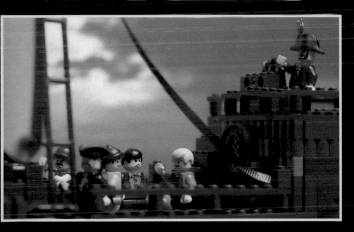

**GONZALO**
He'll be hang'd yet,
Though every drop of water swear against it
And gape at widest to glut him.
**ANTONIO**
Let's all sink with the king.

**SEBASTIAN**
Let's take leave of him.
**GONZALO**
Now would I give a thousand furlongs of sea for an
acre of barren ground, long heath, brown furze, any
thing. The wills above be done! but I would fain
die a dry death.

# ACT I. Scene II (1–305).

MIRANDA

If by your art, my dearest father, you have
Put the wild waters in this roar, allay them.
The sky, it seems, would pour down stinking pitch,
But that the sea, mounting to the welkin's cheek,
Dashes the fire out. O, I have suffered
With those that I saw suffer: a brave vessel,
Who had, no doubt, some noble creature in her,
Dash'd all to pieces. O, the cry did knock
Against my very heart. Poor souls, they perish'd.
Had I been any god of power, I would
Have sunk the sea within the earth or ere
It should the good ship so have swallow'd and
The fraughting souls within her.

PROSPERO
Be collected:
No more amazement: tell your piteous heart
There's no harm done.

MIRANDA
O, woe the day!
PROSPERO
No harm.
I have done nothing but in care of thee,
Of thee, my dear one, thee, my daughter, who
Art ignorant of what thou art, nought knowing
Of whence I am, nor that I am more better
Than Prospero, master of a full poor cell,
And thy no greater father.
MIRANDA
More to know
Did never meddle with my thoughts.

PROSPERO
'Tis time
I should inform thee farther. Lend thy hand,
And pluck my magic garment from me. So:
Lie there, my art. Wipe thou thine eyes; have comfort.
The direful spectacle of the wreck, which touch'd
The very virtue of compassion in thee,
I have with such provision in mine art
So safely ordered that there is no soul—
No, not so much perdition as an hair
Betid to any creature in the vessel
Which thou heard'st cry, which thou saw'st sink. Sit down;
For thou must now know farther.

MIRANDA
You have often
Begun to tell me what I am, but stopp'd
And left me to a bootless inquisition,
Concluding "Stay: not yet."
PROSPERO
The hour's now come;
The very minute bids thee ope thine ear;
Obey and be attentive. Canst thou remember
A time before we came unto this cell?
I do not think thou canst, for then thou wast not
Out three years old.

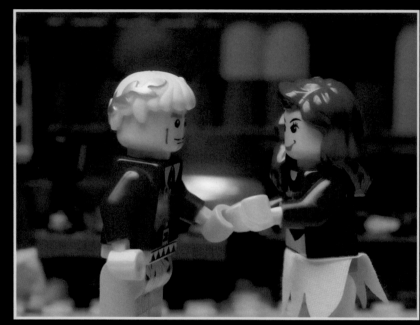

MIRANDA
Certainly, sir, I can.
PROSPERO
By what? by any other house or person?
Of any thing the image tell me that
Hath kept with thy remembrance.

MIRANDA
'Tis far off
And rather like a dream than an assurance
That my remembrance warrants. Had I not
Four or five women once that tended me?

100

PROSPERO
Twelve year since, Miranda, twelve year since,
Thy father was the Duke of Milan and
A prince of power.
MIRANDA
Sir, are not you my father?

PROSPERO
Thou hadst, and more, Miranda. But how is it
That this lives in thy mind? What seest thou else
In the dark backward and abysm of time?
If thou remember'st aught ere thou camest here,
How thou camest here thou mayst.
MIRANDA
But that I do not.

PROSPERO
Thy mother was a piece of virtue, and
She said thou wast my daughter; and thy father
Was Duke of Milan; and thou his only heir
And princess no worse issued.

MIRANDA
O the heavens!
What foul play had we, that we came from thence?
Or blessed was't we did?
PROSPERO
Both, both, my girl:
By foul play, as thou say'st, were we heaved thence,
But blessedly holp hither.

MIRANDA

O, my heart bleeds
To think o' the teen that I have turn'd you to,
Which is from my remembrance! Please you, farther.

PROSPERO

My brother and thy uncle, call'd Antonio—
I pray thee, mark me—that a brother should
Be so perfidious!—he whom next thyself
Of all the world I loved and to him put
The manage of my state; as at that time
Through all the signories it was the first
And Prospero the prime duke, being so reputed
In dignity, and for the liberal arts
Without a parallel; those being all my study,
The government I cast upon my brother
And to my state grew stranger, being transported
And rapt in secret studies. Thy false uncle—
Dost thou attend me?

MIRANDA

Sir, most heedfully.

PROSPERO

Being once perfected how to grant suits,
How to deny them, who to advance and who
To trash for over-topping, new created
The creatures that were mine, I say, or changed 'em,
Or else new form'd 'em; having both the key
Of officer and office, set all hearts i' the state
To what tune pleased his ear; that now he was
The ivy which had hid my princely trunk,
And suck'd my verdure out on't. Thou attend'st not.

MIRANDA

O, good sir, I do.

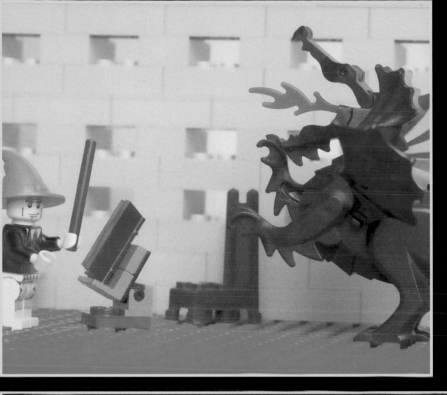

**PROSPERO**

I pray thee, mark me.
I, thus neglecting worldly ends, all dedicated
To closeness and the bettering of my mind
With that which, but by being so retired,
O'er-prized all popular rate, in my false brother
Awaked an evil nature; and my trust,
Like a good parent, did beget of him
A falsehood in its contrary as great
As my trust was; which had indeed no limit,
A confidence sans bound. He being thus lorded,
Not only with what my revenue yielded,
But what my power might else exact, like one
Who having into truth, by telling of it,
Made such a sinner of his memory,
To credit his own lie, he did believe
He was indeed the duke; out o' the substitution
And executing the outward face of royalty,
With all prerogative: hence his ambition growing—
Dost thou hear?

**MIRANDA**
Your tale, sir, would cure deafness.

**PROSPERO**
To have no screen between this part he play'd
And him he play'd it for, he needs will be
Absolute Milan. Me, poor man, my library
Was dukedom large enough: of temporal royalties
He thinks me now incapable; confederates—
So dry he was for sway—wi' the King of Naples
To give him annual tribute, do him homage,
Subject his coronet to his crown and bend
The dukedom yet unbow'd—alas, poor Milan!—
To most ignoble stooping.

MIRANDA
O the heavens!

PROSPERO
Mark his condition and the event; then tell me
If this might be a brother.
MIRANDA
I should sin
To think but nobly of my grandmother:
Good wombs have borne bad sons.

PROSPERO
Now the condition.
The King of Naples, being an enemy
To me inveterate, hearkens my brother's suit;
Which was, that he, in lieu o' the premises
Of homage and I know not how much tribute,
Should presently extirpate me and mine
Out of the dukedom and confer fair Milan
With all the honours on my brother: whereon,
A treacherous army levied, one midnight
Fated to the purpose did Antonio open
The gates of Milan, and, i' the dead of darkness,
The ministers for the purpose hurried thence
Me and thy crying self.

MIRANDA
Alack, for pity!
I, not remembering how I cried out then,
Will cry it o'er again: it is a hint
That wrings mine eyes to't.

PROSPERO
Hear a little further
And then I'll bring thee to the present business
Which now's upon 's; without the which this story
Were most impertinent.
MIRANDA
Wherefore did they not
That hour destroy us?

PROSPERO
Well demanded, wench:
My tale provokes that question. Dear, they durst not,
So dear the love my people bore me, nor set
A mark so bloody on the business, but
With colours fairer painted their foul ends.
In few, they hurried us aboard a bark,
Bore us some leagues to sea; where they prepared
A rotten carcass of a boat, not rigg'd,
Nor tackle, sail, nor mast; the very rats
Instinctively had quit it: there they hoist us,
To cry to the sea that roar'd to us, to sigh
To the winds whose pity, sighing back again,
Did us but loving wrong.

MIRANDA
Alack, what trouble
Was I then to you!
PROSPERO
O, a cherubim
Thou wast that did preserve me. Thou didst smile.
Infused with a fortitude from heaven,
When I have deck'd the sea with drops full salt,
Under my burthen groan'd; which raised in me
An undergoing stomach, to bear up
Against what should ensue.

MIRANDA
How came we ashore?
PROSPERO
By Providence divine.
Some food we had and some fresh water that
A noble Neapolitan, Gonzalo,
Out of his charity, being then appointed
Master of this design, did give us, with
Rich garments, linens, stuffs and necessaries,
Which since have steaded much; so, of his gentleness,
Knowing I loved my books, he furnish'd me
From mine own library with volumes that
I prize above my dukedom.

MIRANDA
Would I might
But ever see that man!
PROSPERO
Now I arise:
Sit still, and hear the last of our sea-sorrow.
Here in this island we arrived; and here
Have I, thy schoolmaster, made thee more profit
Than other princesses can that have more time
For vainer hours and tutors not so careful.

MIRANDA
Heavens thank you for't! And now, I pray you, sir,
For still 'tis beating in my mind, your reason
For raising this sea-storm?

PROSPERO
Know thus far forth.
By accident most strange, bountiful Fortune,
Now my dear lady, hath mine enemies
Brought to this shore; and by my prescience
I find my zenith doth depend upon
A most auspicious star, whose influence
If now I court not but omit, my fortunes
Will ever after droop. Here cease more questions:
Thou art inclined to sleep; 'tis a good dulness,
And give it way: I know thou canst not choose.

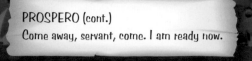

PROSPERO (cont.)

Come away, servant, come. I am ready now.

PROSPERO (cont.)

Approach, my Ariel, come.

ARIEL

All hail, great master! grave sir, hail! I come
To answer thy best pleasure; be't to fly,
To swim, to dive into the fire, to ride
On the curl'd clouds, to thy strong bidding task
Ariel and all his quality.

PROSPERO

Hast thou, spirit,
Perform'd to point the tempest that I bade thee?

ARIEL

To every article.
I boarded the king's ship; now on the beak,
Now in the waist, the deck, in every cabin,
I flamed amazement: sometime I'ld divide,
And burn in many places; on the topmast,
The yards and bowsprit, would I flame distinctly,
Then meet and join.

ARIEL (cont.)

Jove's lightnings, the precursors
O' the dreadful thunder-claps, more momentary
And sight-outrunning were not; the fire and cracks
Of sulphurous roaring the most mighty Neptune
Seem to besiege and make his bold waves tremble,
Yea, his dread trident shake.

PROSPERO

My brave spirit!

Who was so firm, so constant, that this coil

Would not infect his reason?

ARIEL

Not a soul

But felt a fever of the mad and play'd

Some tricks of desperation. All but mariners

Plunged in the foaming brine and quit the vessel,

Then all afire with me: the king's son, Ferdinand,

With hair up-staring,—then like reeds, not hair,—

Was the first man that leap'd; cried, "Hell is empty

And all the devils are here."

PROSPERO

Why that's my spirit!

But was not this nigh shore?

ARIEL

Close by, my master.

PROSPERO

But are they, Ariel, safe?

ARIEL

Not a hair perish'd;

On their sustaining garments not a blemish,

But fresher than before: and, as thou badest me,

In troops I have dispersed them 'bout the isle.

The king's son have I landed by himself;

Whom I left cooling of the air with sighs

In an odd angle of the isle and sitting,

His arms in this sad knot.

PROSPERO

Of the king's ship

The mariners say how thou hast disposed

And all the rest o' the fleet.

ARIEL

Safely in harbour

Is the king's ship; in the deep nook, where once

Thou call'dst me up at midnight to fetch dew

From the still-vex'd Bermoothes, there she's hid:

The mariners all under hatches stow'd;

Who, with a charm join'd to their suffer'd labour,

I have left asleep; and for the rest o' the fleet

Which I dispersed, they all have met again

And are upon the Mediterranean flote,

Bound sadly home for Naples,

Supposing that they saw the king's ship wreck'd

And his great person perish.

**PROSPERO**
Ariel, thy charge
Exactly is perform'd: but there's more work.
What is the time o' the day?
**ARIEL**
Past the mid season.
**PROSPERO**
At least two glasses. The time 'twixt six and now
Must by us both be spent most preciously.

**ARIEL**
Is there more toil? Since thou dost give me pains,
Let me remember thee what thou hast promised,
Which is not yet perform'd me.
**PROSPERO**
How now? moody?
What is't thou canst demand?
**ARIEL**
My liberty.

**PROSPERO**
Before the time be out? no more!
**ARIEL**
I prithee,
Remember I have done thee worthy service;
Told thee no lies, made thee no mistakings, served
Without or grudge or grumblings: thou didst promise
To bate me a full year.

**PROSPERO**
Dost thou forget
From what a torment I did free thee?
**ARIEL**
No.

PROSPERO

Thou dost, and think'st it much to tread the ooze

Of the salt deep,

To run upon the sharp wind of the north,

To do me business in the veins o' the earth

When it is baked with frost.

ARIEL

I do not, sir.

PROSPERO

Thou liest, malignant thing! Hast thou forgot

The foul witch Sycorax, who with age and envy

Was grown into a hoop? hast thou forgot her?

ARIEL

No, sir.

PROSPERO

Thou hast. Where was she born? speak; tell me.

ARIEL

Sir, in Argier.

PROSPERO

O, was she so? I must

Once in a month recount what thou hast been,

Which thou forget'st. This damn'd witch Sycorax,

For mischiefs manifold and sorceries terrible

To enter human hearing, from Argier,

Thou know'st, was banish'd: for one thing she did

They would not take her life. Is not this true?

ARIEL

Ay, sir.

PROSPERO
This blue-eyed hag was hither brought with child
And here was left by the sailors. Thou, my slave,
As thou report'st thyself, wast then her servant;
And, for thou wast a spirit too delicate
To act her earthy and abhorr'd commands,
Refusing her grand hests, she did confine thee,
By help of her more potent ministers
And in her most unmitigable rage,
Into a cloven pine; within which rift
Imprison'd thou didst painfully remain
A dozen years; within which space she died
And left thee there; where thou didst vent thy groans
As fast as mill-wheels strike. Then was this island—
Save for the son that she did litter here,
A freckled whelp hag-born—not honour'd with
A human shape.

ARIEL
Yes, Caliban her son.
PROSPERO
Dull thing, I say so; he, that Caliban
Whom now I keep in service. Thou best know'st
What torment I did find thee in; thy groans
Did make wolves howl and penetrate the breasts
Of ever angry bears: it was a torment
To lay upon the damn'd, which Sycorax
Could not again undo: it was mine art,
When I arrived and heard thee, that made gape
The pine and let thee out.
ARIEL
I thank thee, master.

PROSPERO
If thou more murmur'st, I will rend an oak
And peg thee in his knotty entrails till
Thou hast howl'd away twelve winters.

ARIEL
Pardon, master;
I will be correspondent to command
And do my spiriting gently.

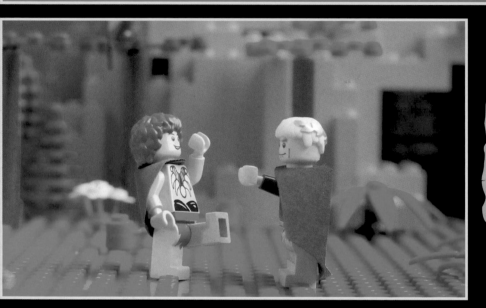

PROSPERO
Do so, and after two days
I will discharge thee.
ARIEL
That's my noble master!
What shall I do? say what; what shall I do?

PROSPERO
Go make thyself like a nymph o' the sea: be subject
To no sight but thine and mine, invisible
To every eyeball else. Go take this shape
And hither come in't: go, hence with diligence!

# ACT I. Scene II (306–375).

T

P rospero sends Ariel on his errand and then wakes Miranda. They are going to visit Caliban.

PROSPERO
Awake, dear heart, awake! thou hast slept well;
Awake!
MIRANDA
The strangeness of your story put
Heaviness in me.

PROSPERO
Shake it off. Come on;
We'll visit Caliban my slave, who never
Yields us kind answer.

MIRANDA
'Tis a villain, sir,
I do not love to look on.
PROSPERO
But, as 'tis,
We cannot miss him: he does make our fire,
Fetch in our wood and serves in offices
That profit us.

PROSPERO (cont.)
What, ho! slave! Caliban!
Thou earth, thou! speak.
CALIBAN
There's wood enough within.
PROSPERO
Come forth, I say! there's other business for thee:
Come, thou tortoise! when?

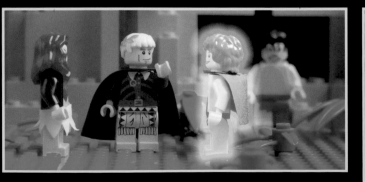

PROSPERO (cont.)
Fine apparition! My quaint Ariel,
Hark in thine ear.

ARIEL
My lord it shall be done.

PROSPERO
Thou poisonous slave, got by the devil himself
Upon thy wicked dam, come forth!

CALIBAN
As wicked dew as e'er my mother brush'd
With raven's feather from unwholesome fen
Drop on you both! a south-west blow on ye
And blister you all o'er!
PROSPERO
For this, be sure, to-night thou shalt have cramps,
Side-stitches that shall pen thy breath up; urchins
Shall, for that vast of night that they may work,
All exercise on thee; thou shalt be pinch'd
As thick as honeycomb, each pinch more stinging
Than bees that made 'em.

CALIBAN
I must eat my dinner.
This island's mine, by Sycorax my mother,
Which thou takest from me. When thou camest first,
Thou strokedst me and madest much of me, wouldst give me
Water with berries in't, and teach me how
To name the bigger light, and how the less,
That burn by day and night: and then I loved thee
And show'd thee all the qualities o' the isle,
The fresh springs, brine-pits, barren place and fertile:
Cursed be I that did so! All the charms
Of Sycorax, toads, beetles, bats, light on you!
For I am all the subjects that you have,
Which first was mine own king: and here you sty me
In this hard rock, whiles you do keep from me
The rest o' the island.

PROSPERO
Thou most lying slave,
Whom stripes may move, not kindness! I have used thee,
Filth as thou art, with human care, and lodged thee
In mine own cell,

**PROSPERO** (cont.)
till thou didst seek to violate
The honour of my child.

**CALIBAN**
O ho, O ho! would 't had been done!
Thou didst prevent me; I had peopled else
This isle with Calibans.

**PROSPERO**
Abhorred slave,
Which any print of goodness wilt not take,
Being capable of all ill! I pitied thee,
Took pains to make thee speak, taught thee each hour
One thing or other: when thou didst not, savage,
Know thine own meaning, but wouldst gabble like
A thing most brutish, I endow'd thy purposes
With words that made them known. But thy vile race,
Though thou didst learn, had that in't which good natures
Could not abide to be with; therefore wast thou
Deservedly confined into this rock,
Who hadst deserved more than a prison.

**CALIBAN**
You taught me language; and my profit on't
Is, I know how to curse. The red plague rid you
For learning me your language!
**PROSPERO**
Hag-seed, hence!
Fetch us in fuel; and be quick, thou'rt best,
To answer other business. Shrug'st thou, malice?
If thou neglect'st or dost unwillingly
What I command, I'll rack thee with old cramps,
Fill all thy bones with aches, make thee roar
That beasts shall tremble at thy din.

**CALIBAN**
No, pray thee.
I must obey: his art is of such power,
It would control my dam's god, Setebos,
and make a vassal of him.
**PROSPERO**
So, slave; hence!

# ACT I. Scene II (376–505).

**A**riel returns, leading young Ferdinand with a song.

**ARIEL:**
Come unto these yellow sands,
And then take hands:
Courtsied when you have and kiss'd
The wild waves whist,
Foot it featly here and there;

And, sweet sprites, the burthen bear.
Hark, hark!
The watch-dogs bark!
Hark, hark! I hear
The strain of strutting chanticleer
Cry, Cock-a-diddle-dow.

**FERDINAND**
Where should this music be? i' the air or the earth?
It sounds no more: and sure, it waits upon
Some god o' the island. Sitting on a bank,
Weeping again the king my father's wreck,
This music crept by me upon the waters,
Allaying both their fury and my passion
With its sweet air: thence I have follow'd it,
Or it hath drawn me rather. But 'tis gone.
No, it begins again.

**ARIEL**
Full fathom five thy father lies;
Of his bones are coral made;
Those are pearls that were his eyes:
Nothing of him that doth fade
But doth suffer a sea-change
Into something rich and strange.
Sea-nymphs hourly ring his knell
Hark! now I hear them,—Ding-dong, bell.

**FERDINAND**
The ditty does remember my drown'd father.
This is no mortal business, nor no sound
That the earth owes. I hear it now above me.

**PROSPERO**
The fringed curtains of thine eye advance
And say what thou seest yond.

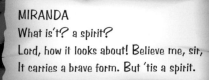

**MIRANDA**
What is't? a spirit?
Lord, how it looks about! Believe me, sir,
It carries a brave form. But 'tis a spirit.

**PROSPERO**
No, wench; it eats and sleeps and hath such senses
As we have, such. This gallant which thou seest
Was in the wreck; and, but he's something stain'd
With grief that's beauty's canker, thou mightst call him
A goodly person: he hath lost his fellows
And strays about to find 'em.

**MIRANDA**
I might call him
A thing divine, for nothing natural
I ever saw so noble.

**PROSPERO**
It goes on, I see,
As my soul prompts it. Spirit, fine spirit! I'll free thee
Within two days for this.

**FERDINAND**
Most sure, the goddess
On whom these airs attend! Vouchsafe my prayer
May know if you remain upon this island;
And that you will some good instruction give
How I may bear me here: my prime request,
Which I do last pronounce, is, O you wonder!
If you be maid or no?

119

MIRANDA
No wonder, sir;
But certainly a maid.

FERDINAND
My language! heavens!
I am the best of them that speak this speech,
Were I but where 'tis spoken.

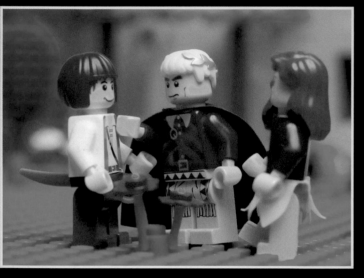

PROSPERO
How? the best?
What wert thou, if the King of Naples heard thee?

FERDINAND
A single thing, as I am now, that wonders
To hear thee speak of Naples. He does hear me;
And that he does I weep: myself am Naples,
Who with mine eyes, never since at ebb, beheld
The king my father wreck'd.

MIRANDA
Alack, for mercy!
FERDINAND
Yes, faith, and all his lords; the Duke of Milan
And his brave son being twain.

PROSPERO
The Duke of Milan
And his more braver daughter could control thee,
If now 'twere fit to do't. At the first sight
They have changed eyes. Delicate Ariel,
I'll set thee free for this.

PROSPERO (cont.)
A word, good sir;
I fear you have done yourself some wrong: a word.

MIRANDA
Why speaks my father so ungently? This
Is the third man that e'er I saw, the first
That e'er I sigh'd for: pity move my father
To be inclined my way!

FERDINAND
O, if a virgin,
And your affection not gone forth, I'll make you
The queen of Naples.

PROSPERO
Soft, sir! one word more.
They are both in either's powers; but this swift business
I must uneasy make, lest too light winning
Make the prize light.

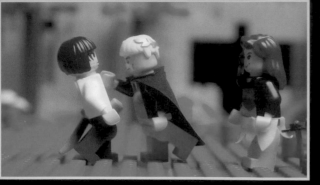

PROSPERO (cont.)
One word more; I charge thee
That thou attend me: thou dost here usurp
The name thou owest not; and hast put thyself
Upon this island as a spy, to win it
From me, the lord on't.

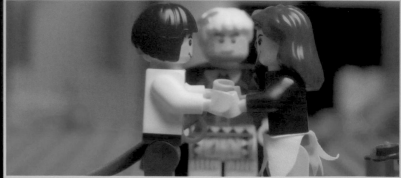

FERDINAND
No, as I am a man.
MIRANDA
There's nothing ill can dwell in such a temple:
If the ill spirit have so fair a house,
Good things will strive to dwell with't.

PROSPERO
Follow me.
Speak not you for him; he's a traitor. Come;
I'll manacle thy neck and feet together:
Sea-water shalt thou drink; thy food shall be
The fresh-brook muscles, wither'd roots and husks
Wherein the acorn cradled. Follow.

FERDINAND
No;
I will resist such entertainment till
Mine enemy has more power.

MIRANDA
O dear father,
Make not too rash a trial of him, for
He's gentle and not fearful.

PROSPERO
What? I say,
My foot my tutor?

PROSPERO (cont.)
Put thy sword up, traitor;
Who makest a show but darest not strike, thy conscience
Is so possess'd with guilt: come from thy ward,
For I can here disarm thee with this stick
And make thy weapon drop.

MIRANDA
Beseech you, father.
PROSPERO
Hence! hang not on my garments.

MIRANDA
Sir, have pity;
I'll be his surety.

PROSPERO
Silence! one word more
Shall make me chide thee, if not hate thee. What!
An advocate for an imposter! hush!
Thou think'st there is no more such shapes as he,
Having seen but him and Caliban: foolish wench!
To the most of men this is a Caliban
And they to him are angels.

MIRANDA
My affections
Are then most humble; I have no ambition
To see a goodlier man.

PROSPERO
Come on; obey:
Thy nerves are in their infancy again
And have no vigour in them.

**FERDINAND**
So they are;
My spirits, as in a dream, are all bound up.
My father's loss, the weakness which I feel,
The wreck of all my friends, nor this man's threats,
To whom I am subdued, are but light to me,
Might I but through my prison once a day
Behold this maid: all corners else o' the earth
Let liberty make use of; space enough
Have I in such a prison.

**PROSPERO**
It works.

**PROSPERO**
Come on.
Thou hast done well, fine Ariel!
Follow me.
Hark what thou else shalt do me.

**MIRANDA**
Be of comfort;
My father's of a better nature, sir,
Than he appears by speech: this is unwonted
Which now came from him.

**PROSPERO**
Thou shalt be free
As mountain winds: but then exactly do
All points of my command.
**ARIEL**
To the syllable.

**PROSPERO**
Come, follow. Speak not for him.

# ACT II. Scene I (186–322).

T

On another part of the island, the other shipwreck victims have found each other and are making their way across the island looking for Ferdinand. They have walked for a while, bickering and chatting. Ariel arrives, unseen by the men, and plays quiet music, bewitching them. All except Alonso, Sebastian, and Antonio lay down to sleep.

ALONSO
What, all so soon asleep! I wish mine eyes
Would, with themselves, shut up my thoughts: I find
They are inclined to do so.

SEBASTIAN
Please you, sir,
Do not omit the heavy offer of it:
It seldom visits sorrow; when it doth,
It is a comforter.
ANTONIO
We two, my lord,
Will guard your person while you take your rest,
And watch your safety.
ALONSO
Thank you. Wondrous heavy.

SEBASTIAN
What a strange drowsiness possesses them!

ANTONIO
It is the quality o' the climate.

SEBASTIAN
Why
Doth it not then our eyelids sink? I find not
Myself disposed to sleep.
ANTONIO
Nor I; my spirits are nimble.
They fell together all, as by consent;
They dropp'd, as by a thunder-stroke. What might,
Worthy Sebastian? O, what might?—No more:—
And yet me thinks I see it in thy face,
What thou shouldst be: the occasion speaks thee, and
My strong imagination sees a crown
Dropping upon thy head.

SEBASTIAN
What, art thou waking?
ANTONIO
Do you not hear me speak?

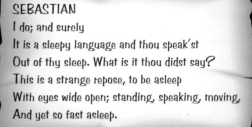

SEBASTIAN
I do; and surely
It is a sleepy language and thou speak'st
Out of thy sleep. What is it thou didst say?
This is a strange repose, to be asleep
With eyes wide open; standing, speaking, moving,
And yet so fast asleep.

ANTONIO
Noble Sebastian,
Thou let'st thy fortune sleep—die, rather; wink'st
Whiles thou art waking.

SEBASTIAN
Thou dost snore distinctly;
There's meaning in thy snores.

ANTONIO
I am more serious than my custom: you
Must be so too, if heed me; which to do
Trebles thee o'er.
SEBASTIAN
Well, I am standing water.

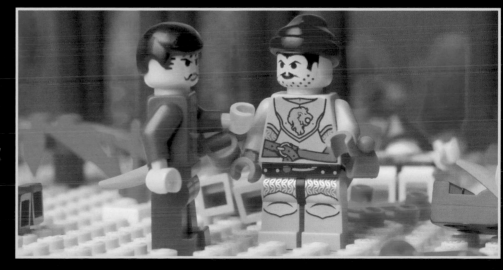

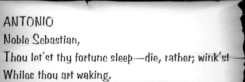

ANTONIO
I'll teach you how to flow.
SEBASTIAN
Do so: to ebb
Hereditary sloth instructs me.
ANTONIO
O,
If you but knew how you the purpose cherish
Whiles thus you mock it! how, in stripping it,
You more invest it! Ebbing men, indeed,
Most often do so near the bottom run
By their own fear or sloth.

SEBASTIAN
Prithee, say on:
The setting of thine eye and cheek proclaim
A matter from thee, and a birth indeed
Which throes thee much to yield.
ANTONIO
Thus, sir:
Although this lord of weak remembrance, this,
Who shall be of as little memory
When he is earth'd, hath here almost persuade,—
For he's a spirit of persuasion, only
Professes to persuade,—the king his son's alive,
'Tis as impossible that he's undrown'd
And he that sleeps here swims.

SEBASTIAN
I have no hope
That he's undrown'd.
ANTONIO
O, out of that "no hope"
What great hope have you! no hope that way is
Another way so high a hope that even
Ambition cannot pierce a wink beyond,
But doubt discovery there. Will you grant with me
That Ferdinand is drown'd?
SEBASTIAN
He's gone.

ANTONIO
Then, tell me,
Who's the next heir of Naples?
SEBASTIAN
Claribel.
ANTONIO
She that is queen of Tunis; she that dwells
Ten leagues beyond man's life; she that from Naples
Can have no note, unless the sun were post—
The man i' the moon's too slow—till new-born chins
Be rough and razorable; she that—from whom?
We all were sea-swallow'd, though some cast again,
And by that destiny to perform an act
Whereof what's past is prologue, what to come
In yours and my discharge.

SEBASTIAN
What stuff is this! how say you?
'Tis true, my brother's daughter's queen of Tunis;
So is she heir of Naples; 'twixt which regions
There is some space.

ANTONIO
A space whose every cubit
Seems to cry out, "How shall that Claribel
Measure us back to Naples? Keep in Tunis,
And let Sebastian wake." Say, this were death
That now hath seized them; why, they were no worse
Than now they are. There be that can rule Naples
As well as he that sleeps; lords that can prate
As amply and unnecessarily
As this Gonzalo; I myself could make
A chough of as deep chat. O, that you bore
The mind that I do! what a sleep were this
For your advancement! Do you understand me?

SEBASTIAN
Methinks I do.
ANTONIO
And how does your content
Tender your own good fortune?

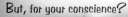

SEBASTIAN
I remember
You did supplant your brother Prospero.
ANTONIO
True:
And look how well my garments sit upon me;
Much feater than before: my brother's servants
Were then my fellows; now they are my men.
SEBASTIAN
But, for your conscience?

ANTONIO
Ay, sir; where lies that? if 'twere a kibe,
'Twould put me to my slipper: but I feel not
This deity in my bosom: twenty consciences,
That stand 'twixt me and Milan, candied be they
And melt ere they molest!

ANTONIO (cont.)
Here lies your brother,
No better than the earth he lies upon,
If he were that which now he's like, that's dead;
Whom I, with this obedient steel, three inches of it,
Can lay to bed for ever; whiles you, doing thus,
To the perpetual wink for aye might put
This ancient morsel, this Sir Prudence, who
Should not upbraid our course. For all the rest,
They'll take suggestion as a cat laps milk;
They'll tell the clock to any business that
We say befits the hour.

SEBASTIAN
Thy case, dear friend,
Shall be my precedent; as thou got'st Milan,
I'll come by Naples. Draw thy sword: one stroke
Shall free thee from the tribute which thou payest;
And I the king shall love thee.
ANTONIO
Draw together;
And when I rear my hand, do you the like,
To fall it on Gonzalo.
SEBASTIAN
O, but one word.

ARIEL

My master through his art foresees the danger
That you, his friend, are in; and sends me forth—
For else his project dies—to keep them living.

ARIEL (cont.)
While you here do snoring lie,
Open-eyed conspiracy
His time doth take.
If of life you keep a care,
Shake off slumber, and beware:
Awake, awake!
ANTONIO
Then let us both be sudden.

GONZALO
Now, good angels
Preserve the king.

ALONSO
Why, how now? ho, awake! Why are you drawn?
Wherefore this ghastly looking?
GONZALO
What's the matter?

SEBASTIAN
Whiles we stood here securing your repose,
Even now, we heard a hollow burst of bellowing
Like bulls, or rather lions: did not wake you?
It struck mine ear most terribly.

**ALONSO**
I heard nothing.

**ANTONIO**
O, 'twas a din to fright a monster's ear,
To make an earthquake! sure, it was the roar
Of a whole herd of lions.

**ALONSO**
Heard you this, Gonzalo?
**GONZALO**
Upon mine honour, sir, I heard a humming,
And that a strange one too, which did awake me:
I shaked you, sir, and cried: as mine eyes open'd,
I saw their weapons drawn: there was a noise,
That's verily. 'Tis best we stand upon our guard,
Or that we quit this place; let's draw our weapons.

**ALONSO**
Lead off this ground; and let's make further search
For my poor son.
**GONZALO**
Heavens keep him from these beasts!
For he is, sure, i' the island.
**ALONSO**
Lead away.

**ARIEL**
Prospero my lord shall know what I have done:
So, king, go safely on to seek thy son.

T

*C*aliban has been sent to collect firewood for Prospero. He meets some interesting new friends.

CALIBAN

All the infections that the sun sucks up
From bogs, fens, flats, on Prosper fall and make him
By inch-meal a disease! His spirits hear me
And yet I needs must curse. But they'll nor pinch,
Fright me with urchin—shows, pitch me i' the mire,
Nor lead me, like a firebrand, in the dark
Out of my way, unless he bid 'em; but
For every trifle are they set upon me;
Sometime like apes that mow and chatter at me
And after bite me, then like hedgehogs which
Lie tumbling in my barefoot way and mount
Their pricks at my footfall; sometime am I
All wound with adders who with cloven tongues
Do hiss me into madness.

CALIBAN (cont.)

Lo, now, lo!
Here comes a spirit of his, and to torment me
For bringing wood in slowly. I'll fall flat;
Perchance he will not mind me.

TRINCULO

Here's neither bush nor shrub, to bear off
any weather at all, and another storm brewing;
I hear it sing i' the wind: yond same black
cloud, yond huge one, looks like a foul
bombard that would shed his liquor. If it
should thunder as it did before, I know not
where to hide my head: yond same cloud cannot
choose but fall by pailfuls. What have we
here? a man or a fish? dead or alive? A fish:
he smells like a fish; a very ancient and fish-
like smell; a kind of not of the newest Poor-
John. A strange fish! Were I in England now,
as once I was, and had but this fish painted,
not a holiday fool there but would give a piece
of silver: there would this monster make a
man; any strange beast there makes a man:
when they will not give a doit to relieve a lame
beggar, they will lazy out ten to see a dead
Indian. Legged like a man and his fins like
arms!

TRINCULO (cont.)

Warm o' my troth! I do now let loose
my opinion; hold it no longer: this is no fish,
but an islander, that hath lately suffered by a thunderbolt.
Alas, the storm is come again! my best way is to
creep under his gaberdine; there is no other
shelter hereabouts: misery acquaints a man with
strange bed-fellows. I will here shroud till the
dregs of the storm be past.

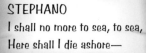

**STEPHANO**
I shall no more to sea, to sea,
Here shall I die ashore—

**STEPHANO (cont.)**
This is a very scurvy tune to sing at a man's
funeral: well, here's my comfort.

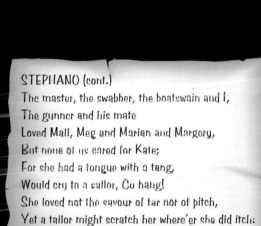

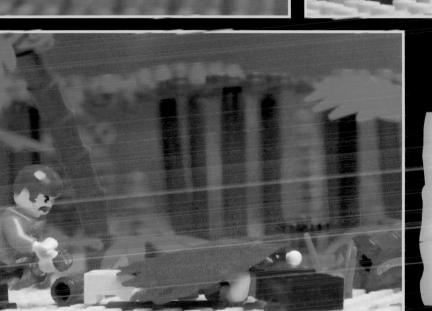

**STEPHANO (cont.)**
The master, the swabber, the boatswain and I,
The gunner and his mate
Loved Mall, Meg and Marian and Margory,
But none of us cared for Kate;
For she had a tongue with a tang,
Would cry to a sailor, Go hang!
She loved not the savour of tar nor of pitch,
Yet a tailor might scratch her where'er she did itch:
Then to sea, boys, and let her go hang!

**STEPHANO (cont.)**
This is a scurvy tune too: but here's my comfort.

**CALIBAN**
Do not torment me: Oh!

CALIBAN
The spirit torments me; Oh!

STEPHANO
This is some monster of the isle with four legs, who hath got, as I take it, an ague. Where the devil should he learn our language? I will give him some relief, if it be but for that. If I can recover him and keep him tame and get to Naples with him, he's a present for any emperor that ever trod on neat's leather.

**CALIBAN**
Do not torment me, prithee; I'll bring my wood home faster.
**STEPHANO**
He's in his fit now and does not talk after the wisest. He shall taste of my bottle: if he have never drunk wine afore will go near to remove his fit. If I can recover him and keep him tame, I will not take too much for him; he shall pay for him that hath him, and that soundly.

**CALIBAN**
Thou dost me yet but little hurt; thou will anon, I know it by thy trembling: now Prosper works upon thee.
**STEPHANO**
Come on your ways; open your mouth; here is that which will give language to you, cat: open your mouth; this will shake your shaking, I can tell you, and that soundly: you cannot tell who's your friend: open your chaps again.

**TRINCULO**
I should know that voice: it should be—but he is drowned; and these are devils: O defend me!

**STEPHANO**
Four legs and two voices: a most delicate monster! His forward voice now is to speak well of his friend; his backward voice is to utter foul speeches and to detract. If all the wine in my bottle will recover him, I will help his ague. Come. Amen! I will pour some in thy other mouth.

**TRINCULO**
Stephano!
**STEPHANO**
Doth thy other mouth call me? Mercy, mercy! This is a devil, and no monster: I will leave him; I have no long spoon.
**TRINCULO**
Stephano! If thou beest Stephano, touch me and speak to me: for I am Trinculo—be not afeard—thy good friend Trinculo.

**STEPHANO**
If thou beest Trinculo, come forth: I'll pull thee by the lesser legs: if any be Trinculo's legs, these are they. Thou art very Trinculo indeed! How camest thou to be the siege of this moon-calf? can he vent Trinculos?
**TRINCULO**
I took him to be killed with a thunder-stroke. But art thou not drowned, Stephano? I hope now thou art not drowned. Is the storm overblown? I hid me under the dead moon-calf's gaberdine for fear of the storm. And art thou living, Stephano? O Stephano, two Neapolitans 'scaped!
**STEPHANO**
Prithee, do not turn me about; my stomach is not constant.

CALIBAN
These be fine things, an if they be not sprites.
That's a brave god and bears celestial liquor.
I will kneel to him.

STEPHANO
How didst thou 'scape? How camest thou hither?
swear by this bottle how thou camest hither. I
escaped upon a butt of sack which the sailors
heaved o'erboard, by this bottle; which I made of
the bark of a tree with mine own hands since I was
cast ashore.

CALIBAN
I'll swear upon that bottle to be thy true subject;
for the liquor is not earthly.
STEPHANO
Here; swear then how thou escapedst.

TRINCULO
Swum ashore. man, like a duck: I can swim like a
duck, I'll be sworn.

**STEPHANO**
Here, kiss the book. Though thou canst swim like a duck, thou art made like a goose.

**TRINCULO**
O Stephano, hast any more of this?

**STEPHANO**
The whole butt, man: my cellar is in a rock by the sea-side where my wine is hid. How now, moon-calf! how does thine ague?

**CALIBAN**
Hast thou not dropp'd from heaven?

**STEPHANO**
Out o' the moon, I do assure thee: I was the man i' the moon when time was.

**CALIBAN**
I have seen thee in her and I do adore thee: My mistress show'd me thee and thy dog and thy bush.

**STEPHANO**
Come, swear to that; kiss the book: I will furnish it anon with new contents swear.

**TRINCULO**
By this good light, this is a very shallow monster! I afeard of him! A very weak monster! The man i' the moon! A most poor credulous monster! Well drawn, monster, in good sooth!

CALIBAN
I'll show thee every fertile inch o' th' island;
And I will kiss thy foot: I prithee, be my god.
TRINCULO
By this light, a most perfidious and drunken
monster! when 's god's asleep, he'll rob his bottle.
CALIBAN
I'll kiss thy foot; I'll swear myself thy subject.
STEPHANO
Come on then; down, and swear.

TRINCULO
I shall laugh myself to death at this puppy-headed
monster. A most scurvy monster! I could find in my
heart to beat him,—
STEPHANO
Come, kiss.
TRINCULO
But that the poor monster's in drink: an abominable monster!

CALIBAN
I'll show thee the best springs; I'll pluck thee berries;
I'll fish for thee and get thee wood enough.
A plague upon the tyrant that I serve!
I'll bear him no more sticks, but follow thee,
Thou wondrous man.
TRINCULO
A most ridiculous monster, to make a wonder of a
Poor drunkard!

**STEPHANO**
I prithee now, lead the way without any more talking. Trinculo, the king and all our company else being drowned, we will inherit here: here; bear my bottle: fellow Trinculo, we'll fill him by and by again.

**CALIBAN**
Farewell master; farewell, farewell!

**TRINCULO**
A howling monster: a drunken monster!

**CALIBAN**
I prithee, let me bring thee where crabs grow;
And I with my long nails will dig thee pignuts;
Show thee a jay's nest and instruct thee how
To snare the nimble marmoset; I'll bring thee
To clustering filberts and sometimes I'll get thee
Young scamels from the rock. Wilt thou go with me?

**CALIBAN**
No more dams I'll make for fish
Nor fetch in firing
At requiring;
Nor scrape trencher, nor wash dish
'Ban, 'Ban, Cacaliban
Has a new master: get a new man.
Freedom, hey-day! hey-day, freedom! freedom,
hey-day, freedom!

**STEPHANO**
O brave monster! Lead the way.

# ACT III. Scene III (1–110).

T

**P**rospero's plan is moving smoothly on all fronts. He has pressed Ferdinand
into servitude, which has given Ferdinand and Miranda time to speak
together and fall quickly in love. Ariel is keeping an eye on Caliban and the
drunken fools Stephano and Trinculo, who have gotten even drunker and have
now decided to kill the master of the island, take the island for their own, and
take his daughter as well. Ariel pranks them and makes them fight, but the
fools are hardly a threat. Meanwhile, Alonso and the men continue their search
for Ferdinand, while Sebastian and Antonio await their chance to kill him and
Gonzalo.

GONZALO

By'r lakin, I can go no further, sir;
My old bones ache: here's a maze trod indeed
Through forth-rights and meanders! By your patience,
I needs must rest me.

ALONSO

Old lord, I cannot blame thee,
Who am myself attach'd with weariness,
To the dulling of my spirits: sit down, and rest.
Even here I will put off my hope and keep it
No longer for my flatterer: he is drown'd
Whom thus we stray to find, and the sea mocks
Our frustrate search on land. Well, let him go.

ANTONIO

I am right glad that he's so out of hope.
Do not, for one repulse, forego the purpose
That you resolved to effect.

SEBASTIAN

The next advantage
Will we take throughly.

ANTONIO

Let it be to-night;
For, now they are oppress'd with travel, they
Will not, nor cannot, use such vigilance
As when they are fresh.

SEBASTIAN

I say, to-night: no more.

ALONSO

What harmony is this? My good friends, hark!

GONZALO

Marvellous sweet music!

ALONSO

Give us kind keepers, heavens! What were these?

SEBASTIAN

A living drollery. Now I will believe
That there are unicorns, that in Arabia
There is one tree, the phoenix' throne, one phoenix
At this hour reigning there.

**GONZALO**
If in Naples
I should report this now, would they believe me?
If I should say, I saw such islanders—
For, certes, these are people of the island—
Who, though they are of monstrous shape, yet, note,
Their manners are more gentle-kind than of
Our human generation you shall find
Many, nay, almost any.

**ANTONIO**
I'll believe both;
And what does else want credit, come to me,
And I'll be sworn 'tis true: Travellers ne'er did lie,
Though fools at home condemn 'em.

**PROSPERO**
Honest lord,
Thou hast said well; for some of you there present
Are worse than devils.

**ALONSO**
I cannot too much muse
Such shapes, such gesture and such sound, expressing,
Although they want the use of tongue, a kind
Of excellent dumb discourse.

**PROSPERO**
Praise in departing.

**FRANCISCO**
They vanish'd strangely.

**SEBASTIAN**
No matter, since
They have left their viands behind; for we have stomachs.
Will't please you taste of what is here?

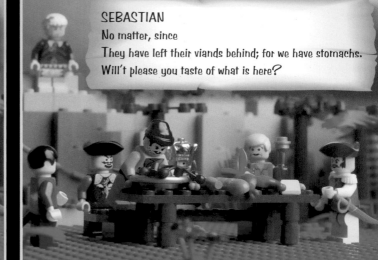

**ALONSO**
Not I.
**GONZALO**
Faith, sir, you need not fear. When we were boys,
Who would believe that there were mountaineers
Dew-lapp'd like bulls, whose throats had hanging at 'em
Wallets of flesh? or that there were such men
Whose heads stood in their breasts? which now we find
Each putter-out of five for one will bring us
Good warrant of.

ALONSO
I will stand to and feed,
Although my last: no matter, since I feel
The best is past. Brother, my lord the duke,
Stand to and do as we.

ARIEL
You are three men of sin, whom Destiny,
That hath to instrument this lower world
And what is in't, the never-surfeited sea
Hath caused to belch up you; and on this island
Where man doth not inhabit; you 'mongst men
Being most unfit to live. I have made you mad;
And even with such-like valour men hang and drown
Their proper selves.

ARIEL (cont.)
You fools! I and my fellows
Are ministers of Fate: the elements,
Of whom your swords are temper'd, may as well
Wound the loud winds, or with bemock'd-at stabs
Kill the still-closing waters, as diminish
One dowle that's in my plume: my fellow-ministers
Are like invulnerable.

ARIEL (cont.)
If you could hurt,
Your swords are now too massy for your strengths
And will not be uplifted. But remember—
For that's my business to you—that you three
From Milan did supplant good Prospero;
Exposed unto the sea, which hath requit it,
Him and his innocent child: for which foul deed
The powers, delaying, not forgetting, have
Incensed the seas and shores, yea, all the creatures,
Against your peace.

ARIEL (cont.)
Thee of thy son, Alonso,
They have bereft; and do pronounce by me:
Lingering perdition, worse than any death
Can be at once, shall step by step attend
You and your ways; whose wraths to guard you from—
Which here, in this most desolate isle, else falls
Upon your heads—is nothing but heart-sorrow
And a clear life ensuing.

PROSPERO
Bravely the figure of this harpy hast thou
Perform'd, my Ariel; a grace it had, devouring:
Of my instruction hast thou nothing bated
In what thou hadst to say: so, with good life
And observation strange, my meaner ministers
Their several kinds have done.

PROSPERO (cont.)
My high charms work
And these mine enemies are all knit up
In their distractions; they now are in my power;
And in these fits I leave them, while I visit
Young Ferdinand, whom they suppose is drown'd,
And his and mine loved darling.

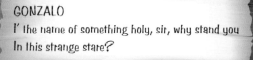

GONZALO
I' the name of something holy, sir, why stand you
In this strange stare?

ALONSO
O, it is monstrous, monstrous:
Methought the billows spoke and told me of it;
The winds did sing it to me, and the thunder,
That deep and dreadful organ-pipe, pronounced
The name of Prosper: it did bass my trespass.
Therefore my son i' the ooze is bedded, and
I'll seek him deeper than e'er plummet sounded
And with him there lie mudded.

SEBASTIAN
But one fiend at a time,
I'll fight their legions o'er.
ANTONIO
I'll be thy second.

GONZALO
All three of them are desperate: their great guilt,
Like poison given to work a great time after,
Now 'gins to bite the spirits. I do beseech you
That are of suppler joints, follow them swiftly
And hinder them from what this ecstasy
May now provoke them to.
ADRIAN
Follow, I pray you.

# ACT IV. Scene I (lines 165–264).

*P*rospero returns to Ferdinand and Miranda, who have meanwhile fallen in love (just as Prospero planned it!). Prospero gives Ferdinand his fatherly blessing to marry his daughter, then he then calls in his spirits to put on a special show for the couple. They are dazzled by the spectacle, but they are soon interrupted by Ariel, who reminds Prospero that Caliban and the drunken fools are on their way to kill him. Prospero ends the magic show abruptly to deal with them.

PROSPERO
Spirit,
We must prepare to meet with Caliban.
ARIEL
Ay, my commander: when I presented Ceres,
I thought to have told thee of it, but I fear'd
Lest I might anger thee.

ARIEL
Thy thoughts I cleave to. What's thy pleasure?

PROSPERO
Say again, where didst thou leave these varlets?
ARIEL
I told you, sir, they were red-hot with drinking;
So full of valour that they smote the air
For breathing in their faces; beat the ground
For kissing of their feet; yet always bending
Towards their project. Then I beat my tabour;
At which, like unback'd colts, they prick'd their ears,
Advanced their eyelids, lifted up their noses
As they smelt music:

ARIEL (cont.)
so I charm'd their ears
That calf-like they my lowing follow'd through
Tooth'd briers, sharp furzes, pricking goss and thorns,
Which entered their frail shins: at last I left them
I' the filthy-mantled pool beyond your cell,
There dancing up to the chins, that the foul lake
O'erstunk their feet.

PROSPERO
This was well done, my bird.
Thy shape invisible retain thou still:
The trumpery in my house, go bring it hither,
For stale to catch these thieves.
ARIEL
I go, I go.
PROSPERO
A devil, a born devil, on whose nature
Nurture can never stick; on whom my pains,
Humanely taken, all, all lost, quite lost;
And as with age his body uglier grows,
So his mind cankers.

PROSPERO (cont.)
I will plague them all,
Even to roaring. Come, hang them on this line.

CALIBAN
Pray you, tread softly, that the blind mole may not
Hear a foot fall: we now are near his cell.
STEPHANO
Monster, your fairy, which you say is
a harmless fairy, has done little better than
played the Jack with us.
TRINCULO
Monster, I do smell all horse-piss; at
which my nose is in great indignation.

STEPHANO
So is mine. Do you hear, monster? If I should take
a displeasure against you, look you,—
TRINCULO
Thou wert but a lost monster.

CALIBAN
Good my lord, give me thy favour still.
Be patient, for the prize I'll bring thee to
Shall hoodwink this mischance: therefore speak softly.
All's hush'd as midnight yet.
TRINCULO
Ay, but to lose our bottles in the pool,—

STEPHANO
There is not only disgrace and dishonour in that, monster, but
an infinite loss.
TRINCULO
That's more to me than my wetting: yet this is your harmless
fairy, monster.
STEPHANO
I will fetch off my bottle, though I be o'er ears for my labour.

**CALIBAN**
Prithee, my king, be quiet. Seest thou here,
This is the mouth o' the cell: no noise, and enter.
Do that good mischief which may make this island
Thine own for ever, and I, thy Caliban,
For aye thy foot-licker.

**STEPHANO**
Give me thy hand. I do begin to have bloody thoughts.
**TRINCULO**
O King Stephano! O peer! O worthy Stephano! look what a
wardrobe here is for thee!

**CALIBAN**
Let it alone, thou fool; it is but trash.

TRINCULO
O, ho, monster! we know what belongs to a frippery. O King Stephano!

STEPHANO
Put off that gown, Trinculo; by this hand, I'll have that gown.

TRINCULO
Thy grace shall have it.

CALIBAN
The dropsy drown this fool! What do you mean
To dote thus on such luggage? Let's alone
And do the murder first: if he awake,
From toe to crown he'll fill our skins with pinches,
Make us strange stuff.

STEPHANO
Be you quiet, monster. Mistress line, is not this my jerkin? Now is the jerkin under the line: now, jerkin, you are like to lose your hair and prove a bald jerkin.

TRINCULO
Do, do: we steal by line and level, an't like your grace.

STEPHANO
I thank thee for that jest; here's a garment for't: wit shall not go unrewarded while I am king of this country. "Steal by line and level" is an excellent pass of pate; there's another garment for't.

TRINCULO
Monster, come, put some lime upon your fingers, and away with the rest.

CALIBAN
I will have none on't: we shall lose our time,
And all be turn'd to barnacles, or to apes
With foreheads villanous low.

STEPHANO
Monster, lay-to your fingers: help to bear this away where my
hogshead of wine is, or I'll turn you out of my kingdom: go to, carry
this.

TRINCULO
And this.
STEPHANO
Ay, and this.

PROSPERO
Hey, Mountain, hey!
ARIEL
Silver! there it goes, Silver!

PROSPERO
Fury, Fury! there, Tyrant, there! hark! hark!
Go charge my goblins that they grind their joints
With dry convulsions, shorten up their sinews
With aged cramps, and more pinch-spotted make them
Than pard or cat o' mountain.
ARIEL
Hark, they roar!

PROSPERO
Let them be hunted soundly. At this hour
Lie at my mercy all mine enemies:
Shortly shall all my labours end, and thou
Shalt have the air at freedom: for a little
Follow, and do me service.

# ACT V. Scene I (lines 1–318).

**T**

**N**ow that Caliban and the fools have been taken care of, Prospero prepares for the final act in his grand plan.

PROSPERO

Now does my project gather to a head:
My charms crack not; my spirits obey; and time
Goes upright with his carriage. How's the day?

ARIEL

On the sixth hour; at which time, my lord,
You said our work should cease.

PROSPERO

I did say so,
When first I raised the tempest. Say, my spirit,
How fares the king and 's followers?

ARIEL

Confined together
In the same fashion as you gave in charge,
Just as you left them; all prisoners, sir,
In the line-grove which weather-fends your cell;
They cannot budge till your release.

ARIEL (cont.)

The king,
His brother and yours, abide all three distracted,
And the remainder mourning over them,
Brimful of sorrow and dismay; but chiefly
Him that you term'd, sir, "The good old lord Gonzalo;"
His tears run down his beard, like winter's drops
From eaves of reeds. Your charm so strongly works 'em
That if you now beheld them, your affections
Would become tender.

PROSPERO

Dost thou think so, spirit?

ARIEL

Mine would, sir, were I human.

PROSPERO

And mine shall.
Hast thou, which art but air, a touch, a feeling
Of their afflictions, and shall not myself,
One of their kind, that relish all as sharply,
Passion as they, be kindlier moved than thou art?
Though with their high wrongs I am struck to the quick,
Yet with my nobler reason 'gainst my fury
Do I take part: the rarer action is
In virtue than in vengeance: they being penitent,
The sole drift of my purpose doth extend
Not a frown further. Go release them, Ariel:
My charms I'll break, their senses I'll restore,
And they shall be themselves.

ARIEL

I'll fetch them, sir.

PROSPERO

Ye elves of hills, brooks, standing lakes and groves,
And ye that on the sands with printless foot
Do chase the ebbing Neptune and do fly him
When he comes back; you demi-puppets that
By moonshine do the green sour ringlets make,
Whereof the ewe not bites, and you whose pastime
Is to make midnight mushrooms, that rejoice
To hear the solemn curfew; by whose aid,
Weak masters though ye be, I have bedimm'd
The noontide sun, call'd forth the mutinous winds,
And 'twixt the green sea and the azured vault
Set roaring war: to the dread rattling thunder

PROSPERO (cont.)

Have I given fire and rifted Jove's stout oak
With his own bolt; the strong-based promontory
Have I made shake and by the spurs pluck'd up
The pine and cedar: graves at my command
Have waked their sleepers, oped, and let 'em forth
By my so potent art. But this rough magic
I here abjure, and, when I have required
Some heavenly music, which even now I do,
To work mine end upon their senses that
This airy charm is for, I'll break my staff,

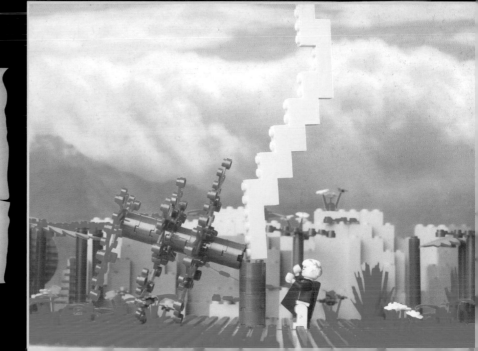

PROSPERO (cont.)
Bury it certain fathoms in the earth,
And deeper than did ever plummet sound
I'll drown my book.

PROSPERO (cont.)
A solemn air and the best comforter
To an unsettled fancy cure thy brains,
Now useless, boil'd within thy skull! There stand,
For you are spell-stopp'd.
Holy Gonzalo, honourable man,
Mine eyes, even sociable to the show of thine,
Fall fellowly drops. The charm dissolves apace,
And as the morning steals upon the night,
Melting the darkness, so their rising senses
Begin to chase the ignorant fumes that mantle
Their clearer reason. O good Gonzalo,
My true preserver, and a loyal sir
To him you follow'st! I will pay thy graces
Home both in word and deed.

PROSPERO (cont.)
Most cruelly
Didst thou, Alonso, use me and my daughter:
Thy brother was a furtherer in the act.
Thou art pinch'd for it now, Sebastian. Flesh and blood,
You, brother mine, that entertain'd ambition,
Expell'd remorse and nature; who, with Sebastian,
Whose inward pinches therefore are most strong,
Would here have kill'd your king; I do forgive thee,
Unnatural though thou art.

**PROSPERO (cont.)**
Their understanding
Begins to swell, and the approaching tide
Will shortly fill the reasonable shore
That now lies foul and muddy. Not one of them
That yet looks on me, or would know me Ariel,
Fetch me the hat and rapier in my cell:
I will discase me, and myself present
As I was sometime Milan: quickly, spirit;
Thou shalt ere long be free.

**ARIEL**
Where the bee sucks. there suck I:
In a cowslip's bell I lie;
There I couch when owls do cry.
On the bat's back I do fly
After summer merrily.
Merrily, merrily shall I live now
Under the blossom that hangs on the bough.

**PROSPERO**
Why, that's my dainty Ariel! I shall miss thee:
But yet thou shalt have freedom: so, so, so.
To the king's ship, invisible as thou art:
There shalt thou find the mariners asleep
Under the hatches; the master and the boatswain
Being awake, enforce them to this place,
And presently, I prithee.

163

**ARIEL**
I drink the air before me, and return
Or ere your pulse twice beat.

**GONZALO**
All torment, trouble, wonder and amazement
Inhabits here: some heavenly power guide us
Out of this fearful country!

**PROSPERO**
Behold, sir king,
The wronged Duke of Milan, Prospero:
For more assurance that a living prince
Does now speak to thee, I embrace thy body;
And to thee and thy company I bid
A hearty welcome.

**ALONSO**
Whether thou be'st he or no,
Or some enchanted trifle to abuse me,
As late I have been, I not know: thy pulse
Beats as of flesh and blood; and, since I saw thee,
The affliction of my mind amends, with which,
I fear, a madness held me: this must crave,
An if this be at all, a most strange story.
Thy dukedom I resign and do entreat
Thou pardon me my wrongs. But how should Prospero
Be living and be here?

**PROSPERO**
First, noble friend,
Let me embrace thine age, whose honour cannot
Be measured or confined.

**GONZALO**
Whether this be
Or be not, I'll not swear.
**PROSPERO**
You do yet taste
Some subtilties o' the isle, that will not let you
Believe things certain. Welcome, my friends all!

PROSPERO (cont.)
But you, my brace of lords, were I so minded,
I here could pluck his highness' frown upon you
And justify you traitors: at this time
I will tell no tales.

SEBASTIAN
The devil speaks in him.

PROSPERO
No.
For you, most wicked sir, whom to call brother
Would even infect my mouth, I do forgive
Thy rankest fault; all of them; and require
My dukedom of thee, which perforce, I know,
Thou must restore.

ALONSO
If thou be'st Prospero,
Give us particulars of thy preservation;
How thou hast met us here, who three hours since
Were wreck'd upon this shore; where I have lost—
How sharp the point of this remembrance is!—
My dear son Ferdinand.

PROSPERO
I am woe for't, sir.
ALONSO
Irreparable is the loss, and patience
Says it is past her cure.

PROSPERO
I rather think
You have not sought her help, of whose soft grace
For the like loss I have her sovereign aid
And rest myself content.
ALONSO
You the like loss!
PROSPERO
As great to me as late; and, supportable
To make the dear loss, have I means much weaker
Than you may call to comfort you, for I
Have lost my daughter.

**ALONSO**

A daughter?
O heavens, that they were living both in Naples,
The king and queen there! that they were, I wish
Myself were mudded in that oozy bed
Where my son lies. When did you lose your daughter?

**PROSPERO**

In this last tempest. I perceive these lords
At this encounter do so much admire
That they devour their reason and scarce think
Their eyes do offices of truth, their words
Are natural breath: but, howsoe'er you have
Been justled from your senses, know for certain
That I am Prospero and that very duke
Which was thrust forth of Milan, who most strangely
Upon this shore, where you were wreck'd, was landed,
To be the lord on't.

**PROSPERO (cont.)**

No more yet of this;
For 'tis a chronicle of day by day,
Not a relation for a breakfast nor
Befitting this first meeting. Welcome, sir;
This cell's my court: here have I few attendants
And subjects none abroad: pray you, look in.
My dukedom since you have given me again,
I will requite you with as good a thing;
At least bring forth a wonder, to content ye
As much as me my dukedom.

**MIRANDA**
Sweet lord, you play me false.
**FERDINAND**
No, my dear'st love,
I would not for the world.
**MIRANDA**
Yes, for a score of kingdoms you should wrangle,
And I would call it fair play.

**ALONSO**
If this prove
A vision of the Island, one dear son
Shall I twice lose.
**SEBASTIAN**
A most high miracle!

**FERDINAND**
Though the seas threaten, they are merciful;
I have cursed them without cause.
**ALONSO**
Now all the blessings
Of a glad father compass thee about!
Arise, and say how thou camest here.

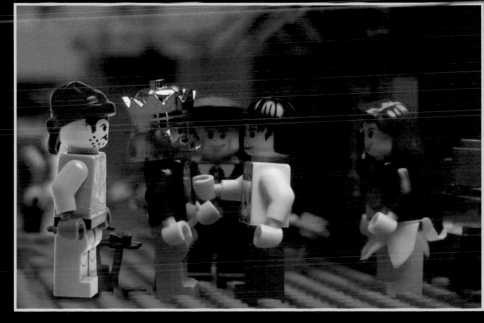

MIRANDA
O, wonder!
How many goodly creatures are there here!
How beauteous mankind is! O brave new world,
That has such people in't!
PROSPERO
'Tis new to thee.

ALONSO
What is this maid with whom thou wast at play?
Your eld'st acquaintance cannot be three hours:
Is she the goddess that hath sever'd us,
And brought us thus together?
FERDINAND
Sir, she is mortal;
But by immortal Providence she's mine:
I chose her when I could not ask my father
For his advice, nor thought I had one. She
Is daughter to this famous Duke of Milan,
Of whom so often I have heard renown,
But never saw before; of whom I have
Received a second life; and second father
This lady makes him to me.

ALONSO
I am hers:
But, O, how oddly will it sound that I
Must ask my child forgiveness!
PROSPERO
There, sir, stop:
Let us not burthen our remembrance with
A heaviness that's gone.

GONZALO
I have inly wept,
Or should have spoke ere this. Look down, you gods,
And on this couple drop a blessed crown!
For it is you that have chalk'd forth the way
Which brought us hither.

ALONSO
I say, Amen, Gonzalo!

GONZALO
Was Milan thrust from Milan, that his issue
Should become kings of Naples? O, rejoice
Beyond a common joy, and set it down
With gold on lasting pillars: In one voyage
Did Claribel her husband find at Tunis,
And Ferdinand, her brother, found a wife
Where he himself was lost, Prospero his dukedom
In a poor isle and all of us ourselves
When no man was his own.

ALONSO
Give me your hands:
Let grief and sorrow still embrace his heart
That doth not wish you joy!

GONZALO
Be it so! Amen!
O, look, sir, look, sir! here is more of us:
I prophesied, if a gallows were on land,
This fellow could not drown. Now, blasphemy,
That swear'st grace o'erboard, not an oath on shore?
Hast thou no mouth by land? What is the news?

BOATSWAIN
The best news is, that we have safely found
Our king and company; the next, our ship—
Which, but three glasses since, we gave out split—
Is tight and yare and bravely rigg'd as when
We first put out to sea.

ARIEL
Sir, all this service
Have I done since I went.
PROSPERO
My tricksy spirit!

ALONSO
These are not natural events; they strengthen
From strange to stranger. Say, how came you hither?
BOATSWAIN
If I did think, sir, I were well awake,
I'ld strive to tell you. We were dead of sleep,
And—how we know not—all clapp'd under hatches;
Where but even now with strange and several noises
Of roaring, shrieking, howling, jingling chains,
And more diversity of sounds, all horrible,
We were awaked; straightway, at liberty;
Where we, in all her trim, freshly beheld
Our royal, good and gallant ship, our master
Capering to eye her: on a trice, so please you,
Even in a dream, were we divided from them
And were brought moping hither.

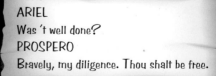

ARIEL
Was 't well done?
PROSPERO
Bravely, my diligence. Thou shalt be free.

**ALONSO**

This is as strange a maze as e'er men trod
And there is in this business more than nature
Was ever conduct of: some oracle
Must rectify our knowledge.

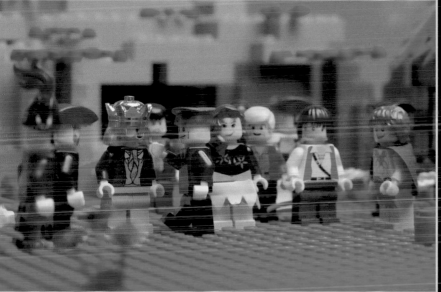

**PROSPERO**

Sir, my liege,
Do not infest your mind with beating on
The strangeness of this business; at pick'd leisure
Which shall be shortly, single I'll resolve you,
Which to you shall seem probable, of every
These happen'd accidents; till when, be cheerful
And think of each thing well.

**PROSPERO (cont.)**

Come hither, spirit:
Set Caliban and his companions free;
Untie the spell.

PROSPERO (cont.)
How fares my gracious sir?
There are yet missing of your company
Some few odd lads that you remember not.
STEPHANO
Every man shift for all the rest, and
let no man take care for himself; for all is
but fortune. Coragio, bully-monster, coragio!
TRINCULO
If these be true spies which I wear in my head,
here's a goodly sight.

CALIBAN
O Setebos, these be brave spirits indeed!
How fine my master is! I am afraid
He will chastise me.

SEBASTIAN
Ha, ha!
What things are these, my lord Antonio?
Will money buy 'em?
ANTONIO
Very like; one of them
Is a plain fish, and, no doubt, marketable.
PROSPERO
Mark but the badges of these men, my lords,
Then say if they be true. This mis-shapen knave,
His mother was a witch, and one so strong
That could control the moon, make flows and ebbs,
And deal in her command without her power.
These three have robb'd me; and this demi-devil—
For he's a bastard one—had plotted with them
To take my life. Two of these fellows you
Must know and own; this thing of darkness!
Acknowledge mine.
CALIBAN
I shall be pinch'd to death.

ALONSO
Is not this Stephano, my drunken butler?
SEBASTIAN
He is drunk now: where had he wine?
ALONSO
And Trinculo is reeling ripe: where should they
Find this grand liquor that hath gilded 'em?
How camest thou in this pickle?

TRINCULO
I have been in such a pickle since I
saw you last that, I fear me, will never out of
my bones: I shall not fear fly-blowing.
SEBASTIAN
Why, how now, Stephano!
STEPHANO
O, touch me not; I am not Stephano, but a cramp.

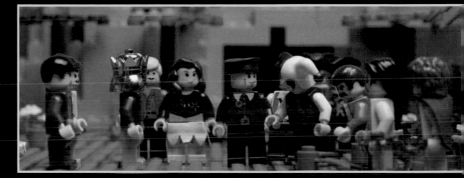

PROSPERO
You'ld be king o' the isle, sirrah?
STEPHANO
I should have been a sore one then.
ALONSO
This is a strange thing as e'er I look'd on.
PROSPERO
He is as disproportion'd in his manners
As in his shape. Go, sirrah, to my cell;
Take with you your companions; as you look
To have my pardon, trim it handsomely.

CALIBAN
Ay, that I will; and I'll be wise hereafter
And seek for grace. What a thrice-double ass
Was I, to take this drunkard for a god
And worship this dull fool!

PROSPERO
Go to; away!
ALONSO
Hence, and bestow your luggage where you found it.
SEBASTIAN
Or stole it, rather.
PROSPERO
Sir, I invite your highness and your train
To my poor cell, where you shall take your rest
For this one night; which, part of it, I'll waste
With such discourse as, I not doubt, shall make it
Go quick away; the story of my life
And the particular accidents gone by
Since I came to this isle: and in the morn
I'll bring you to your ship and so to Naples,
Where I have hope to see the nuptial
Of these our dear-beloved solemnized;
And thence retire me to my Milan, where
Every third thought shall be my grave.
ALONSO
I long
To hear the story of your life, which must
Take the ear strangely.
PROSPERO
I'll deliver all;
And promise you calm seas, auspicious gales
And sail so expeditious that shall catch
Your royal fleet far off.

PROSPERO (cont.)
My Ariel, chick,
That is thy charge: then to the elements
Be free, and fare thou well! Please you, draw near.

# EPILOGUE

T

### PROSPERO

Now my charms are all o'erthrown,
And what strength I have's mine own,
Which is most faint: now, 'tis true,
I must be here confined by you,
Or sent to Naples. Let me not,
Since I have my dukedom got
And pardon'd the deceiver, dwell
In this bare island by your spell;
But release me from my bands
With the help of your good hands:
Gentle breath of yours my sails
Must fill, or else my project fails,
Which was to please. Now I want
Spirits to enforce, art to enchant,
And my ending is despair,
Unless I be relieved by prayer,
Which pierces so that it assaults
Mercy itself and frees all faults.
As you from crimes would pardon'd be,
Let your indulgence set me free.

# Much Ado About Nothing

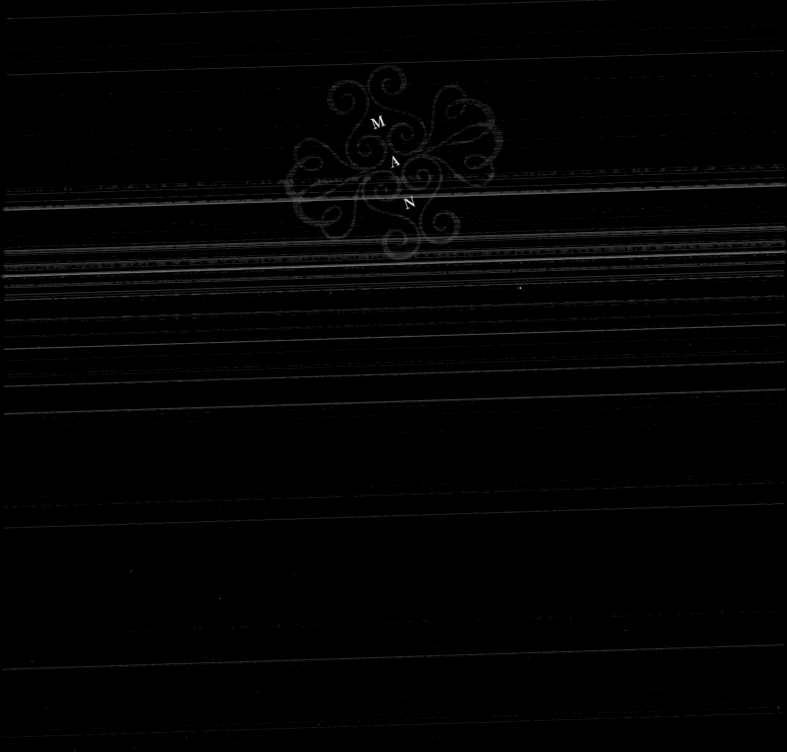

William Shakespeare's play *Much Ado About Nothing* set the standard for contemporary romantic comedies. First penned between 1598 and 1599, and published in the First Folio in 1623, it is written almost entirely in prose. Set in Messina, Italy, the play follows the courtships of two couples and the mix of funny misadventures and underhanded sabotage that follow closely behind them. Balancing cheerful banter with serious moral dilemmas, this play explores how misinformation and mischief-makers—try as they might—can never overthrow love.

In keeping with comic style, *Much Ado About Nothing* is witty with wordplay, slapstick in action, and none of the characters die. What makes this play classically Shakespearean, however, is that this storyline is just a plot twist away from a tragedy like *Romeo & Juliet*. The character Don Pedro, the good-hearted Prince of Aragon, acts as a matchmaker to the couples, while his troublemaker brother, Don John, does his best to undo all of Don Pedro's hard work. The accusations against Claudio's bride, Hero, are so gravely serious that she can only be pardoned through staged horrific consequences. It is only because these consequences are so fleeting that the play is allowed to end as a comedy and not as a tragedy.

The tragic overtones of the play's plot are also softened by the characters' chirpy dialogue and silly mishaps. Some of the Bard's finest crafted wit and wordplay are spoken through the reluctant sweethearts Beatrice and Benedick and the dutiful watchmen, Dogberry and Verges. Beatrice and Benedick's clever and spitfire dialogue is so magnetic that they are often cited as the founding couple of the contemporary romantic comedy. Dogberry and Verges, the bumbling watchmen and the defenders of justice and malapropism, also help keep the play light. While these characters appear both hopeless and oddly effective in their pursuit of justice, their distracted banter and amusing misuse of language has since given rise to the term, "Dogberryism." Both sets of characters are the guiding forces of comedy throughout the play.

Shakespeare's iconic *Much Ado About Nothing* presents an intermingling of tragic and charmingly comic events. Deception and sabotage nearly cause the downfall of each of the characters, but the essence of the play—that love conquers all—sets the tone so that such negative forces are comically overpowered. The cumbersome events, mixed with merry back-and-forth and authentic love, lend *Much Ado About Nothing* a special kind of depth, which helps to cement its legacy as one of Shakespeare's most loved theatrical comedies.

**DON PEDRO, Prince of Aragon**

**DON JOHN, his bastard brother**

**CLAUDIO, a young Lord of Florence**

**BENEDICK, a young Lord of Padua**

**LEONATO, Governor of Messina**

**ANTONIO, an old man, Leonato's brother**

**BORACHIO, follower of Don John**

**CONRADE, follower of Don John**

**FRIAR FRANCIS**

**DOGBERRY, a Constable**

**VERGES, a Headborough**

**A SEXTON**

**HERO, daughter to Leonato**

**BEATRICE, niece to Leonato**

**MARGARET, waiting gentlewoman attending on Hero**

**URSULA, waiting gentlewoman attending on Hero**

**FIRST WATCHMAN**

**SECOND WATCHMAN**

**SEACOLE**

# ACT I. Scene I (82–139).

M
A
N

**M**uch *Ado About Nothing* begins with a messenger carrying a letter to the governor of Messina, Leonato. The letter explains that after a long battle, Don Pedro (the Prince of Aragon) and his men will be arriving to Leonato's home to celebrate their victory. The letter mentions that a Florentine soldier named Claudio—who was given special honors for his role in the battle—will be among the army men. Leonato's daughter, Hero, and his niece, Beatrice, have been off to the side listening to the exchange with the messenger. Beatrice chimes in, asking the messenger about a particular soldier named Benedick. She proceeds on a long rant about how much she dislikes him, which only serves to prove the opposite. The army of men arrives on the scene, including Don Pedro, Claudio, Benedick, Balthasar, and Don John, Don Pedro's illegitimate half-brother, whom they call "The Bastard."

**DON PEDRO**
Good Signior Leonato, you are come to meet your trouble: the fashion of the world is to avoid cost, and you encounter it.

**LEONATO**
Never came trouble to my house in the likeness of your grace: for trouble being gone, comfort should remain; but when you depart from me, sorrow abides and happiness takes his leave.

**DON PEDRO**
You embrace your charge too willingly. I think this is your daughter.

**LEONATO**
Her mother hath many times told me so.

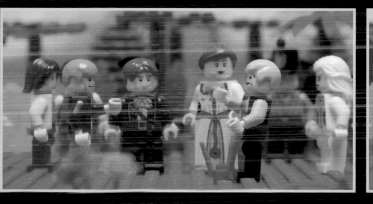

**BENEDICK**
Were you in doubt, sir, that you asked her?

**LEONATO**
Signior Benedick, no; for then were you a child.

**DON PEDRO**
You have it full, Benedick: we may guess by this what you are, being a man. Truly, the lady fathers herself. Be happy, lady; for you are like an honourable father.

**BENEDICK**
If Signior Leonato be her father, she would not have his head on her shoulders for all Messina, as like him as she is.

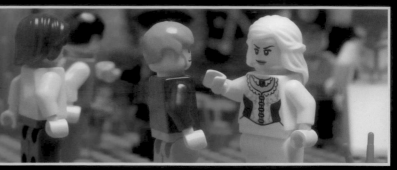

**BEATRICE**
I wonder that you will still be talking, Signior
Benedick: nobody marks you.
**BENEDICK**
What, my dear Lady Disdain! are you yet living?

**BEATRICE**
Is it possible disdain should die while she hath
such meet food to feed it as Signior Benedick?
Courtesy itself must convert to disdain, if you come
in her presence.

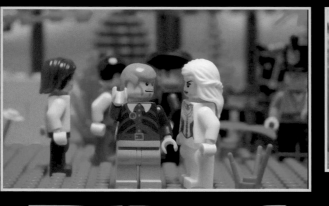

**BENEDICK**
Then is courtesy a turncoat. But it is certain I
am loved of all ladies, only you excepted: and I
would I could find in my heart that I had not a hard
heart; for, truly, I love none.

**BEATRICE**
A dear happiness to women: they would else have
been troubled with a pernicious suitor. I thank God
and my cold blood, I am of your humour for that: I
had rather hear my dog bark at a crow than a man
swear he loves me.

**BENEDICK**
God keep your ladyship still in that mind! so some
gentleman or other shall 'scape a predestinate
scratched face.
**BEATRICE**
Scratching could not make it worse, an 'twere such
a face as yours were.

**BENEDICK**
Well, you are a rare parrot-teacher.
**BEATRICE**
A bird of my tongue is better than a beast of yours.

BENEDICK
I would my horse had the speed of your tongue, and so good a continuer. But keep your way, i' God's name; I have done.
BEATRICE
You always end with a jade's trick: I know you of old.

DON PEDRO
That is the sum of all, Leonato. Signior Claudio and Signior Benedick, my dear friend Leonato hath invited you all. I tell him we shall stay here at the least a month; and he heartily prays some occasion may detain us longer. I dare swear he is no hypocrite, but prays from his heart.
LEONATO
If you swear, my lord, you shall not be forsworn.

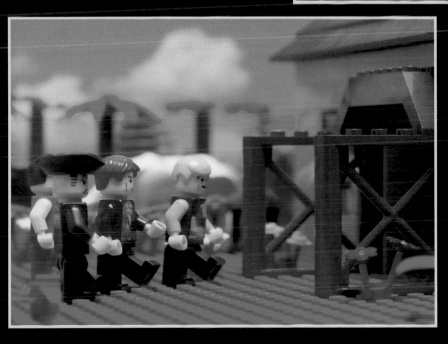

LEONATO (cont.)
Let me bid you welcome, my lord: being reconciled to the prince your brother, I owe you all duty.
DON JOHN
I thank you: I am not of many words, but I thank you.
LEONATO
Please it your grace lead on?
DON PEDRO
Your hand, Leonato; we will go together.

# ACT I. Scene I (257–291).

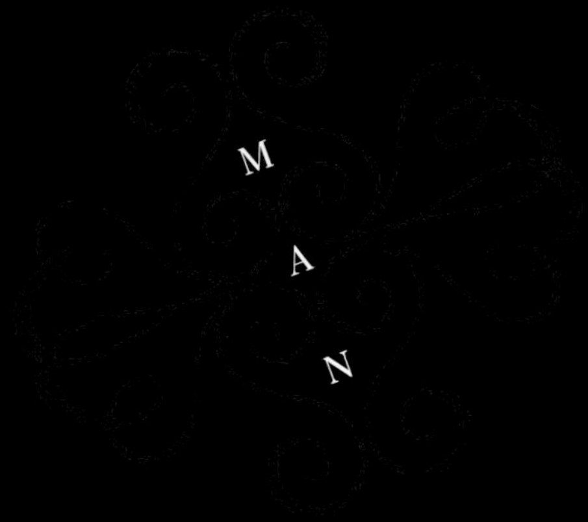

M

A

N

As the others exit, Claudio and Benedick are left to discuss their gentlemanly pursuits. Claudio indicates that he has fallen in love with Hero and looks to Benedick for his thoughts on the situation. Benedick, who does not have an especially high opinion of women or marriage, tells Claudio marriage is like putting his "neck into a yoke" (I.i.175), or in other words, losing his freedom to a wife and becoming another member of the marital herd. Don Pedro enters and encourages Claudio to pursue Hero, finding them worthy of one another. Benedick continues to criticize marriage, but Don Pedro says that "in time the savage bull doth bear the yoke" (I.i.228) as well, meaning that even the most ardent bachelor will find a wife to tame him.

CLAUDIO
Hath Leonato any son, my lord?
DON PEDRO
No child but Hero; she's his only heir.
Dost thou affect her, Claudio?

CLAUDIO
O, my lord,
When you went onward on this ended action,
I look'd upon her with a soldier's eye,
That liked, but had a rougher task in hand
Than to drive liking to the name of love:
But now I am return'd and that war-thoughts
Have left their places vacant, in their rooms
Come thronging soft and delicate desires,
All prompting me how fair young Hero is,
Saying, I liked her ere I went to wars.

DON PEDRO
Thou wilt be like a lover presently
And tire the hearer with a book of words.
If thou dost love fair Hero, cherish it,
And I will break with her and with her father,
And thou shalt have her. Was't not to this end
That thou began'st to twist so fine a story?

CLAUDIO
How sweetly you do minister to love,
That know love's grief by his complexion!
But lest my liking might too sudden seem,
I would have salved it with a longer treatise.
DON PEDRO
What need the bridge much broader than the flood?
The fairest grant is the necessity.
Look, what will serve is fit: 'tis once, thou lovest,
And I will fit thee with the remedy.
I know we shall have revelling to-night:
I will assume thy part in some disguise
And tell fair Hero I am Claudio,
And in her bosom I'll unclasp my heart
And take her hearing prisoner with the force
And strong encounter of my amorous tale:
Then after to her father will I break;
And the conclusion is, she shall be thine.
In practise let us put it presently.

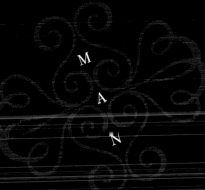

*A*s the house prepares for the evening's party, Antonio seeks out Leonato to share some news. His trusted servant, having overheard only a portion of Claudio and Don Pedro's plot to woo Hero, gives Antonio misinformation, which Antonio passes on to Leonato. He explains that Don Pedro is deeply in love with Hero and plans to win her over at the party. Leonato accepts this to be true, and tells Antonio to let Hero know so she can prepare.

Meanwhile, Don John "The Bastard" and Conrade are in another room, discussing Don John's hatred of his brother, Don Pedro, for having more power and for limiting his own. As he stews, he describes himself as a "plain-dealing villain" (I.ii.27–8), implying that while he may be malignant, he never pretends to be otherwise. He remains in sour spirits until Borachio joins them and explains that he has overheard Claudio and Don Pedro's true plan to woo Hero. Don John sees this as a wonderful opportunity to stir up trouble for Don Pedro—whom he would like to overthrow—and Claudio—whom he sees as the only person to stand in his way. They head off to the feast as they begin their scheme.

At the party, Beatrice discusses her disdain for men and marriage, while Leonato prods Hero to get ready to accept the Prince's courtship. A mask-donning Don Pedro does approach Hero, asking her to dance, and he begins to amuse her on behalf of Claudio. Wearing masks, the attendees of the gathering dance and chatter with one another, including one of Don John's counterparts with an equal of Hero's, and Beatrice with Benedick. While Benedick knows the identity of his dance partner, the same is not true for Beatrice. She inevitably releases a series of pointed insults regarding Benedick, who is left feeling rather scorned. Claudio tries to pretend he is Benedick in front of Don John to glean more about Don Pedro's progress with Hero. Realizing the ruse and taking advantage of it, Don John tells "Benedick" that Don Pedro is wooing Hero for himself and not for Claudio. Don John leaves Claudio to put the pieces together, thinking his friend has betrayed him.

BENEDICK
Count Claudio?
CLAUDIO
Yea, the same.
BENEDICK
Come, will you go with me?
CLAUDIO
Whither?

BENEDICK
Even to the next willow, about your own business,
county. What fashion will you wear the garland of?
about your neck, like an usurer's chain? or under
your arm, like a lieutenant's scarf? You must wear
it one way, for the prince hath got your Hero.
CLAUDIO
I wish him joy of her.

BENEDICK
Why, that's spoken like an honest drovier: so they
sell bullocks. But did you think the prince would
have served you thus?
CLAUDIO
I pray you, leave me.

BENEDICK
Ho! now you strike like the blind man: 'twas the
boy that stole your meat, and you'll beat the post.
CLAUDIO
If it will not be, I'll leave you.

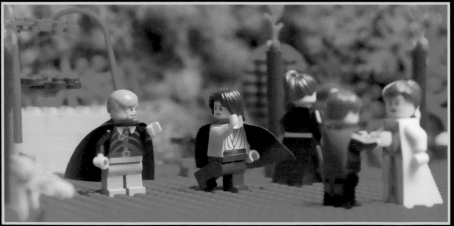

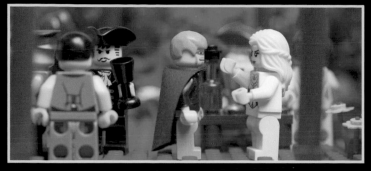

**BENEDICK**

Alas, poor hurt fowl! now will he creep into sedges.
But that my Lady Beatrice should know me, and not
know me! The prince's fool! Ha? It may be I go
under that title because I am merry. Yea, but so I
am apt to do myself wrong; I am not so reputed: it
is the base, though bitter, disposition of Beatrice
that puts the world into her person and so gives me
out. Well, I'll be revenged as I may.

**DON PEDRO**

Now, signior, where's the count? did you see him?

**BENEDICK**

Troth, my lord, I have played the part of Lady Fame.
I found him here as melancholy as a lodge in a
warren: I told him, and I think I told him true,
that your grace had got the good will of this young
lady; and I offered him my company to a willow-tree,
either to make him a garland, as being forsaken, or
to bind him up a rod, as being worthy to be whipped.

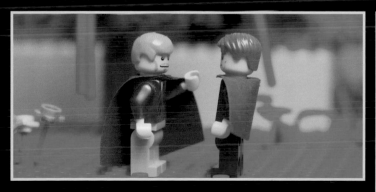

**DON PEDRO**

Wilt thou make a trust a transgression? The
transgression is in the stealer.

**DON PEDRO**

To be whipped! What's his fault?

**BENEDICK**

The flat transgression of a schoolboy, who, being
overjoyed with finding a birds' nest, shows it his
companion, and he steals it.

**BENEDICK**
Yet it had not been amiss the rod had been made, and the garland too; for the garland he might have worn himself, and the rod he might have bestowed on you, who, as I take it, have stolen his birds' nest.

**DON PEDRO**
I will but teach them to sing, and restore them to the owner.

**BENEDICK**
If their singing answer your saying, by my faith, you say honestly.

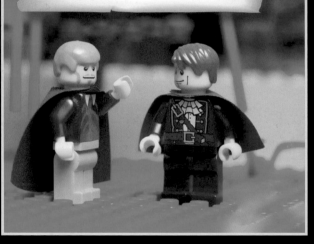

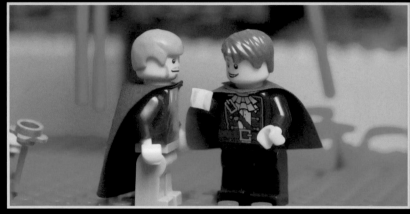

**DON PEDRO**
The Lady Beatrice hath a quarrel to you: the gentleman that danced with her told her she is much wronged by you.

**BENEDICK**
O, she misused me past the endurance of a block! an oak but with one green leaf on it would have answered her; my very visor began to assume life and scold with her. She told me, not thinking I had been myself, that I was the prince's jester, that I was duller than a great thaw; huddling jest upon jest with such impossible conveyance upon me that I stood like a man at a mark, with a whole army shooting at me.

**BENEDICK (cont.)**
She speaks poniards, and every word stabs:
if her breath were as terrible as her terminations,
there were no living near her; she would infect to
the north star. I would not marry her, though she
were endowed with all that Adam had left him before
he transgressed: she would have made Hercules have
turned spit, yea, and have cleft his club to make
the fire too. Come, talk not of her: you shall find
her the infernal Ate in good apparel. I would to God
some scholar would conjure her; for certainly, while
she is here, a man may live as quiet in hell as in a
sanctuary; and people sin upon purpose, because they
would go thither; so, indeed, all disquiet, horror
and perturbation follows her.

**DON PEDRO**
Look, here she comes.

**BENEDICK**
O God, sir, here's a dish I love not: I cannot
endure my Lady Tongue.

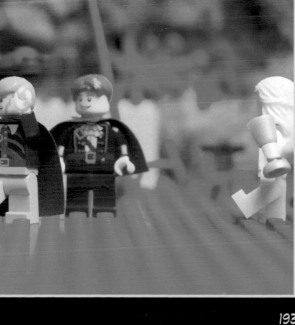

**BENEDICK**
Will your grace command me any service to the
world's end? I will go on the slightest errand now
to the Antipodes that you can devise to send me on;
I will fetch you a tooth-picker now from the
furthest inch of Asia, bring you the length of
Prester John's foot, fetch you a hair off the great
Cham's beard, do you any embassage to the Pigmies,
rather than hold three words' conference with this
harpy. You have no employment for me?
**DON PEDRO**
None, but to desire your good company.

**DON PEDRO**
Come, lady, come; you have lost the heart of
Signior Benedick.
**BEATRICE**
Indeed, my lord, he lent it me awhile; and I gave
him use for it, a double heart for his single one:
marry, once before he won it of me with false dice,
therefore your grace may well say I have lost it.

**DON PEDRO**
You have put him down, lady, you have put him down.
**BEATRICE**
So I would not he should do me, my lord, lest I
should prove the mother of fools. I have brought
Count Claudio, whom you sent me to seek.

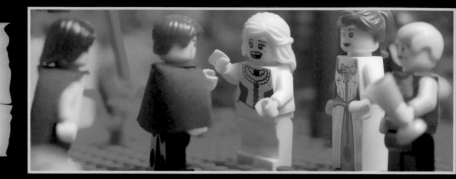

**DON PEDRO**
Why, how now, count! wherefore are you sad?
**CLAUDIO**
Not sad, my lord.
**DON PEDRO**
How then? sick?
**CLAUDIO**
Neither, my lord.

**BEATRICE**
The count is neither sad, nor sick, nor merry, nor
well; but civil count, civil as an orange, and
something of that jealous complexion.

**DON PEDRO**
I' faith, lady, I think your blazon to be true; though, I'll be sworn, if he be so, his conceit is false. Here, Claudio, I have wooed in thy name, and fair Hero is won: I have broke with her father, and his good will obtained: name the day of marriage, and God give thee joy!

**LEONATO**
Count, take of me my daughter, and with her my fortunes: his grace hath made the match, and all grace say Amen to it.

**BEATRICE**
Speak, count, 'tis your cue.

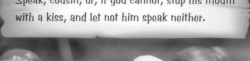

**CLAUDIO**
Silence is the perfectest herald of joy: I were
but little happy, if I could say how much. Lady, as
you are mine, I am yours: I give away myself for
you and dote upon the exchange.

**DON PEDRO**
In faith, lady, you have a merry heart.
**BEATRICE**
Yea, my lord; I thank it, poor fool, it keeps on
the windy side of care. My cousin tells him in his
ear that he is in her heart.

**CLAUDIO**
And so she doth, cousin.
**BEATRICE**
Good Lord, for alliance! Thus goes every one to the
world but I, and I am sunburnt; I may sit in a
corner and cry heigh-ho for a husband!

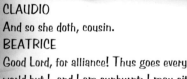

**DON PEDRO**
Lady Beatrice, I will get you one.
**BEATRICE**
I would rather have one of your father's getting.
Hath your grace ne'er a brother like you? Your
father got excellent husbands, if a maid could come by them.
**DON PEDRO**
Will you have me, lady?

**BEATRICE**
No, my lord, unless I might have another for working-days: your grace is too costly to wear every day. But, I beseech your grace, pardon me: I was born to speak all mirth and no matter.

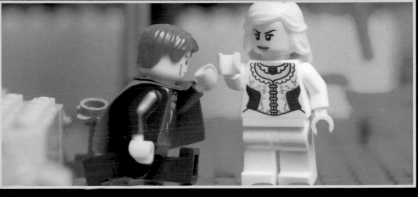

**DON PEDRO**
Your silence most offends me, and to be merry best becomes you; for, out of question, you were born in a merry hour.
**BEATRICE**
No, sure, my lord, my mother cried; but then there was a star danced, and under that was I born. Cousins, God give you joy!

**LEONATO**
Niece, will you look to those things I told you of?
**BEATRICE**
I cry you mercy, uncle. By your grace's pardon.

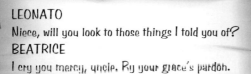

**DON PEDRO**
By my troth, a pleasant-spirited lady.
**LEONATO**
There's little of the melancholy element in her, my lord: she is never sad but when she sleeps, and not ever sad then; for I have heard my daughter say, she hath often dreamed of unhappiness and waked herself with laughing.
**DON PEDRO**
She cannot endure to hear tell of a husband.

**LEONATO**
O, by no means: she mocks all her wooers out of suit.
**DON PEDRO**
She were an excellent wife for Benedick.
**LEONATO**
O Lord, my lord, if they were but a week married, they would talk themselves mad.
**DON PEDRO**
County Claudio, when mean you to go to church?

CLAUDIO
To-morrow, my lord: time goes on crutches till love have all his rites.
LEONATO
Not till Monday, my dear son, which is hence a just seven-night; and a time too brief, too, to have all things answer my mind.

DON PEDRO
Come, you shake the head at so long a breathing: but, I warrant thee, Claudio, the time shall not go dully by us. I will in the interim undertake one of Hercules' labours; which is, to bring Signior Benedick and the Lady Beatrice into a mountain of affection the one with the other. I would fain have it a match, and I doubt not but to fashion it, if you three will but minister such assistance as I shall give you direction.

LEONATO
My lord, I am for you, though it cost me ten nights' watchings.
CLAUDIO
And I, my lord.

DON PEDRO
And you too, gentle Hero?
HERO
I will do any modest office, my lord, to help my cousin to a good husband.
DON PEDRO
And Benedick is not the unhopefullest husband that I know. Thus far can I praise him; he is of a noble strain, of approved valour and confirmed honesty. I will teach you how to humour your cousin, that she shall fall in love with Benedick; and I, with your two helps, will so practise on Benedick that, in despite of his quick wit and his queasy stomach, he shall fall in love with Beatrice. If we can do this, Cupid is no longer an archer: his glory shall be ours, for we are the only love-gods. Go in with me, and I will tell you my drift.

*T*he match between Claudio and Hero has been made, making Don
John's plan of sabotage just a little bit harder. Borachio eases his fears
by producing an elaborate set of scenarios to tarnish Hero's name. While Don
John is to convince Don Pedro that he has set Claudio up with a wolf in sheep's
clothing, Borachio will charm Hero's attendant, Margaret, all the way to Hero's
bedroom window and pose as if Hero were being unfaithful to Claudio.

Over in the orchard, Benedick ponders the changes he sees in Claudio, who
went from a man who laughed at the things others did for love to becoming one
of them. He promises himself that he will never become a fool to love unless
the woman he desires is the true embodiment of perfection. Benedick sees Don
Pedro, Claudio, and Leonato wander into the orchard and immediately hides so
they do not know he is there. Both Claudio and Don Pedro know that Benedick
is hiding, and they listen to Balthasar poorly sing while they grab Benedick's
attention. Balthasar leaves, and the two reel Benedick in to eavesdrop on their
private discussion.

**DON PEDRO**
Come hither, Leonato. What was it you told me of to-day, that your niece Beatrice was in love with Signior Benedick?

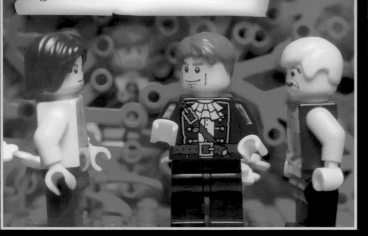

**CLAUDIO**
O, ay: stalk on, stalk on; the fowl sits. I did never think that lady would have loved any man.

**LEONATO**
No, nor I neither; but most wonderful that she should so dote on Signior Benedick, whom she hath in all outward behaviors seemed ever to abhor.

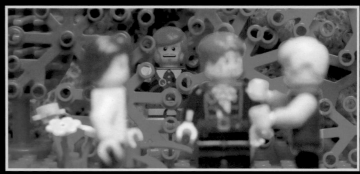

**BENEDICK**
Is't possible? Sits the wind in that corner?

**LEONATO**
By my troth, my lord, I cannot tell what to think of it but that she loves him with an enraged affection: it is past the infinite of thought.
**DON PEDRO**
May be she doth but counterfeit.
**CLAUDIO**
Faith, like enough.

**LEONATO**
O God, counterfeit! There was never counterfeit of passion came so near the life of passion as she discovers it.
**DON PEDRO**
Why, what effects of passion shows she?

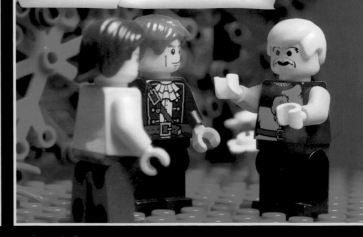

**CLAUDIO**
Bait the hook well; this fish will bite.

**LEONATO**
What effects, my lord? She will sit you, you heard my daughter tell you how.
**CLAUDIO**
She did, indeed.
**DON PEDRO**
How, how, pray you? You amaze me: I would have thought her spirit had been invincible against all assaults of affection.
**LEONATO**
I would have sworn it had, my lord; especially against Benedick.

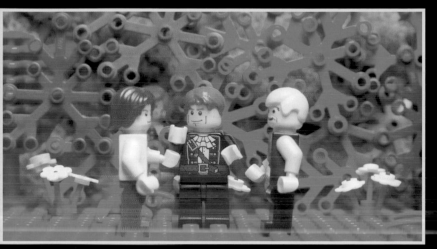

**BENEDICK**
I should think this a gull, but that the white-bearded fellow speaks it: knavery cannot, sure, hide himself in such reverence.

**CLAUDIO**
He hath ta'en the infection: hold it up.
**DON PEDRO**
Hath she made her affection known to Benedick?
**LEONATO**
No; and swears she never will: that's her torment.
**CLAUDIO**
'Tis true, indeed; so your daughter says: "Shall I," says she, "that have so oft encountered him with scorn, write to him that I love him?"

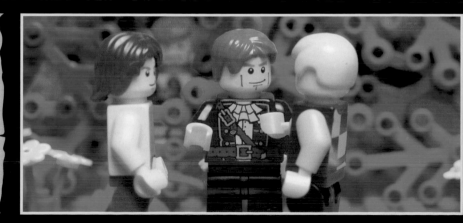

LEONATO
This says she now when she is beginning to write to him; for she'll be up twenty times a night, and there will she sit in her smock till she have writ a sheet of paper: my daughter tells us all.
CLAUDIO
Now you talk of a sheet of paper, I remember a pretty jest your daughter told us of.
LEONATO
O, when she had writ it and was reading it over, she found Benedick and Beatrice between the sheet?
CLAUDIO
That.

LEONATO
O, she tore the letter into a thousand halfpence; railed at herself, that she should be so immodest to write to one that she knew would flout her; "I measure him," says she, "by my own spirit; for I should flout him, if he writ to me; yea, though I love him, I should."

CLAUDIO
Then down upon her knees she falls, weeps, sobs, beats her heart, tears her hair, prays, curses; "O sweet Benedick! God give me patience!"
LEONATO
She doth indeed; my daughter says so: and the ecstasy hath so much overborne her that my daughter is sometime afeared she will do a desperate outrage to herself: it is very true.

DON PEDRO
It were good that Benedick knew of it by some other, if she will not discover it.
CLAUDIO
To what end? He would make but a sport of it and torment the poor lady worse.

**DON PEDRO**
An he should, it were an alms to hang him. She's an excellent sweet lady; and, out of all suspicion, she is virtuous.

**CLAUDIO**
And she is exceeding wise.

**DON PEDRO**
In every thing but in loving Benedick.

**LEONATO**
O, my lord, wisdom and blood combating in so tender a body, we have ten proofs to one that blood hath the victory. I am sorry for her, as I have just cause, being her uncle and her guardian.

**DON PEDRO**
I would she had bestowed this dotage on me: I would have daffed all other respects and made her half myself. I pray you, tell Benedick of it, and hear what a' will say.

**LEONATO**
Were it good, think you?

**CLAUDIO**
Hero thinks surely she will die; for she says she will die, if he love her not, and she will die, ere she make her love known, and she will die, if he woo her, rather than she will bate one breath of her accustomed crossness.

**DON PEDRO**
She doth well: if she should make tender of her love, 'tis very possible he'll scorn it; for the man, as you know all, hath a contemptible spirit.
**CLAUDIO**
He is a very proper man.
**DON PEDRO**
He hath indeed a good outward happiness.

**CLAUDIO**
Before God! and, in my mind, very wise.
**DON PEDRO**
He doth indeed show some sparks that are like wit.
**CLAUDIO**
And I take him to be valiant.
**DON PEDRO**
As Hector, I assure you: and in the managing of quarrels you may say he is wise; for either he avoids them with great discretion, or undertakes them with a most Christian-like fear.

LEONATO

If he do fear God, a' must necessarily keep peace: if he break the peace, he ought to enter into a quarrel with fear and trembling.

DON PEDRO

And so will he do; for the man doth fear God, howsoever it seems not in him by some large jests he will make. Well I am sorry for your niece. Shall we go seek Benedick, and tell him of her love?

CLAUDIO

Never tell him, my lord: let her wear it out with good counsel.

LEONATO

Nay, that's impossible: she may wear her heart out first.

DON PEDRO

Well, we will hear further of it by your daughter: let it cool the while. I love Benedick well; and I could wish he would modestly examine himself, to see how much he is unworthy so good a lady.

LEONATO

My lord, will you walk? dinner is ready.

CLAUDIO

If he do not dote on her upon this, I will never trust my expectation.

DON PEDRO

Let there be the same net spread for her; and that must your daughter and her gentlewomen carry. The sport will be, when they hold one an opinion of another's dotage, and no such matter: that's the scene that I would see, which will be merely a dumb-show. Let us send her to call him in to dinner.

BENEDICK

This can be no trick: the conference was sadly borne. They have the truth of this from Hero. They seem to pity the lady: it seems her affections have their full bent. Love me! why, it must be requited. I hear how I am censured: they say I will bear myself proudly, if I perceive the love come from her; they say too that she will rather die than give any sign of affection. I did never think to marry: I must not seem proud: happy are they that hear their detractions and can put them to mending. They say the lady is fair; 'tis a truth, I can bear them witness; and virtuous; 'tis so, I cannot reprove it; and wise, but for loving me; by my troth, it is no addition to her wit, nor no great argument of her folly, for I will be horribly in love with her.

BENEDICK (cont.)

I may chance have some odd quirks and remnants of wit broken on me, because I have railed so long against marriage: but doth not the appetite alter? a man loves the meat in his youth that he cannot endure in his age. Shall quips and sentences and these paper bullets of the brain awe a man from the career of his humour? No, the world must be peopled. When I said I would die a bachelor, I did not think I should live till I were married.

BENEDICK (cont.)

Here comes Beatrice. By this day! she's a fair lady: I do spy some marks of love in her.

BEATRICE

Against my will I am sent to bid you come in to dinner.

BENEDICK

Fair Beatrice, I thank you for your pains.

BEATRICE
I took no more pains for those thanks than you take pains to thank me: if it had been painful, I would not have come.
BENEDICK
You take pleasure then in the message?

BEATRICE
Yea, just so much as you may take upon a knife's point and choke a daw withal. You have no stomach, signior: fare you well.

BENEDICK
Ha! "Against my will I am sent to bid you come in to dinner;" there's a double meaning in that "I took no more pains for those thanks than you took pains to thank me." That's as much as to say, "Any pains that I take for you is as easy as thanks." If I do not take pity of her, I am a villain; if I do not love her, I am a Jew. I will go get her picture.

# ACT III. Scene I (1–115).

HERO

Good Margaret, run thee to the parlor;
There shalt thou find my cousin Beatrice
Proposing with the prince and Claudio:
Whisper her ear and tell her, I and Ursula
Walk in the orchard and our whole discourse
Is all of her; say that thou overheard'st us;
And bid her steal into the pleached bower,
Where honeysuckles, ripen'd by the sun,
Forbid the sun to enter, like favourites,
Made proud by princes, that advance their pride
Against that power that bred it: there will she hide her,
To listen our purpose. This is thy office;
Bear thee well in it and leave us alone.

MARGARET

I'll make her come, I warrant you, presently.

HERO

Now, Ursula, when Beatrice doth come,
As we do trace this alley up and down,
Our talk must only be of Benedick.
When I do name him, let it be thy part
To praise him more than ever man did merit:
My talk to thee must be how Benedick
Is sick in love with Beatrice. Of this matter
Is little Cupid's crafty arrow made,
That only wounds by hearsay.

HERO (cont.)

Now begin;
For look where Beatrice, like a lapwing, runs
Close by the ground, to hear our conference.

URSULA

The pleasant'st angling is to see the fish
Cut with her golden oars the silver stream,
And greedily devour the treacherous bait:
So angle we for Beatrice; who even now
Is couched in the woodbine coverture.
Fear you not my part of the dialogue.

HERO
Then go we near her, that her ear lose nothing
Of the false sweet bait that we lay for it.

HERO (cont.)
No, truly, Ursula, she is too disdainful;
I know her spirits are as coy and wild
As haggerds of the rock.

URSULA
But are you sure
That Benedick loves Beatrice so entirely?
HERO
So says the prince and my new-trothed lord.
URSULA
And did they bid you tell her of it, madam?

HERO
They did entreat me to acquaint her of it;
But I persuaded them, if they loved Benedick,
To wish him wrestle with affection,
And never to let Beatrice know of it.
URSULA
Why did you so? Doth not the gentleman
Deserve as full as fortunate a bed
As ever Beatrice shall couch upon?
HERO
O god of love! I know he doth deserve
As much as may be yielded to a man:
But Nature never framed a woman's heart
Of prouder stuff than that of Beatrice;
Disdain and scorn ride sparkling in her eyes,
Misprising what they look on, and her wit
Values itself so highly that to her
All matter else seems weak: she cannot love,
Nor take no shape nor project of affection,
She is so self-endeared.

URSULA
Sure, I think so;
And therefore certainly it were not good
She know his love, lest she make sport at it.

HERO
Why, you speak truth. I never yet saw man,
How wise, how noble, young, how rarely featured,
But she would spell him backward: if fair-faced,
She would swear the gentleman should be her sister;
If black, why, Nature, drawing of an antique,
Made a foul blot; if tall, a lance ill-headed;
If low, an agate very vilely cut;
If speaking, why, a vane blown with all winds;
If silent, why, a block moved with none.
So turns she every man the wrong side out
And never gives to truth and virtue that
Which simpleness and merit purchaseth.

URSULA
Sure, sure, such carping is not commendable.

HERO
No, not to be so odd and from all fashions
As Beatrice is, cannot be commendable:
But who dare tell her so? If I should speak,
She would mock me into air; O, she would laugh me
Out of myself, press me to death with wit.
Therefore let Benedick, like cover'd fire,
Consume away in sighs, waste inwardly:
It were a better death than die with mocks,
Which is as bad as die with tickling.

URSULA
Yet tell her of it: hear what she will say.

HERO
No; rather I will go to Benedick
And counsel him to fight against his passion.
And, truly, I'll devise some honest slanders
To stain my cousin with: one doth not know
How much an ill word may empoison liking.

**URSULA**

O, do not do your cousin such a wrong.
She cannot be so much without true judgment—
Having so swift and excellent a wit
As she is prized to have—as to refuse
So rare a gentleman as Signior Benedick.

**HERO**

He is the only man of Italy.
Always excepted my dear Claudio.

**URSULA**

I pray you, be not angry with me, madam,
Speaking my fancy: Signior Benedick,
For shape, for bearing, argument and valour,
Goes foremost in report through Italy.

**HERO**

Indeed, he hath an excellent good name.

**URSULA**

His excellence did earn it, ere he had it.
When are you married, madam?

**HERO**

Why, every day, to-morrow. Come, go in:
I'll show thee some attires, and have thy counsel
Which is the best to furnish me to-morrow.

**URSULA**

She's limed, I warrant you: we have caught her, madam.

**HERO**

If it proves so, then loving goes by haps:
Some Cupid kills with arrows, some with traps.

**BEATRICE**

What fire is in mine ears? Can this be true?
Stand I condemn'd for pride and scorn so much?
Contempt, farewell! and maiden pride, adieu!
No glory lives behind the back of such.
And, Benedick, love on; I will requite thee,
Taming my wild heart to thy loving hand:
If thou dost love, my kindness shall incite thee
To bind our loves up in a holy band;
For others say thou dost deserve, and I
Believe it better than reportingly.

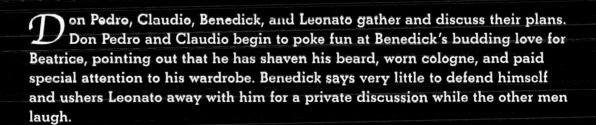

*D*on Pedro, Claudio, Benedick, and Leonato gather and discuss their plans. Don Pedro and Claudio begin to poke fun at Benedick's budding love for Beatrice, pointing out that he has shaven his beard, worn cologne, and paid special attention to his wardrobe. Benedick says very little to defend himself and ushers Leonato away with him for a private discussion while the other men laugh.

DON JOHN
My lord and brother, God save you!
DON PEDRO
Good den, brother.
DON JOHN
If your leisure served, I would speak with you.

DON PEDRO
In private?
DON JOHN
If it please you: yet Count Claudio may hear; for what I would speak of concerns him.
DON PEDRO
What's the matter?

DON JOHN
Means your lordship to be married to-morrow?
DON PEDRO
You know he does.
DON JOHN
I know not that, when he knows what I know.

**CLAUDIO**
If there be any impediment, I pray you discover it.

**DON JOHN**
You may think I love you not: let that appear hereafter, and aim better at me by that I now will manifest. For my brother, I think he holds you well, and in dearness of heart hath holp to effect your ensuing marriage;—surely suit ill spent and labour ill bestowed.
**DON PEDRO**
Why, what's the matter?

**DON JOHN**
I came hither to tell you; and, circumstances shortened, for she has been too long a talking of, the lady is disloyal.
**CLAUDIO**
Who, Hero?
**DON PEDRO**
Even she; Leonato's Hero, your Hero, every man's Hero:
**CLAUDIO**
Disloyal?

**DON JOHN**
The word is too good to paint out her wickedness; I could say she were worse: think you of a worse title, and I will fit her to it. Wonder not till further warrant: go but with me to-night, you shall see her chamber-window entered, even the night before her wedding-day: if you love her then, to-morrow wed her; but it would better fit your honour to change your mind.

**CLAUDIO**
May this be so?

**DON PEDRO**
I will not think it.

**DON JOHN**
If you dare not trust that you see, confess not that you know: if you will follow me, I will show you enough; and when you have seen more and heard more, proceed accordingly.

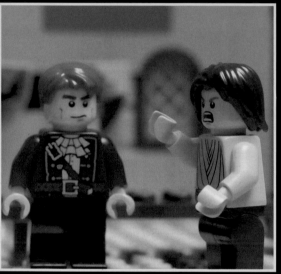

**CLAUDIO**
If I see any thing to-night why I should not marry her to-morrow in the congregation, where I should wed, there will I shame her.

**DON PEDRO**
And, as I wooed for thee to obtain her, I will join with thee to disgrace her.

**DON JOHN**
I will disparage her no farther till you are my witnesses: bear it coldly but till midnight, and let the issue show itself.

**DON PEDRO**
O day untowardly turned!

**CLAUDIO**
O mischief strangely thwarting!

**DON JOHN**
O plague right well prevented! so will you say when you have seen the sequel.

# ACT III. Scene III (1–87).

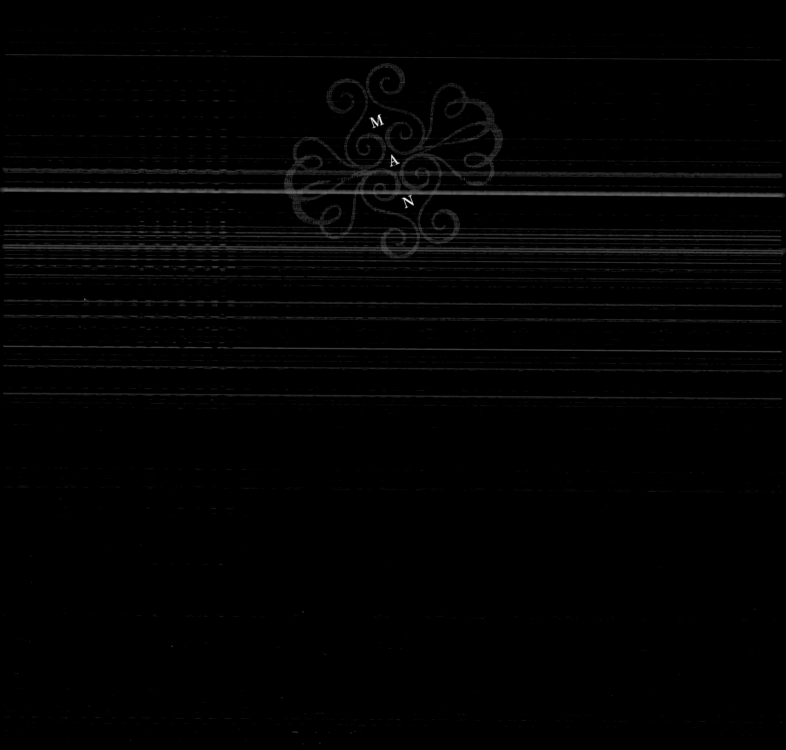

DOGBERRY
Are you good men and true?

VERGES
Yea, or else it were pity but they should suffer salvation, body and soul.

DOGBERRY
Nay, that were a punishment too good for them, if they should have any allegiance in them, being chosen for the prince's watch.

VERGES
Well, give them their charge, neighbour Dogberry.

DOGBERRY
First, who think you the most desertless man to be constable?

FIRST WATCHMAN
Hugh Otecake, sir, or George Seacole; for they can write and read.

DOGBERRY
Come hither, neighbour Seacole. God hath blessed you with a good name: to be a well-favoured man is the gift of fortune; but to write and read comes by nature.

SECOND WATCHMAN
Both which, master constable,—

**DOGBERRY**
You have: I knew it would be your answer. Well, for your favour, sir, why, give God thanks, and make no boast of it; and for your writing and reading, let that appear when there is no need of such vanity. You are thought here to be the most senseless and fit man for the constable of the watch; therefore bear you the lantern. This is your charge: you shall comprehend all vagrom men; you are to bid any man stand, in the prince's name.

**SECOND WATCHMAN**
How if a' will not stand?

**DOGBERRY**
Why, then, take no note of him, but let him go; and presently call the rest of the watch together and thank God you are rid of a knave.

**VERGES**
If he will not stand when he is bidden, he is none of the prince's subjects.

**DOGBERRY**
True, and they are to meddle with none but the prince's subjects. You shall also make no noise in the streets; for, for the watch to babble and to talk is most tolerable and not to be endured.

**SECOND WATCHMAN**
We will rather sleep than talk: we know what belongs to a watch.

DOGBERRY
Why, you speak like an ancient and most quiet watchman; for I cannot see how sleeping should offend: only, have a care that your bills be not stolen. Well, you are to call at all the ale-houses, and bid those that are drunk get them to bed.

SECOND WATCHMAN
How if they will not?
DOGBERRY
Why, then, let them alone till they are sober: if they make you not then the better answer, you may say they are not the men you took them for.
SECOND WATCHMAN
Well, sir.
DOGBERRY
If you meet a thief, you may suspect him, by virtue of your office, to be no true man; and, for such kind of men, the less you meddle or make with them, why the more is for your honesty.

SECOND WATCHMAN
If we know him to be a thief, shall we not lay hands on him?
DOGBERRY
Truly, by your office, you may; but I think they that touch pitch will be defiled: the most peaceable way for you, if you do take a thief, is to let him show himself what he is and steal out of your company.

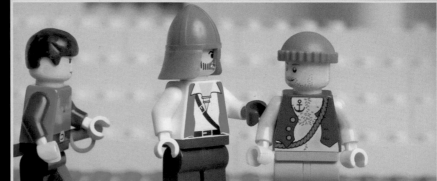

VERGES
You have been always called a merciful man, partner.
DOGBERRY
Truly, I would not hang a dog by my will, much more a man who hath any honesty in him.

**VERGES**

If you hear a child cry in the night, you must call to the nurse and bid her still it.

**SECOND WATCHMAN**

How if the nurse be asleep and will not hear us?

**DOGBERRY**

Why, then, depart in peace, and let the child wake her with crying; for the ewe that will not hear her lamb when it baes will never answer a calf when he bleats.

**VERGES**

'Tis very true.

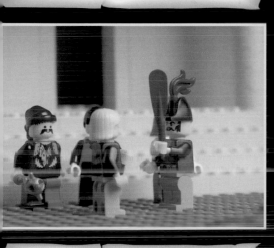

**DOGBERRY**

This is the end of the charge:—you, constable, are to present the prince's own person: it you meet the prince in the night, you may stay him.

**VERGES**

Nay, by'r our lady, that I think a' cannot.

**DOGBERRY**

Five shillings to one on't, with any man that knows the statutes, he may stay him: marry, not without the prince be willing; for, indeed, the watch ought to offend no man; and it is an offence to stay a man against his will.

**VERGES**

By'r lady, I think it be so.

**DOGBERRY**

Ha, ha, ha! Well, masters, good night: an there be any matter of weight chances, call up me: keep your fellows' counsels and your own; and good night. Come, neighbour.

**SECOND WATCHMAN**

Well, masters, we hear our charge: let us go sit here upon the church-bench till two, and then all to bed.

**DOGBERRY**

One word more, honest neighbours. I pray you watch about Signior Leonato's door; for the wedding being there to-morrow, there is a great coil to-night. Adieu: be vigitant, I beseech you.

MAN

*T*he watchmen look on from the shadows and listen as Borachio tells Conrade of his villainous success. Just as they had planned, Claudio and Don Pedro mistake Margaret for Hero and, in seeing her with another man, fly into a rage and vow to humiliate Hero at her own wedding. Hearing this, the watchmen spring forth from their hiding place and take Borachio and Conrade into custody.

Hero prepares for the wedding with Margaret and Beatrice. They merrily trade explicit jokes, and Beatrice volunteers that she is not feeling well. Margaret suggests that Beatrice finds some "carduus benedictus" (III.iv.65) to ease her heart, which steers the conversation to a more serious place, suggesting that Beatrice embrace her love for Benedick. Ursula, Hero's attendant, arrives and hurries them to leave for the church.

The watchmen Dogberry and Verges approach Leonato and humorously stumble into their explanation of the criminal events of Messina. The pair spends so much time bantering back and forth that Leonato rushes off to the wedding before he can hear what Dogberry and Verges are about to tell him—that Don John and his men have allowed events to unfold that will tarnish his good daughter's name.

LEONATO
Come, Friar Francis, be brief; only to the plain form of marriage, and you shall recount their particular duties afterwards.

FRIAR FRANCIS
You come hither, my lord, to marry this lady.
CLAUDIO
No.

LEONATO
To be married to her: friar, you come to marry her.

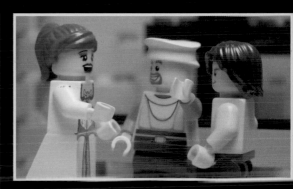

FRIAR FRANCIS
Lady, you come hither to be married to this count.
HERO
I do.
FRIAR FRANCIS
If either of you know any inward impediment why you should not be conjoined, charge you, on your souls, to utter it.

CLAUDIO
Know you any, Hero?

HERO
None, my lord.
FRIAR FRANCIS
Know you any, count?

**LEONATO**
I dare make his answer, none.

**CLAUDIO**
O, what men dare do! what men may do! what men daily do, not knowing what they do!

**BENEDICK**
How now! interjections? Why, then, some be of laughing, as, ah, ha, he!

**CLAUDIO**
Stand thee by, friar. Father, by your leave:
Will you with free and unconstrained soul
Give me this maid, your daughter?

**LEONATO**
As freely, son, as God did give her me.

**CLAUDIO**
And what have I to give you back, whose worth
May counterpoise this rich and precious gift?

DON PEDRO
Nothing, unless you render her again.

CLAUDIO
Sweet prince, you learn me noble thankfulness.
There, Leonato, take her back again:
Give not this rotten orange to your friend;
She's but the sign and semblance of her honour.
Behold how like a maid she blushes here!

CLAUDIO (cont.)
O, what authority and show of truth
Can cunning sin cover itself withal!
Comes not that blood as modest evidence
To witness simple virtue? Would you not swear,
All you that see her, that she were a maid,
By these exterior shows? But she is none:
She knows the heat of a luxurious bed;
Her blush is guiltiness, not modesty.

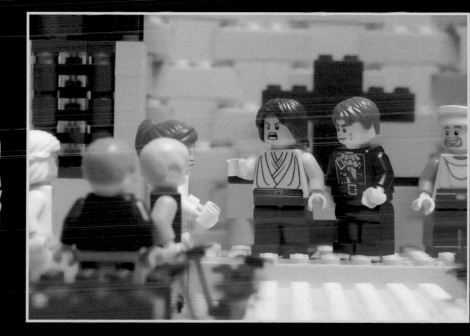

LEONATO
What do you mean, my lord?

CLAUDIO
Not to be married,
Not to knit my soul to an approved wanton.
LEONATO
Dear my lord, if you, in your own proof,
Have vanquish'd the resistance of her youth,
And made defeat of her virginity,—

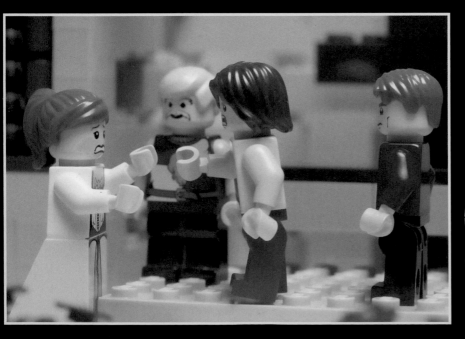

CLAUDIO
I know what you would say: if I have known her,
You will say she did embrace me as a husband,
And so extenuate the 'forehand sin:
No, Leonato,
I never tempted her with word too large;
But, as a brother to his sister, show'd
Bashful sincerity and comely love.
HERO
And seem'd I ever otherwise to you?

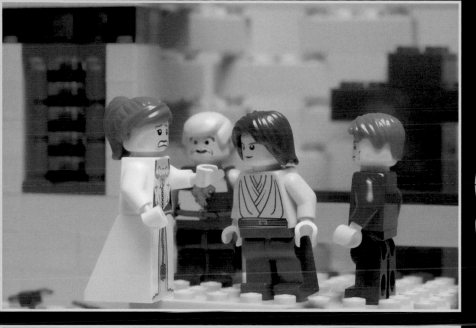

CLAUDIO
Out on thee! Seeming! I will write against it:
You seem to me as Dian in her orb,
As chaste as is the bud ere it be blown;
But you are more intemperate in your blood
Than Venus, or those pamper'd animals
That rage in savage sensuality.
HERO
Is my lord well, that he doth speak so wide?

LEONATO
Sweet prince, why speak not you?
DON PEDRO
What should I speak?
I stand dishonour'd, that have gone about
To link my dear friend to a common stale.

LEONATO
Are these things spoken, or do I but dream?
DON JOHN
Sir, they are spoken, and these things are true.

227

BENEDICK
This looks not like a nuptial.
HERO
True! O God!

CLAUDIO
Leonato, stand I here?
Is this the prince? is this the prince's brother?
Is this face Hero's? are our eyes our own?
LEONATO
All this is so: but what of this, my lord?
CLAUDIO
Let me but move one question to your daughter;
And, by that fatherly and kindly power
That you have in her, bid her answer truly.
LEONATO
I charge thee do so, as thou art my child.

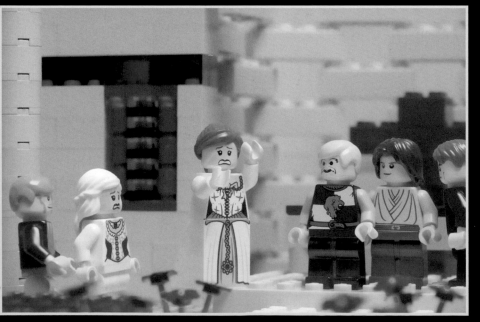

HERO
O, God defend me! how am I beset!
What kind of catechising call you this?
CLAUDIO
To make you answer truly to your name.
HERO
Is it not Hero? Who can blot that name
With any just reproach?
CLAUDIO
Marry, that can Hero;
Hero itself can blot out Hero's virtue.
What man was he talk'd with you yesternight
Out at your window betwixt twelve and one?
Now, if you are a maid, answer to this.
HERO
I talk'd with no man at that hour, my lord.

**DON PEDRO**
Why, then are you no maiden. Leonato,
I am sorry you must hear: upon mine honour,
Myself, my brother and this grieved count
Did see her, hear her, at that hour last night
Talk with a ruffian at her chamber-window
Who hath indeed, most like a liberal villain,
Confess'd the vile encounters they have had
A thousand times in secret.

**DON JOHN**
Fie, fie! they are not to be named, my lord,
Not to be spoke of;
There is not chastity enough in language
Without offence to utter them. Thus, pretty lady,
I am sorry for thy much misgovernment.

**CLAUDIO**
O Hero, what a Hero hadst thou been,
If half thy outward graces had been placed
About thy thoughts and counsels of thy heart!
But fare thee well, most foul, most fair! farewell,
Thou pure impiety and impious purity!
For thee I'll lock up all the gates of love,
And on my eyelids shall conjecture hang,
To turn all beauty into thoughts of harm,
And never shall it more be gracious.

**LEONATO**
Hath no man's dagger here a point for me?

**BEATRICE**
Why, how now, cousin! wherefore sink you down?

**DON JOHN**
Come, let us go. These things, come thus to light,
Smother her spirits up.

**BENEDICK**
How doth the lady?
**BEATRICE**
Dead, I think. Help, uncle!
Hero! why, Hero! Uncle! Signior Benedick! Friar!

**LEONATO**
O Fate! take not away thy heavy hand.
Death is the fairest cover for her shame
That may be wish'd for.

**BEATRICE**
How now, cousin Hero!

# ACT IV. Scene I (253–326).

M
A
N

With the Princes and Claudio gone, Hero stirs from her fainting spell, and Leonato begs her not to wake up. Believing the accusations, he despairs that he was given a shameful daughter whose supposed actions have made her irreversibly tainted in his eyes. Beatrice defends her cousin, crying slander, Friar Francis bets her chastity against his piety, and Hero arises to plead to her father to believe her. Benedick suggests that this could all just be the doing of Don John the Bastard, "whose spirits toil in frame of villainies" and who may have simply misled the Don Pedro and Claudio. Friar Francis comes up with a plan to determine whether or not Hero is falsely accused: since the Princes and Claudio left Hero for dead at the altar, the family will continue on as if she has actually died, which he hopes will bring out those who falsely accused her from sorrow and guilt. Claudio would forgive his dead betrothed, and Hero would be vindicated. They agree to keep the secret until the moment of clarity arrives.

BENEDICK
Lady Beatrice, have you wept all this while?
BEATRICE
Yea, and I will weep a while longer.

BENEDICK
I will not desire that.
BEATRICE
You have no reason; I do it freely.

BENEDICK
Surely I do believe your fair cousin is wronged.
BEATRICE
Ah, how much might the man deserve of me that would right her!

BENEDICK
Is there any way to show such friendship?
BEATRICE
A very even way, but no such friend.

BENEDICK
May a man do it?
BEATRICE
It is a man's office, but not yours.

BENEDICK
I do love nothing in the world so well as you: is not that strange?

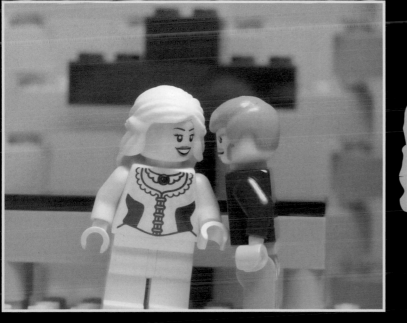

BEATRICE
As strange as the thing I know not. It were as possible for me to say I loved nothing so well as you: but believe me not; and yet I lie not; I confess nothing, nor I deny nothing. I am sorry for my cousin.

BENEDICK

By my sword, Beatrice, thou lovest me.

BEATRICE

Do not swear, and eat it.

BENEDICK

I will swear by it that you love me; and I will make him eat it that says I love not you.

BEATRICE

Will you not eat your word?

BENEDICK

With no sauce that can be devised to it. I protest I love thee.

BEATRICE

Why, then, God forgive me!

BENEDICK

What offence, sweet Beatrice?

BEATRICE

You have stayed me in a happy hour: I was about to protest I loved you.

BENEDICK

And do it with all thy heart.

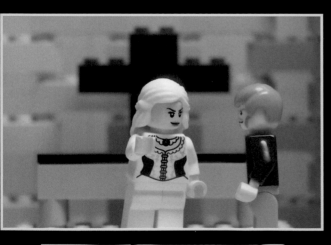

BEATRICE

I love you with so much of my heart that none is left to protest.

BENEDICK

Come, bid me do any thing for thee.

BEATRICE

Kill Claudio.

BENEDICK
Ha! not for the wide world.
BEATRICE
You kill me to deny it. Farewell.

BENEDICK
Tarry, sweet Beatrice.
BEATRICE
I am gone, though I am here: there is no love in
you: nay, I pray you, let me go.
BENEDICK
Beatrice,—

BEATRICE
In faith, I will go.
BENEDICK
We'll be friends first.
BEATRICE
You dare easier be friends with me than fight with mine enemy.
BENEDICK
Is Claudio thine enemy?

BEATRICE
Is he not approved in the height a villain, that
hath slandered, scorned, dishonoured my kinswoman? O
that I were a man! What, bear her in hand until they
come to take hands; and then, with public
accusation, uncovered slander, unmitigated rancour,
—O God, that I were a man! I would eat his heart
in the market-place.

BENEDICK
Hear me, Beatrice,—
BEATRICE
Talk with a man out at a window! A proper saying!
BENEDICK
Nay, but, Beatrice,—
BEATRICE
Sweet Hero! She is wronged, she is slandered, she is undone.
BENEDICK
Beat—

BEATRICE
Princes and counties! Surely, a princely testimony, a goodly count, Count Comfect; a sweet gallant, surely! O that I were a man for his sake! or that I had any friend would be a man for my sake! But manhood is melted into courtesies, valour into compliment, and men are only turned into tongue, and trim ones too: he is now as valiant as Hercules that only tells a lie and swears it. I cannot be a man with wishing, therefore I will die a woman with grieving.

BENEDICK
Tarry, good Beatrice. By this hand, I love thee.
BEATRICE
Use it for my love some other way than swearing by it.
BENEDICK
Think you in your soul the Count Claudio hath wronged Hero?
BEATRICE
Yea, as sure as I have a thought or a soul.

BENEDICK
Enough, I am engaged; I will challenge him. I will kiss your hand, and so I leave you. By this hand, Claudio shall render me a dear account. As you hear of me, so think of me. Go, comfort your cousin: I must say she is dead: and so, farewell.

# ACT IV. Scene II (1–81).

DOGBERRY
Is our whole dissembly appeared?
VERGES
O, a stool and a cushion for the sexton.
SEXTON
Which be the malefactors?

DOGBERRY
Marry, that am I and my partner.
VERGES
Nay, that's certain; we have the exhibition to examine.

SEXTON
But which are the offenders that are to be
examined? let them come before master constable.

DOGBERRY
Yea, marry, let them come before me.

CONRADE
I am a gentleman, sir, and my name is Conrade.

DOGBERRY (cont.)
What is your name, friend?
BORACHIO
Borachio.
DOGBERRY
Pray, write down, Borachio. Yours, sirrah?

**DOGBERRY**
Write down, master gentleman Conrade. Masters, do you serve God?

**CONRADE and BORACHIO**
Yea, sir, we hope.

**DOGBERRY**
Write down, that they hope they serve God: and write God first; for God defend but God should go before such villains! Masters, It is proved already that you are little better than false knaves; and it will go near to be thought so shortly. How answer you for yourselves?

**CONRADE**
Marry, sir, we say we are none.

**DOGBERRY**
A marvellous witty fellow, I assure you: but I will go about with him. Come you hither, sirrah; a word in your ear: sir, I say to you, it is thought you are false knaves.

**BORACHIO**
Sir, I say to you we are none.

**DOGBERRY**
Well, stand aside. 'Fore God, they are both in a tale. Have you writ down, that they are none?

**SEXTON**
Master constable, you go not the way to examine: you must call forth the watch that are their accusers.

**DOGBERRY**
Yea, marry, that's the eftest way. Let the watch come forth. Masters, I charge you, in the prince's name, accuse these men.

**FIRST WATCHMAN**
This man said, sir, that Don John, the prince's brother, was a villain.

**DOGBERRY**
Write down Prince John a villain. Why, this is flat perjury, to call a prince's brother villain.

**BORACHIO**
Master constable,—
**DOGBERRY**
Pray thee, fellow, peace: I do not like thy look, I promise thee.

**SEXTON**
What heard you him say else?
**SECOND WATCHMAN**
Marry, that he had received a thousand ducats of Don John for accusing the Lady Hero wrongfully.
**DOGBERRY**
Flat burglary as ever was committed.
**VERGES**
Yea, by mass, that it is.

SEXTON
What else, fellow?
FIRST WATCHMAN
And that Count Claudio did mean, upon his words, to
disgrace Hero before the whole assembly, and not marry her.
DOGBERRY
O villain! thou wilt be condemned into everlasting
redemption for this.
SEXTON
What else?
WATCHMEN
This is all.

SEXTON
And this is more, masters, than you can deny.
Prince John is this morning secretly stolen away;
Hero was in this manner accused, in this very manner
refused, and upon the grief of this suddenly died.
Master constable, let these men be bound, and
brought to Leonato's: I will go before and show
him their examination.
DOGBERRY
Come, let them be opinioned.

VERGES
Let them be in the hands—
CONRADE
Off, coxcomb!

241

**DOGBERRY**
God's my life, where's the sexton? let him write down the prince's officer coxcomb. Come, bind them. Thou naughty varlet!

**CONRADE**
Away! you are an ass, you are an ass.

**DOGBERRY**
Dost thou not suspect my place? dost thou not suspect my years? O that he were here to write me down an ass! But, masters, remember that I am an ass; though it be not written down, yet forget not that I am an ass. No, thou villain, thou art full of piety, as shall be proved upon thee by good witness. I am a wise fellow, and, which is more, an officer, and, which is more, a householder, and, which is more, as pretty a piece of flesh as any is in Messina, and one that knows the law, go to; and a rich fellow enough, go to; and a fellow that hath had losses, and one that hath two gowns and every thing handsome about him. Bring him away. O that I had been writ down an ass!

242

# ACT V Scene I (112–324).

M
A
N

**W**hile preparations are made to determine Hero's innocence, Leonato has come unraveled in his anguish. Antonio attempts to console and advise him, but it is to no avail. Don Pedro and Claudio enter the scene, and Leonato berates the men for having "killed" his daughter by weapon of slander. Don Pedro and Claudio are saddened and apologetic but continue to stand by their assertions that Hero was untrue. Just as Benedick comes across the group, Leonato and Antonio storm off.

**CLAUDIO**
Now, signior, what news?

**BENEDICK**
Good day, my lord.

**DON PEDRO**
Welcome, signior: you are almost come to part almost a fray.

**CLAUDIO**
We had like to have had our two noses snapped off with two old men without teeth.

**DON PEDRO**
Leonato and his brother. What thinkest thou? Had we fought, I doubt we should have been too young for them.

**BENEDICK**
In a false quarrel there is no true valour. I came to seek you both.

**CLAUDIO**
We have been up and down to seek thee; for we are high-proof melancholy and would fain have it beaten away. Wilt thou use thy wit?

**BENEDICK**
It is in my scabbard: shall I draw it?

**DON PEDRO**
Dost thou wear thy wit by thy side?

**CLAUDIO**
Never any did so, though very many have been beside their wit. I will bid thee draw, as we do the minstrels; draw, to pleasure us.

**DON PEDRO**
As I am an honest man, he looks pale. Art thou sick, or angry?

**CLAUDIO**
What, courage, man! What though care killed a cat, thou hast mettle enough in thee to kill care.

**BENEDICK**
Sir, I shall meet your wit in the career, and you charge it against me. I pray you choose another subject.

**CLAUDIO**
Nay, then, give him another staff: this last was broke cross.

**DON PEDRO**
By this light, he changes more and more: I think he be angry indeed.

CLAUDIO

If he be, he knows how to turn his girdle.

BENEDICK

Shall I speak a word in your ear?

CLAUDIO

God bless me from a challenge!

BENEDICK

You are a villain; I jest not:
I will make it good how you dare, with what you
dare, and when you dare. Do me right, or I will
protest your cowardice. You have killed a sweet
lady, and her death shall fall heavy on you. Let me
hear from you.

CLAUDIO

Well, I will meet you, so I may have good cheer.

DON PEDRO

What, a feast, a feast?

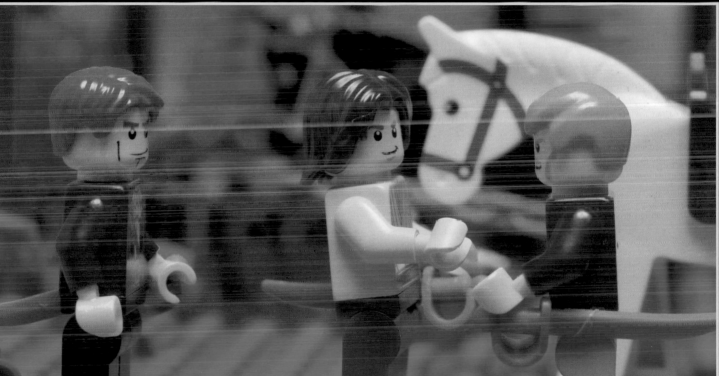

CLAUDIO

I' faith, I thank him; he hath bid me to a calf's
head and a capon; the which if I do not carve most
curiously, say my knife's naught. Shall I not find
a woodcock too?

BENEDICK

Sir, your wit ambles well; it goes easily.

DON PEDRO

I'll tell thee how Beatrice praised thy wit the
other day. I said, thou hadst a fine wit: "True,"
said she, "a fine little one." "No," said I, "a
great wit:" "Right," says she, "a great gross one."

"Nay," said I, "a good wit:" "Just," said she, "it
hurts nobody." "Nay," said I, "the gentleman
is wise:" "Certain," said she, "a wise gentleman."
"Nay," said I, "he hath the tongues:" "That I
believe," said she, "for he swore a thing to me on
Monday night, which he forswore on Tuesday morning;
there's a double tongue; there's two tongues." Thus
did she, an hour together, transshape thy particular
virtues: yet at last she concluded with a sigh, thou
wast the properest man in Italy.

CLAUDIO

For the which she wept heartily and said she cared not.

DON PEDRO

Yea, that she did: but yet, for all that, an if she did not hate him deadly, she would love him dearly: the old man's daughter told us all.

CLAUDIO

All, all; and, moreover, God saw him when he was hid in the garden.

DON PEDRO

But when shall we set the savage bull's horns on the sensible Benedick's head?

CLAUDIO

Yea, and text underneath, "Here dwells Benedick the married man"?

BENEDICK

Fare you well, boy: you know my mind. I will leave you now to your gossip-like humour: you break jests as braggarts do their blades, which God be thanked, hurt not. My lord, for your many courtesies I thank you: I must discontinue your company: your brother the bastard is fled from Messina: you have among you killed a sweet and innocent lady. For my Lord Lackbeard there, he and I shall meet: and, till then, peace be with him.

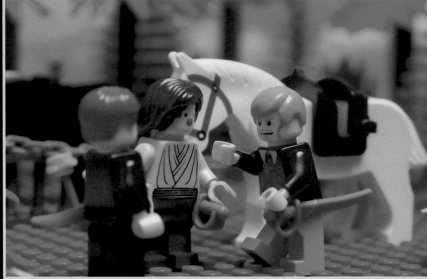

DON PEDRO

He is in earnest.

CLAUDIO

In most profound earnest; and, I'll warrant you, for the love of Beatrice.

DON PEDRO

And hath challenged thee.

CLAUDIO

Most sincerely.

DON PEDRO

What a pretty thing man is when he goes in his doublet and hose and leaves off his wit!

CLAUDIO

He is then a giant to an ape; but then is an ape a doctor to such a man.

DON PEDRO

But, soft you, let me be: pluck up, my heart, and be sad. Did he not say, my brother was fled?

**DOGBERRY**
Come you, sir: if justice cannot tame you, she
shall ne'er weigh more reasons in her balance: nay,
an you be a cursing hypocrite once, you must be looked to.

**DON PEDRO**
How now? two of my brother's men bound! Borachio
one!

**CLAUDIO**
Hearken after their offence, my lord.

**DON PEDRO**
Officers, what offence have these men done?

**DOGBERRY**
Marry, sir, they have committed false report;
moreover, they have spoken untruths; secondarily,
they are slanders; sixth and lastly, they have
belied a lady; thirdly, they have verified unjust
things; and, to conclude, they are lying knaves.

**DON PEDRO**
First, I ask thee what they have done; thirdly, I ask thee what's their offence; sixth and lastly, why they are committed; and, to conclude, what you lay to their charge.

**CLAUDIO**
Rightly reasoned, and in his own division: and, by my troth, there's one meaning well suited.

**DON PEDRO**
Who have you offended, masters, that you are thus bound to your answer? this learned constable is too cunning to be understood: what's your offence?

**BORACHIO**
Sweet prince, let me go no farther to mine answer: do you hear me, and let this count kill me. I have deceived even your very eyes: what your wisdoms could not discover, these shallow fools have brought to light: who in the night overheard me confessing to this man how Don John your brother incensed me to slander the Lady Hero, how you were brought into the orchard and saw me court Margaret in Hero's garments, how you disgraced her, when you should marry her: my villany they have upon record; which I had rather seal with my death than repeat over to my shame. The lady is dead upon mine and my master's false accusation; and, briefly, I desire nothing but the reward of a villain.

**DON PEDRO**
Runs not this speech like iron through your blood?

**CLAUDIO**
I have drunk poison whiles he utter'd it.

**DON PEDRO**
But did my brother set thee on to this?

**BORACHIO**
Yea, and paid me richly for the practise of it.

**DON PEDRO**
He is composed and framed of treachery:
And fled he is upon this villany.

**CLAUDIO**
Sweet Hero! now thy image doth appear
In the rare semblance that I loved it first.

**DOGBERRY**
Come, bring away the plaintiffs: by this time our sexton hath reformed Signior Leonato of the matter: and, masters, do not forget to specify, when time and place shall serve, that I am an ass.

**VERGES**
Here, here comes master Signior Leonato, and the Sexton too.

LEONATO
Which is the villain? let me see his eyes,
That, when I note another man like him,
I may avoid him: which of these is he?

BORACHIO
If you would know your wronger, look on me.
LEONATO
Art thou the slave that with thy breath hast kill'd
Mine innocent child?
BORACHIO
Yea, even I alone.
LEONATO
No, not so, villain; thou beliest thyself:
Here stand a pair of honourable men;
A third is fled, that had a hand in it.
I thank you, princes, for my daughter's death:
Record it with your high and worthy deeds:
'Twas bravely done, if you bethink you of it.

CLAUDIO
I know not how to pray your patience;
Yet I must speak. Choose your revenge yourself;
Impose me to what penance your invention
Can lay upon my sin: yet sinn'd I not
But in mistaking.
DON PEDRO
By my soul, nor I:
And yet, to satisfy this good old man,
I would bend under any heavy weight
That he'll enjoin me to.
LEONATO
I cannot bid you bid my daughter live;
That were impossible: but, I pray you both,
Possess the people in Messina here
How innocent she died;

**LEONATO (cont.)**
and if your love
Can labour ought in sad invention,
Hang her an epitaph upon her tomb
And sing it to her bones, sing it to-night:

**LEONATO (cont.)**
To-morrow morning come you to my house,
And since you could not be my son-in-law,
Be yet my nephew: my brother hath a daughter,
Almost the copy of my child that's dead,
And she alone is heir to both of us:
Give her the right you should have given her cousin,
And so dies my revenge.

**CLAUDIO**
O noble sir,
Your over-kindness doth wring tears from me!
I do embrace your offer; and dispose
For henceforth of poor Claudio.

**LEONATO**
To-morrow then I will expect your coming;
To-night I take my leave. This naughty man
Shall face to face be brought to Margaret,
Who I believe was pack'd in all this wrong,
Hired to it by your brother.

**BORACHIO**
No, by my soul, she was not,
Nor knew not what she did when she spoke to me,
But always hath been just and virtuous
In any thing that I do know by her.

**DOGBERRY**
Moreover, sir, which indeed is not under white and
black, this plaintiff here, the offender, did call
me ass: I beseech you, let it be remembered in his
punishment. And also, the watch heard them talk of
one Deformed: they say he wears a key in his ear and
a lock hanging by it, and borrows money in God's
name, the which he hath used so long and never paid
that now men grow hard-hearted and will lend nothing
for God's sake: pray you, examine him upon that point.

LEONATO
I thank thee for thy care and honest pains.
DOGBERRY
Your worship speaks like a most thankful and reverend youth; and I praise God for you.
LEONATO
There's for thy pains.
DOGBERRY
God save the foundation!
LEONATO
Go, I discharge thee of thy prisoner, and I thank thee.

DOGBERRY
I leave an arrant knave with your worship, which I beseech your worship to correct yourself, for the example of others. God keep your worship! I wish your worship well; God restore you to health! I humbly give you leave to depart; and if a merry meeting may be wished, God prohibit it! Come, neighbour.

LEONATO
Until to-morrow morning, lords, farewell.
ANTONIO
Farewell, my lords: we look for you to-morrow.
DON PEDRO
We will not fail.
CLAUDIO
To-night I'll mourn with Hero.
LEONATO
Bring you these fellows on. We'll talk with Margaret, How her acquaintance grew with this lewd fellow.

$\mathcal{B}$enedick works on scribing a love poem for Beatrice and asks Margaret for help. Instead, she calls for Beatrice and Benedick explains that he has challenged Claudio to a duel in defense of Hero and Beatrice. They dance around their feelings for one another, still continuing to verbally spar back and forth. Ursula enters and tells them that Hero has been vindicated and the culprit, Don John, has run away. They immediately head to Leonato's to see what will happen.

Don Pedro and Claudio enter Leonato's family tomb in order to pay respects to Hero, whom they still believe to be dead. By her tomb, Claudio sees Hero's epitaph, which reads that she was "done to death by slanderous tongues" (V.iii.3). Claudio expresses his profound sadness and promises to honor Hero's memory. Claudio and Don Pedro then leave for Leonato's house so that Claudio can fulfill Leonato's wishes.

**FRIAR FRANCIS**
Did I not tell you she was innocent?
**LEONATO**
So are the prince and Claudio, who accused her
Upon the error that you heard debated:
But Margaret was in some fault for this,
Although against her will, as it appears
In the true course of all the question.
**ANTONIO**
Well, I am glad that all things sort so well.

**BENEDICK**
And so am I,

**BENEDICK** (cont.)
being else by faith enforced
To call young Claudio to a reckoning for it.

**LEONATO**
Well, daughter, and you gentle-women all,
Withdraw into a chamber by yourselves,
And when I send for you, come hither mask'd.

**LEONATO** (cont.)
The prince and Claudio promised by this hour
To visit me. You know your office, brother:
You must be father to your brother's daughter
And give her to young Claudio.
**ANTONIO**
Which I will do with confirm'd countenance.

BENEDICK
Friar, I must entreat your pains, I think.
FRIAR FRANCIS
To do what, signior?
BENEDICK
To bind me, or undo me; one of them.

BENEDICK (cont.)
Signior Leonato, truth it is, good signior,
Your niece regards me with an eye of favour.
LEONATO
That eye my daughter lent her: 'tis most true.
BENEDICK
And I do with an eye of love requite her.
LEONATO
The sight whereof I think you had from me,
From Claudio and the prince: but what's your will?
BENEDICK
Your answer, sir, is enigmatical:
But, for my will, my will is your good will
May stand with ours, this day to be conjoin'd
In the state of honourable marriage:
In which, good friar, I shall desire your help.
LEONATO
My heart is with your liking.

FRIAR FRANCIS
And my help.
Here comes the prince and Claudio.
DON PEDRO
Good morrow to this fair assembly.
LEONATO
Good morrow, prince; good morrow, Claudio:
We here attend you. Are you yet determined
To-day to marry with my brother's daughter?

CLAUDIO
I'll hold my mind, were she an Ethiope.

LEONATO
Call her forth, brother; here's the friar ready.

DON PEDRO
Good morrow, Benedick. Why, what's the matter,
That you have such a February face,
So full of frost, of storm and cloudiness?
CLAUDIO
I think he thinks upon the savage bull.
Tush, fear not, man; we'll tip thy horns with gold
And all Europa shall rejoice at thee,
As once Europa did at lusty Jove,
When he would play the noble beast in love.

CLAUDIO (cont.)
Which is the lady I must seize upon?

BENEDICK
Bull Jove, sir, had an amiable low;
And some such strange bull leap'd your father's cow,
And got a calf in that same noble feat
Much like to you, for you have just his bleat.
CLAUDIO
For this I owe you: here comes other reckonings.

ANTONIO
This same is she, and I do give you her.

CLAUDIO
Why, then she's mine. Sweet, let me see your face.
LEONATO
No, that you shall not, till you take her hand
Before this friar and swear to marry her.

CLAUDIO
Give me your hand: before this holy friar,
I am your husband, if you like of me.
HERO
And when I lived, I was your other wife:

HERO (cont.)
And when you loved, you were my other husband.

CLAUDIO
Another Hero!

DON PEDRO
The former Hero! Hero that is dead!

HERO
Nothing certainer:
One Hero died defiled, but I do live,
And surely as I live, I am a maid.

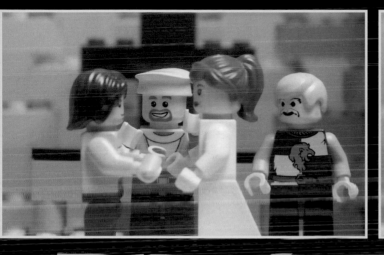

LEONATO
She died, my lord, but whiles her slander lived.
FRIAR FRANCIS
All this amazement can I qualify:
When after that the holy rites are ended,
I'll tell you largely of fair Hero's death:
Meantime let wonder seem familiar,
And to the chapel let us presently.

BENEDICK
Soft and fair, friar. Which is Beatrice?
BEATRICE
I answer to that name. What is your will?
BENEDICK
Do not you love me?
BEATRICE
Why, no; no more than reason.

BENEDICK
Why, then your uncle and the prince and Claudio
Have been deceived; they swore you did.
BEATRICE
Do not you love me?
BENEDICK
Troth, no; no more than reason.
BEATRICE
Why, then my cousin Margaret and Ursula
Are much deceived; for they did swear you did.

257

**BENEDICK**
They swore that you were almost sick for me.
**BEATRICE**
They swore that you were well-nigh dead for me.
**BENEDICK**
'Tis no such matter. Then you do not love me?
**BEATRICE**
No, truly, but in friendly recompense.

**LEONATO**
Come, cousin, I am sure you love the gentleman.
**CLAUDIO**
And I'll be sworn upon't that he loves her;
For here's a paper written in his hand,
A halting sonnet of his own pure brain,
Fashion'd to Beatrice.
**HERO**
And here's another
Writ in my cousin's hand, stolen from her pocket,
Containing her affection unto Benedick.

**BENEDICK**
A miracle! here's our own hands against our hearts.
Come, I will have thee; but, by this light, I take
thee for pity.
**BEATRICE**
I would not deny you; but, by this good day, I yield
upon great persuasion; and partly to save your life,
for I was told you were in a consumption.
**BENEDICK**
Peace! I will stop your mouth.

**DON PEDRO**
How dost thou, Benedick, the married man?

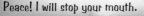

**BENEDICK**

I'll tell thee what, prince; a college of wit-crackers cannot flout me out of my humour. Dost thou think I care for a satire or an epigram? No: if a man will be beaten with brains, a' shall wear nothing handsome about him. In brief, since I do purpose to marry, I will think nothing to any purpose that the world can say against it; and therefore never flout at me for what I have said against it; for man is a giddy thing, and this is my conclusion. For thy part, Claudio, I did think to have beaten thee, but in that thou art like to be my kinsman, live unbruised and love my cousin.

**CLAUDIO**

I had well hoped thou wouldst have denied Beatrice, that I might have cudgelled thee out of thy single life, to make thee a double-dealer; which, out of question, thou wilt be, if my cousin do not look exceedingly narrowly to thee.

**BENEDICK**

Come, come, we are friends: let's have a dance ere we are married, that we may lighten our own hearts and our wives' heels.

**LEONATO**

We'll have dancing afterward.

**MESSENGER**

My lord, your brother John is ta'en in flight,
And brought with armed men back to Messina.

**BENEDICK**

Think not on him till to-morrow:
I'll devise thee brave punishments for him.
Strike up, pipers.

# The Taming of the Shrew

*T*he Taming of the Shrew is one of Shakespeare's most well-known and frequently adapted comedies. First scrawled sometime between 1590 and 1592, this play depicts one man's attempt at domesticating the wild-hearted and outspoken Katharina and the suitors who stumble over one another to marry her younger sister. The play explores the more businesslike aspects of marriage and uses silly disguises and comic role-playing to reflect on and explore the social rules in Elizabethan times.

The play centers on two sisters, Katharina and Bianca. Many wealthy and impressive men want the chance to marry beautiful Bianca, but her overbearing father says that her older sister must be married first. The determined Petruchio takes on the task to marry the "shrew" Katharina, but mostly because the idea of "taming" an unconventional woman seems like an amusing contest to be won. Petruchio mirrors Katharina's dominant and blunt personality to trick her into becoming more submissive and agreeable. The wordplay with these interactions is funny and borders on the ridiculous, but it is somewhat disappointing from a modern perspective to watch the defeat of the independent Katharina. Bianca's potential husbands, Hortensio and Lucentio, dress up as scholars to spend more time with her right under her father's nose. The role-playing and dress-up of the characters make great slapstick comedy and witty dialogue but also give them the rare opportunity to shift between social classes in their attempts to get what they want.

*The Taming of the Shrew* departs from most of Shakespeare's comedies, as the central focus is not on the romances between the main characters but on the commerce of marriage itself. Since the play continues on after the wedding day—the typical marker of a happy ending in Shakespearean comedies—the play shows that the *happily ever after* is instead a long and sometimes amusing negotiation of how to survive a marriage. *The Taming of the Shrew* is an unconventional comedy that is both entertaining and thought provoking. While concepts like dowries and servitude are outdated, larger themes like gender roles and relationships still ring true for today's audiences, and the play is still a favorite to be adapted, modernized, and played out on stage and screen.

**BAPTISTA Minola,**
a rich man of Padua

**VINCENTIO,** an old
gentleman of Pisa

**LUCENTIO,** son to
Vincentio; in love
with Bianca

**LUCENTIO**
as Cambio

**PETRUCHIO,**
a gentleman of Verona;
suitor to Katharina

**GREMIO,** suitor to
Bianca

**HORTENSIO,** suitor
to Bianca

**HORTENSIO**
as musician

**TRANIO,** servant
to Lucentio

**TRANIO** as Lucentio

**BIONDELLO,**
servant to Lucentio

**GRUMIO,** servant to
Petruchio

**KATHARINA,**
the shrew, older
daughter to Baptista

**BIANCA,** younger
daughter to Baptista

**WIDOW**

**TAILOR**

**HABERDASHER**

## Not Pictured

**PERSONS IN THE INDUCTION**

A Lord
CHRISTOPHER SLY, a tinker
Hostess
Page
Players
Huntsmen
Servants

CURTIS, servant to Petruchio
PEDANT, set up to personate Vincentio

Servants attending on Baptista and Petruchio

# ACT I. Scene I (1–244).

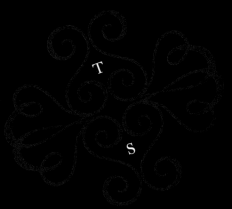

*T*he *Taming of the Shrew* begins with an Induction, which presents characters that are independent from the play itself in an effort to set a literal stage for the story to come. Christopher Sly, a poor drunkard who has caused a ruckus at a local watering hole, unceremoniously passes out as the tavern mistress is chiding him for his behavior. A rich Lord walks into the tavern and, amused to find Sly lacquered with alcohol and unconscious, decides to play a trick on him. The Lord has his attendants bring Sly to the nicest room in the inn, bathe him, dress him in the finest clothes, and adorn him with jewelry. Upon his waking, they are instructed to convince Sly that he is a wealthy nobleman who has been asleep for fifteen years.

As the plan unfolds and the servants prepare for Sly to rouse from his drunken sleep, a troop of actors arrives at the tavern to perform for the Lord. Finding this to be opportune, the Lord convinces the actors to perform for "nobleman" Sly and to do their best not to betray their amusement at any of his uncouth behavior. He goes on to instruct his servant, Bartholomew, to dress up as Sly's distraught wife who will fawn over him once he wakes. Sly awakes sputtering for his next ale, belligerently expressing his confusion about the servants attending to him and the wealthy treatment. The Lord and his attendants tell Sly of his over-the-top and lavish lifestyle, and that he has come down with a hallucinatory illness that makes him think he is a peasant, and he slowly begins to believe them. He quickly embraces his status, going so far as to make sexual inferences to his faux wife. The attendants inform him that the actors are there, and that doctors have prescribed a comedy for his viewing, which will prevent him from going insane again. Sly and his noble wife cozy up and begin to watch the actors perform *The Taming of the Shrew*.

## LUCENTIO

Tranio, since for the great desire I had
To see fair Padua, nursery of arts,
I am arrived for fruitful Lombardy,
The pleasant garden of great Italy;
And by my father's love and leave am arm'd
With his good will and thy good company,
My trusty servant, well approved in all,
Here let us breathe and haply institute
A course of learning and ingenious studies.
Pisa renown'd for grave citizens
Gave me my being and my father first,
A merchant of great traffic through the world,
Vincetino come of Bentivolii.
Vincetino's son brought up in Florence
It shall become to serve all hopes conceived,
To deck his fortune with his virtuous deeds:
And therefore, Tranio, for the time I study,
Virtue and that part of philosophy
Will I apply that treats of happiness
By virtue specially to be achieved.
Tell me thy mind; for I have Pisa left
And am to Padua come, as he that leaves
A shallow plash to plunge him in the deep
And with satiety seeks to quench his thirst.

## TRANIO

Mi perdonato, gentle master mine,
I am in all affected as yourself;
Glad that you thus continue your resolve
To suck the sweets of sweet philosophy.
Only, good master, while we do admire
This virtue and this moral discipline,
Let's be no stoics nor no stocks, I pray;
Or so devote to Aristotle's cheques
As Ovid be an outcast quite abjured:
Balk logic with acquaintance that you have
And practise rhetoric in your common talk;
Music and poesy use to quicken you;
The mathematics and the metaphysics,
Fall to them as you find your stomach serves you;
No profit grows where is no pleasure ta'en:
In brief, sir, study what you most affect.

**LUCENTIO**
Gramercies, Tranio, well dost thou advise.
If, Biondello, thou wert come ashore,
We could at once put us in readiness,
And take a lodging fit to entertain
Such friends as time in Padua shall beget.

**LUCENTIO** (cont.)
But stay a while: what company is this?
**TRANIO**
Master, some show to welcome us to town.

**BAPTISTA**
Gentlemen, importune me no farther,
For how I firmly am resolved you know;
That is, not bestow my youngest daughter
Before I have a husband for the elder:
If either of you both love Katharina,
Because I know you well and love you well,
Leave shall you have to court her at your pleasure.

GREMIO

To cart her rather: she's too rough for me.
There, there, Hortensio, will you any wife?

KATHARINA

I pray you, sir, is it your will
To make a stale of me amongst these mates?

HORTENSIO

Mates, maid! how mean you that? no mates for you,
Unless you were of gentler, milder mould.

KATHARINA

I' faith, sir, you shall never need to fear:
Iwis it is not half way to her heart;
But if it were, doubt not her care should be
To comb your noddle with a three-legg'd stool
And paint your face and use you like a fool.

HORTENSIO

From all such devils, good Lord deliver us!

GREMIO

And me too, good Lord!

TRANIO

Hush, master! here's some good pastime toward:
That wench is stark mad or wonderful froward.

LUCENTIO

But in the other's silence do I see
Maid's mild behavior and sobriety.
Peace, Tranio!

TRANIO

Well said, master; mum! and gaze your fill.

BAPTISTA

Gentlemen, that I may soon make good
What I have said, Bianca, get you in:
And let it not displease thee, good Bianca,
For I will love thee ne'er the less, my girl.

KATHARINA

A pretty peat! it is best
Put finger in the eye, an she knew why.

BIANCA

Sister, content you in my discontent.
Sir, to your pleasure humbly I subscribe:
My books and instruments shall be my company,
On them to look and practise by myself.

**LUCENTIO**
Hark, Tranio! thou may'st hear Minerva speak.

**HORTENSIO**
Signior Baptista, will you be so strange?
Sorry am I that our good will effects
Bianca's grief.
**GREMIO**
Why will you mew her up,
Signior Baptista, for this fiend of hell,
And make her bear the penance of her tongue?

**BAPTISTA**
Gentlemen, content ye; I am resolved:
Go in, Bianca:

**BAPTISTA (cont.)**
And for I know she taketh most delight
In music, instruments and poetry,
Schoolmasters will I keep within my house,
Fit to instruct her youth. If you, Hortensio,
Or Signior Gremio, you, know any such,
Prefer them hither; for to cunning men
I will be very kind, and liberal
To mine own children in good bringing up:
And so farewell.

269

KATHARINA
Why, and I trust I may go too, may I not? What, shall I be appointed hours; as though, belike, I knew not what to take and what to leave, ha?

BAPTISTA (cont.)
Katharina, you may stay;
For I have more to commune with Bianca.

GREMIO
You may go to the devil's dam: your gifts are so good, here's none will hold you. Their love is not so great, Hortensio, but we may blow our nails together, and fast it fairly out: our cakes dough on both sides. Farewell: yet for the love I bear my sweet Bianca, if I can by any means light on a fit man to teach her that wherein she delights, I will wish him to her father.

HORTENSIO
So will I, Signior Gremio: but a word, I pray. Though the nature of our quarrel yet never brooked parle, know now, upon advice, it toucheth us both, that we may yet again have access to our fair mistress and be happy rivals in Bianco's love, to labour and effect one thing specially.
GREMIO
What's that, I pray?
HORTENSIO
Marry, sir, to get a husband for her sister.
GREMIO
A husband! a devil.
HORTENSIO
I say, a husband.

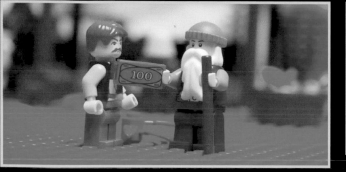

**GREMIO**
I say, a devil. Thinkest thou, Hortensio, though her father be very rich, any man is so very a fool to be married to hell'?

**HORTENSIO**
Tush, Gremio, though it pass your patience and mine to endure her loud alarums, why, man, there be good fellows in the world, an a man could light on them, would take her with all faults, and money enough.

**GREMIO**
I cannot tell; but I had as lief take her dowry with this condition, to be whipped at the high cross every morning.

**HORTENSIO**
Faith, as you say, there's small choice in rotten apples. But come; since this bar in law makes us friends, it shall be so far forth friendly maintained all by helping Baptista's eldest daughter to a husband we set his youngest free for a husband, and then have to't a fresh. Sweet Bianca! Happy man be his dole! He that runs fastest gets the ring. How say you, Signior Gremio?

**GREMIO**
I am agreed; and would I had given him the best horse in Padua to begin his wooing that would thoroughly woo her, wed her and bed her and rid the house of her! Come on.

**TRANIO**
I pray, sir, tell me, is it possible
That love should of a sudden take such hold?

**LUCENTIO**
O Tranio, till I found it to be true,
I never thought it possible or likely;
But see, while idly I stood looking on,
I found the effect of love in idleness:
And now in plainness do confess to thee,
That art to me as secret and as dear
As Anna to the queen of Carthage was,
Tranio, I burn, I pine, I perish, Tranio,
If I achieve not this young modest girl.
Counsel me, Tranio, for I know thou canst;
Assist me, Tranio, for I know thou wilt.

**TRANIO**
Master, it is no time to chide you now;
Affection is not rated from the heart:
If love have touch'd you, nought remains but so,
"Redime te captum quam queas minimo."

**LUCENTIO**
Gramercies, lad, go forward; this contents:
The rest will comfort, for thy counsel's sound.
**TRANIO**
Master, you look'd so longly on the maid,
Perhaps you mark'd not what's the pith of all.

**LUCENTIO**
O yes, I saw sweet beauty in her face,
Such as the daughter of Agenor had,
That made great Jove to humble him to her hand.
When with his knees he kiss'd the Cretan strand.

**TRANIO**
Saw you no more? mark'd you not how her sister
Began to scold and raise up such a storm
That mortal ears might hardly endure the din?

**LUCENTIO**
Tranio, I saw her coral lips to move
And with her breath she did perfume the air:
Sacred and sweet was all I saw in her.
**TRANIO**
Nay, then, 'tis time to stir him from his trance.
I pray, awake, sir: if you love the maid,
Bend thoughts and wits to achieve her. Thus it stands:
Her eldest sister is so curst and shrewd
That till the father rid his hands of her,
Master, your love must live a maid at home;
And therefore has he closely mew'd her up,
Because she will not be annoy'd with suitors.

LUCENTIO
Ah, Tranio, what a cruel father's he!
But art thou not advised, he took some care
To get her cunning schoolmasters to instruct her?
TRANIO
Ay, marry, am I, sir; and now 'tis plotted.

LUCENTIO
I have it, Tranio.
TRANIO
Master, for my hand,
Both our inventions meet and jump in one.
LUCENTIO
Tell me thine first.

TRANIO
You will be schoolmaster
And undertake the teaching of the maid:
That's your device.
LUCENTIO
It is: may it be done?

TRANIO
Not possible; for who shall bear your part,
And be in Padua here Vincentio's son,
Keep house and ply his book, welcome his friends,
Visit his countrymen and banquet them?

**LUCENTIO**
Basta; content thee, for I have it full.
We have not yet been seen in any house,
Nor can we lie distinguish'd by our faces
For man or master; then it follows thus;
Thou shalt be master, Tranio, in my stead,
Keep house and port and servants as I should:

**LUCENTIO (cont.)**
I will some other be, some Florentine,
Some Neapolitan, or meaner man of Pisa.
'Tis hatch'd and shall be so: Tranio, at once
Uncase thee; take my colour'd hat and cloak:
When Biondello comes, he waits on thee;
But I will charm him first to keep his tongue.

**TRANIO**
So had you need.
In brief, sir, sith it your pleasure is,
And I am tied to be obedient;
For so your father charged me at our parting,
"Be serviceable to my son," quoth he,
Although I think 'twas in another sense;
I am content to be Lucentio,
Because so well I love Lucentio.
**LUCENTIO**
Tranio, be so, because Lucentio loves:
And let me be a slave, to achieve that maid
Whose sudden sight hath thrall'd my wounded eye.
Here comes the rogue.

**LUCENTIO (cont.)**
Sirrah, where have you been?
**BIONDELLO**
Where have I been! Nay, how now! where are you?
Master, has my fellow Tranio stolen your clothes? Or
you stolen his? or both? pray, what's the news?

**LUCENTIO**

Sirrah, come hither: 'tis no time to jest,
And therefore frame your manners to the time.
Your fellow Tranio here, to save my life,
Puts my apparel and my countenance on,
And I for my escape have put on his;
For in a quarrel since I came ashore
I kill'd a man and fear I was descried:
Wait you on him, I charge you, as becomes,
While I make way from hence to save my life:
You understand me?

**BIONDELLO**

I, sir! ne'er a whit.

**LUCENTIO**

And not a jot of Tranio in your mouth:
Tranio is changed into Lucentio.

**BIONDELLO**

The better for him: would I were so too!

**TRANIO**

So could I, faith, boy, to have the next wish after,
That Lucentio indeed had Baptista's youngest daughter.
But, sirrah, not for my sake, but your master's, I advise
You use your manners discreetly in all kind of companies:
When I am alone, why, then I am Tranio;
But in all places else your master Lucentio.

**LUCENTIO**

Tranio, let's go: one thing more rests, that
thyself execute, to make one among these wooers: if
thou ask me why, sufficeth, my reasons are both good
and weighty.

# ACT II. Scene I (1–404).

T
S

*A*t the conclusion of the first scene, the spotlight returns fleetingly to the characters from the Induction. Christopher Sly is nodding off to sleep, and his noble "wife" and "servant" are prodding him to keep awake and enjoy the performance. He sleepily responds that he loves it and wishes it were over.

The second scene opens with Petruchio and his servant, Grumio, arriving at Hortensio's house from Verona. Grumio perceives everything Petruchio says in a literal sense, which leads to much misunderstanding, comic banter, and Grumio being pulled by the ears. Petruchio explains at length that he has come to Padua to find a wife, so long as she is exceedingly rich. Hortensio knows of a beautiful and wealthy young woman named Katharina for him to marry, but he warns that she is a quarrelsome, "intolerable curst" (I.i.86) whom even he would not marry for all the gold in a mine. Hortensio urges Petruchio to aid him in his own quest for love, as he has eyes for the shrew's sister. The sisters' father, Baptista, has declared that the younger Bianca cannot wed until Katharina has married. Hortensio decides that he will dress up as a music tutor so that during private lessons he can properly court Bianca. At the same time, Lucentio dresses up as the Latin teacher "Cambio" under the guise that he will help another old man of Padua, Gremio, to win Bianca. Petruchio agrees to pursue Katharina so that Hortensio and Gremio can compete for Bianca's affections. In yet another twist, Lucentio has instructed his servant Tranio to dress up as Lucentio and also compete for Bianca.

**BIANCA**
Good sister, wrong me not, nor wrong yourself,
To make a bondmaid and a slave of me;
That I disdain: but for these other gawds,
Unbind my hands, I'll pull them off myself,
Yea, all my raiment, to my petticoat;
Or what you will command me will I do,
So well I know my duty to my elders.

**KATHARINA**
Of all thy suitors, here I charge thee, tell
Whom thou lovest best: see thou dissemble not.

**BIANCA**
Believe me, sister, of all the men alive
I never yet beheld that special face
Which I could fancy more than any other.

KATHARINA
Minion, thou liest. Is't not Hortensio?
BIANCA
If you affect him, sister, here I swear
I'll plead for you myself, but you shall have him.

KATHARINA
O then, belike, you fancy riches more:
You will have Gremio to keep you fair.
BIANCA
Is it for him you do envy me so?
Nay then you jest, and now I well perceive
You have but jested with me all this while:
I prithee, sister Kate, untie my hands.

KATHARINA
If that be jest, then all the rest was so.

BAPTISTA
Why, how now, dame! whence grows this insolence?
Bianca, stand aside. Poor girl! she weeps.
Go ply thy needle; meddle not with her.
For shame, thou helding of a devilish spirit,
Why dost thou wrong her that did ne'er wrong thee?
When did she cross thee with a bitter word?

KATHARINA
What, will you not suffer me? Nay, now I see
She is your treasure, she must have a husband;
I must dance bare-foot on her wedding day
And for your love to her lead apes in hell.

KATHARINA (cont.)
Talk not to me: I will go sit and weep
Till I can find occasion of revenge.

**BAPTISTA**
Was ever gentleman thus grieved as I?
But who comes here?

**GREMIO**
Good morrow, neighbour Baptista.
**BAPTISTA**
Good morrow, neighbour Gremio.
God save you, gentlemen!

**PETRUCHIO**
And you, good sir! Pray, have you not a daughter
Call'd Katharina, fair and virtuous?

**BAPTISTA**
I have a daughter, sir, called Katharina.

**GREMIO**
You are too blunt: go to it orderly.

281

**PETRUCHIO**
You wrong me, Signior Gremio: give me leave.
I am a gentleman of Verona, sir,
That, hearing of her beauty and her wit,
Her affability and bashful modesty,
Her wondrous qualities and mild behavior,
Am bold to show myself a forward guest
Within your house, to make mine eye the witness
Of that report which I so oft have heard.
And, for an entrance to my entertainment,

**PETRUCHIO (cont.)**
I do present you with a man of mine,
Cunning in music and the mathematics,
To instruct her fully in those sciences,
Whereof I know she is not ignorant:
Accept of him, or else you do me wrong:
His name is Litio, born in Mantua.

**BAPTISTA**
You're welcome, sir; and he, for your good sake.
But for my daughter Katharina, this I know,
She is not for your turn, the more my grief.
**PETRUCHIO**
I see you do not mean to part with her,
Or else you like not of my company.
**BAPTISTA**
Mistake me not; I speak but as I find.
Whence are you, sir? what may I call your name?

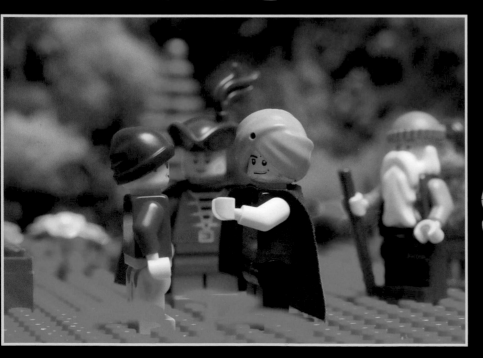

**PETRUCHIO**
Petruchio is my name; Antonio's son,
A man well known throughout all Italy.
**BAPTISTA**
I know him well: you are welcome for his sake.

GREMIO
Saving your tale, Petruchio, I pray,
Let us, that are poor petitioners, speak too:
Baccare! you are marvellous forward.
PETRUCHIO
O, pardon me, Signior Gremio; I would fain be doing.

GREMIO
I doubt it not, sir; but you will curse your
wooing. Neighbour, this is a gift very grateful, I am
sure of it. To express the like kindness, myself,
that have been more kindly beholding to you than
any, freely give unto you this young scholar,
that hath been long studying at Rheims; as cunning
in Greek, Latin, and other languages, as the other
in music and mathematics: his name is Cambio; pray,
accept his service.
BAPTISTA
A thousand thanks, Signior Gremio.
Welcome, good Cambio.

BAPTISTA (cont.)
But, gentle sir, methinks you walk like a stranger:
may I be so bold to know the cause of your coming?
TRANIO
Pardon me, sir, the boldness is mine own,
That, being a stranger in this city here,
Do make myself a suitor to your daughter,
Unto Bianca, fair and virtuous.
Nor is your firm resolve unknown to me,
In the preferment of the eldest sister.
This liberty is all that I request,
That, upon knowledge of my parentage,
I may have welcome 'mongst the rest that woo
And free access and favour as the rest:
And, toward the education of your daughters,
I here bestow a simple instrument,
And this small packet of Greek and Latin books:
If you accept them, then their worth is great.

**BAPTISTA**
Lucentio is your name; of whence, I pray?
**TRANIO**
Of Pisa, sir; son to Vincentio.
**BAPTISTA**
A mighty man of Pisa; by report
I know him well: you are very welcome, sir,
Take you the lute, and you the set of books;
You shall go see your pupils presently.
Holla, within!
Sirrah, lead these gentlemen
To my daughters; and tell them both,
These are their tutors: bid them use them well.
We will go walk a little in the orchard,
And then to dinner. You are passing welcome,
And so I pray you all to think yourselves.

**PETRUCHIO**
Signior Baptista, my business asketh haste,
And every day I cannot come to woo.
You knew my father well, and in him me,
Left solely heir to all his lands and goods,
Which I have better'd rather than decreased:
Then tell me, if I get your daughter's love,
What dowry shall I have with her to wife?
**BAPTISTA**
After my death the one half of my lands,
And in possession twenty thousand crowns.

**PETRUCHIO**

And, for that dowry, I'll assure her of
Her widowhood, be it that she survive me,
In all my lands and leases whatsoever:
Let specialties be therefore drawn between us,
That covenants may be kept on either hand.

**BAPTISTA**

Well mayst thou woo, and happy be thy speed!
But be thou arm'd for some unhappy words.

**PETRUCHIO**

Ay, to the proof; as mountains are for winds,
That shake not, though they blow perpetually.

BAPTISTA
How now, my friend! why dost thou look so pale?
HORTENSIO
For fear, I promise you, if I look pale.

HORTENSIO
Why, no; for she hath broke the lute to me.
I did but tell her she mistook her frets,
And bow'd her hand to teach her fingering;
When, with a most impatient devilish spirit,
"Frets, call you these?" quoth she; "I'll fume with them:"
And, with that word, she struck me on the head,
And through the instrument my pate made way;
And there I stood amazed for a while,
As on a pillory, looking through the lute;
While she did call me rascal fiddler
And twangling Jack; with twenty such vile terms,
As had she studied to misuse me so.

BAPTISTA
What, will my daughter prove a good musician?
HORTENSIO
I think she'll sooner prove a soldier
Iron may hold with her, but never lutes.
BAPTISTA
Why, then thou canst not break her to the lute?

PETRUCHIO
Now, by the world, it is a lusty wench;
I love her ten times more than e'er I did:
O, how I long to have some chat with her!
BAPTISTA
Well, go with me and be not so discomfited:
Proceed in practise with my younger daughter;
She's apt to learn and thankful for good turns.
Signior Petruchio, will you go with us,
Or shall I send my daughter Kate to you?
PETRUCHIO
I pray you do.

PETRUCHIO (cont.)
I will attend her here,
And woo her with some spirit when she comes.
Say that she rail; why then I'll tell her plain
She sings as sweetly as a nightingale:
Say that she frown, I'll say she looks as clear
As morning roses newly wash'd with dew:
Say she be mute and will not speak a word;

Then I'll commend her volubility,
And say she uttereth piercing eloquence:
If she do bid me pack, I'll give her thanks,
As though she bid me stay by her a week:
If she deny to wed, I'll crave the day
When I shall ask the banns and when be married.
But here she comes; and now, Petruchio, speak.

PETRUCHIO (cont.)
Good morrow, Kate; for that's your name, I hear.
KATHARINA
Well have you heard, but something hard of hearing:
They call me Katharina that do talk of me.

PETRUCHIO
You lie, in faith; for you are call'd plain Kate,
And bonny Kate and sometimes Kate the curst;
But Kate, the prettiest Kate in Christendom
Kate of Kate Hall, my super-dainty Kate,
For dainties are all Kates, and therefore, Kate,
Take this of me, Kate of my consolation;
Hearing thy mildness praised in every town,
Thy virtues spoke of, and thy beauty sounded,
Yet not so deeply as to thee belongs,
Myself am moved to woo thee for my wife.

KATHARINA
Moved! in good time: let him that moved you hither
Remove you hence: I knew you at the first
You were a moveable.
PETRUCHIO
Why, what's a moveable?
KATHARINA
A join'd-stool.

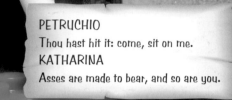

PETRUCHIO
Thou hast hit it: come, sit on me.
KATHARINA
Asses are made to bear, and so are you.

PETRUCHIO
Women are made to bear, and so are you.
KATHARINA
No such jade as you, if me you mean.
PETRUCHIO
Alas! good Kate, I will not burden thee;
For, knowing thee to be but young and light—

KATHARINA
Too light for such a swain as you to catch;
And yet as heavy as my weight should be.
PETRUCHIO
Should be! Should—buzz!
KATHARINA
Well ta'en, and like a buzzard.

PETRUCHIO
O slow-wing'd turtle! shall a buzzard take thee?
KATHARINA
Ay, for a turtle, as he takes a buzzard.
PETRUCHIO
Come, come, you wasp; i' faith, you are too angry.
KATHARINA
If I be waspish, best beware my sting.

PETRUCHIO
My remedy is then, to pluck it out.

KATHARINA
Ay, if the fool could find it where it lies.
PETRUCHIO
Who knows not where a wasp does
wear his sting? In his tail.
KATHARINA
In his tongue.
PETRUCHIO
Whose tongue?

KATHARINA
Yours, if you talk of tails: and so farewell.
PETRUCHIO
What, with my tongue in your tail? nay, come again,
Good Kate; I am a gentleman.

PETRUCHIO
A combless cock, so Kate will be my hen.
KATHARINA
No cock of mine; you crow too like a craven.
PETRUCHIO
Nay, come, Kate, come; you must not look so sour.
KATHARINA
It is my fashion, when I see a crab.
PETRUCHIO
Why, here's no crab; and therefore look not sour.
KATHARINA
There is, there is.
PETRUCHIO
Then show it me.

KATHARINA
Had I a glass, I would.
PETRUCHIO
What, you mean my face?
KATHARINA
Well aim'd of such a young one.
PETRUCHIO
Now, by Saint George, I am too young for you.
KATHARINA
Yet you are wither'd.
PETRUCHIO
'Tis with cares.
KATHARINA
I care not.
PETRUCHIO
Nay, hear you, Kate: in sooth you scape not so.
KATHARINA
I chafe you, if I tarry: let me go.

**PETRUCHIO**

No, not a whit: I find you passing gentle.
'Twas told me you were rough and coy and sullen,
And now I find report a very liar;
For thou are pleasant, gamesome, passing courteous,
But slow in speech, yet sweet as spring-time flowers:
Thou canst not frown, thou canst not look askance,
Nor bite the lip, as angry wenches will,
Nor hast thou pleasure to be cross in talk,
But thou with mildness entertain'st thy wooers,
With gentle conference, soft and affable.
Why does the world report that Kate doth limp?
O slanderous world! Kate like the hazel-twig
Is straight and slender and as brown in hue
As hazel nuts and sweeter than the kernels.
O, let me see thee walk: thou dost not halt.

**KATHARINA**

Go, fool, and whom thou keep'st command.

**PETRUCHIO**

Did ever Dian so become a grove
As Kate this chamber with her princely gait?
O, be thou Dian, and let her be Kate;
And then let Kate be chaste and Dian sportful!

**KATHARINA**

Where did you study all this goodly speech?

**PETRUCHIO**

It is extempore, from my mother-wit.

**KATHARINA**

A witty mother! witless else her son.

**PETRUCHIO**

Am I not wise?

**KATHARINA**

Yes; keep you warm.

**PETRUCHIO**

Marry, so I mean, sweet Katharina, in thy bed:
And therefore, setting all this chat aside,
Thus in plain terms: your father hath consented
That you shall be my wife; your dowry 'greed on;
And, will you, nill you, I will marry you.
Now, Kate, I am a husband for your turn;
For, by this light, whereby I see thy beauty,
Thy beauty, that doth make me like thee well,
Thou must be married to no man but me;
For I am he am born to tame you Kate,
And bring you from a wild Kate to a Kate
Conformable as other household Kates.
Here comes your father: never make denial;
I must and will have Katharina to my wife.

**BAPTISTA**
Now, Signior Petruchio, how speed you with my daughter?
**PETRUCHIO**
How but well, sir? how but well?
It were impossible I should speed amiss.
**BAPTISTA**
Why, how now, daughter Katharina! in your umps?

**KATHARINA**
Call you me daughter? now, I promise you
You have show'd a tender fatherly regard,
To wish me wed to one half lunatic;
A mad-cup ruffian and a swearing Jack,
That thinks with oaths to face the matter out.

**PETRUCHIO**
Father, 'tis thus: yourself and all the world,
That talk'd of her, have talk'd amiss of her:
If she be curst, it is for policy,
For she's not froward, but modest as the dove;
She is not hot, but temperate as the morn;
For patience she will prove a second Grissel,
And Roman Lucrece for her chastity:
And to conclude, we have 'greed so well together,
That upon Sunday is the wedding-day.

**KATHARINA**
I'll see thee hang'd on Sunday first.

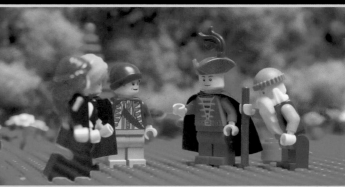

**GREMIO**
Hark, Petruchio; she says she'll see thee hang'd first.
**TRANIO**
Is this your speeding? nay, then, good night our part!

**PETRUCHIO**
Be patient, gentlemen; I choose her for myself:
If she and I be pleased, what's that to you?
'Tis bargain'd 'twixt us twain, being alone,
That she shall still be curst in company.
I tell you, 'tis incredible to believe
How much she loves me: O, the kindest Kate!
She hung about my neck; and kiss on kiss
She vied so fast, protesting oath on oath,
That in a twink she won me to her love.
O, you are novices! 'tis a world to see,
How tame, when men and women are alone,
A meacock wretch can make the curstest shrew.
Give me thy hand, Kate: I will unto Venice,
To buy apparel 'gainst the wedding-day.
Provide the feast, father, and bid the guests;
I will be sure my Katharina shall be fine.

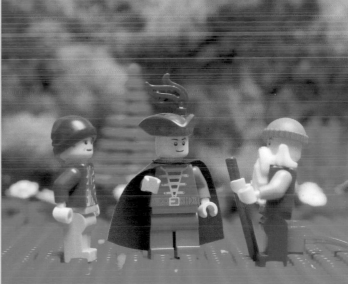

**BAPTISTA**
I know not what to say: but give me your hands;
God send you joy, Petruchio! 'tis a match.
**GREMIO and TRANIO**
Amen, say we: we will be witnesses.
**PETRUCHIO**
Father, and wife, and gentlemen, adieu;
I will to Venice; Sunday comes apace:
We will have rings and things and fine array;
And kiss me, Kate, we will be married o'Sunday.

**GREMIO**
Was ever match clapp'd up so suddenly?
**BAPTISTA**
Faith, gentlemen, now I play a merchant's part,
And venture madly on a desperate mart.
**TRANIO**
'Twas a commodity lay fretting by you:
'Twill bring you gain, or perish on the seas.
**BAPTISTA**
The gain I seek is, quiet in the match.

GREMIO
No doubt but he hath got a quiet catch.
But now, Baptists, to your younger daughter:
Now is the day we long have looked for:
I am your neighbour, and was suitor first.
TRANIO
And I am one that love Bianca more
Than words can witness, or your thoughts can guess.

GREMIO
Youngling, thou canst not love so dear as I.
TRANIO
Graybeard, thy love doth freeze.
GREMIO
But thine doth fry.
Skipper, stand back: 'tis age that nourisheth.
TRANIO
But youth in ladies' eyes that flourisheth.

BAPTISTA
Content you, gentlemen: I will compound this strife:
'Tis deeds must win the prize; and he of both
That can assure my daughter greatest dower
Shall have my Bianca's love.
Say, Signior Gremio, what can you assure her?

**GREMIO**
First, as you know, my house within the city
Is richly furnished with plate and gold;
Basins and ewers to lave her dainty hands;
My hangings all of Tyrian tapestry;
In ivory coffers I have stuff'd my crowns;
In cypress chests my arras counterpoints,
Costly apparel, tents, and canopies,
Fine linen, Turkey cushions boss'd with pearl,
Valance of Venice gold in needlework,
Pewter and brass and all things that belong
To house or housekeeping: then, at my farm
I have a hundred milch-kine to the pail,
Sixscore fat oxen standing in my stalls,
And all things answerable to this portion.
Myself am struck in years, I must confess;
And if I die to-morrow, this is hers,
If whilst I live she will be only mine.

**TRANIO**
That "only" came well in. Sir, list to me:
I am my father's heir and only son:
If I may have your daughter to my wife,
I'll leave her houses three or four as good,
Within rich Pisa walls, as any one
Old Signior Gremio has in Padua;
Besides two thousand ducats by the year
Of fruitful land, all which shall be her jointure.
What, have I pinch'd you, Signior Gremio?
**GREMIO**
Two thousand ducats by the year of land!
My land amounts not to so much in all:
That she shall have; besides an argosy
That now is lying in Marseilles' road.
What, have I choked you with an argosy?

**TRANIO**
Gremio, 'tis known my father hath no less
Than three great argosies; besides two galliases,
And twelve tight galleys: these I will assure her,
And twice as much, whate'er thou offer'st next.
**GREMIO**
Nay, I have offer'd all, I have no more;
And she can have no more than all I have:
If you like me, she shall have me and mine.
**TRANIO**
Why, then the maid is mine from all the world,
By your firm promise: Gremio is out-vied.
**BAPTISTA**
I must confess your offer is the best;
And, let your father make her the assurance,
She is your own; else, you must pardon me,
if you should die before him, where's her dower?

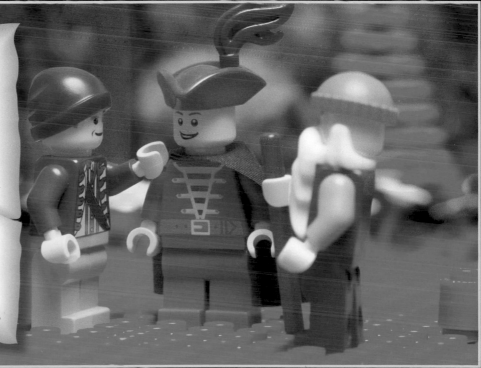

TRANIO
That's but a cavil: he is old, I young.
GREMIO
And may not young men die, as well as old?
BAPTISTA
Well, gentlemen,
I am thus resolved: on Sunday next you know
My daughter Katharina is to be married:
Now, on the Sunday following, shall Bianca
Be bride to you, if you this assurance;
If not, Signior Gremio:
And so, I take my leave, and thank you both.
GREMIO
Adieu, good neighbour.

GREMIO (cont.)
Now I fear thee not:
Sirrah young gamester, your father were a fool
To give thee all, and in his waning age
Set foot under thy table: tut, a toy!
An old Italian fox is not so kind, my boy.

TRANIO
A vengeance on your crafty wither'd hide!
Yet I have faced it with a card of ten.
'Tis in my head to do my master good:
I see no reason but supposed Lucentio
Must get a father, call'd "supposed Vincentio;"
And that's a wonder: fathers commonly
Do get their children; but in this case of wooing,
A child shall get a sire, if I fail not of my cunning.

# ACT III. Scene II (1–248).

$\mathcal{A}$ ct III begins with Hortensio (dressed as Licio) and Lucentio (dressed as Cambio) bickering over who should have preference over Bianca's first lesson. Bianca intervenes and chooses to start with "Cambio" while "Licio" tunes his instrument. Lucentio reveals himself and his motives to Bianca. The two whisper to each other just out of earshot of Hortensio, who struggles to keep up with Lucentio. By the end of the lesson, it is clear that Bianca favors Lucentio.

**BAPTISTA**
Signior Lucentio, this is the 'pointed day.
That Katharina and Petruchio should be married,
And yet we hear not of our son-in-law.
What will be said? what mockery will it be,
To want the bridegroom when the priest attends
To speak the ceremonial rites of marriage!
What says Lucentio to this shame of ours?

**KATHARINA**
No shame but mine: I must, forsooth, be forced
To give my hand opposed against my heart
Unto a mad-brain rudesby full of spleen;
Who woo'd in haste and means to wed at leisure.
I told you, I, he was a frantic fool,
Hiding his bitter jests in blunt behavior:
And, to be noted for a merry man,
He'll woo a thousand, 'point the day of marriage,
Make feasts, invite friends, and proclaim the banns;
Yet never means to wed where he hath woo'd.
Now must the world point at poor Katharina,
And say, "Lo, there is mad Petruchio's wife,
If it would please him come and marry her!"

**TRANIO**
Patience, good Katharina, and Baptista too.
Upon my life, Petruchio means but well,
Whatever fortune stays him from his word:
Though he be blunt, I know him passing wise;
Though he be merry, yet withal he's honest.

**KATHARINA**
Would Katharina had never seen him though!

**BAPTISTA**
Go, girl; I cannot blame thee now to weep;
For such an injury would vex a very saint,
Much more a shrew of thy impatient humour.

BIONDELLO
Master, master! news, old news, and such news as you never heard of!

BAPTISTA
Is it new and old too? how may that be?

BIONDELLO
Why, is it not news, to hear of Petruchio's coming?
BAPTISTA
Is he come?

BIONDELLO
Why, no, sir.

BAPTISTA
What then?

BIONDELLO
He is coming.
BAPTISTA
When will he be here?

**BIONDELLO**
When he stands where I am and sees you there.

**TRANIO**
But say, what to thine old news?

**BIONDELLO**
Why, Petruchio is coming in a new hat and an old jerkin, a pair of old breeches thrice turned, a pair of boots that have been candle-cases, one buckled, another laced, an old rusty sword ta'en out of the town-armory, with a broken hilt, and chapeless; with two broken points: his horse hipped with an old mothy saddle and stirrups of no kindred; besides, possessed with the glanders and like to mose in the chine; troubled with the lampass, infected with the fashions, full of wingdalls, sped with spavins, rayed with yellows, past cure of the fives, stark spoiled with the staggers, begnawn with the bots, swayed in the back and shoulder-shotten; near-legged before and with, a half-chequed bit and a head-stall of sheep's leather which, being restrained to keep him from stumbling, hath been often burst and now repaired with knots; one girth six time pieced and a woman's crupper of velure, which hath two letters for her name fairly set down in studs, and here and there pieced with packthread.

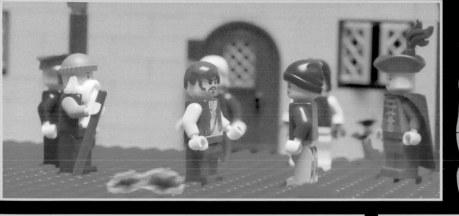

BAPTISTA
Who comes with him?
BIONDELLO
O, sir, his lackey, for all the world caparisoned like the horse; with a linen stock on one leg and a kersey boot-hose on the other, gartered with a red and blue list; an old hat and "the humour of forty fancies" pricked in't for a feather: a monster, a very monster in apparel, and not like a Christian footboy or a gentleman's lackey.

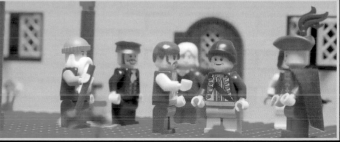

TRANIO
'Tis some odd humour pricks him to this fashion;
Yet oftentimes he goes but mean-apparell'd.

BAPTISTA
I am glad he's come, howsoe'er he comes.
BIONDELLO
Why, sir, he comes not.

BAPTISTA
Didst thou not say he comes?
BIONDELLO
Who? that Petruchio came?

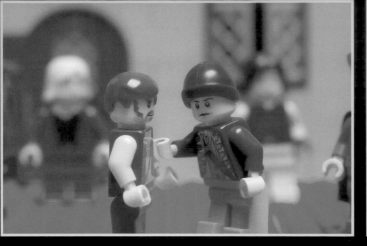

BAPTISTA

Ay, that Petruchio came.

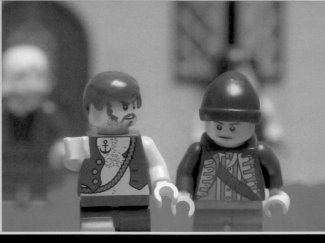

BIONDELLO

No, sir, I say his horse comes, with him on his back.

BAPTISTA

Why, that's all one.

BIONDELLO

Nay, by Saint Jamy,
I hold you a penny,
A horse and a man
Is more than one,
And yet not many.

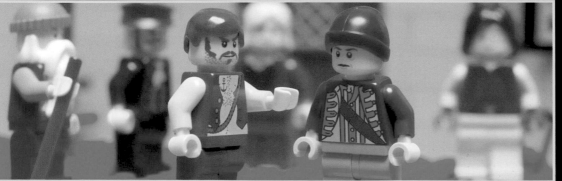

**PETRUCHIO**
Come, where be these gallants? who's at home?

**BAPTISTA**
You are welcome, sir.

**BAPTISTA**
And yet you halt not.

**PETRUCHIO**
And yet I come not well.

**TRANIO**
Not so well apparell'd
As I wish you were.

**PETRUCHIO**
Were it better, I should rush in thus.
But where is Kate? where is my lovely bride?
How does my father? Gentles, methinks you frown:
And wherefore gaze this goodly company,
As if they saw some wondrous monument,
Some comet or unusual prodigy?

**BAPTISTA**
Why, sir, you know this is your wedding-day:
First were we sad, fearing you would not come;
Now sadder, that you come so unprovided.
Fie, doff this habit, shame to your estate,
An eye-sore to our solemn festival!

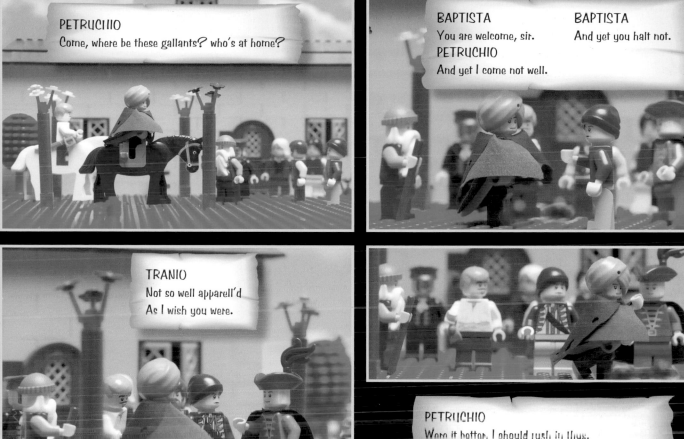

TRANIO
And tells us, what occasion of import
Hath all so long detain'd you from your wife,
And sent you hither so unlike yourself?

TRANIO
And tells us, what occasion of import
Hath all so long detain'd you from your wife,
And sent you hither so unlike yourself?

PETRUCHIO
Tedious it were to tell, and harsh to hear:
Sufficeth I am come to keep my word,
Though in some part enforced to digress;
Which, at more leisure, I will so excuse
As you shall well be satisfied withal.
But where is Kate? I stay too long from her:
The morning wears, 'tis time we were at church.

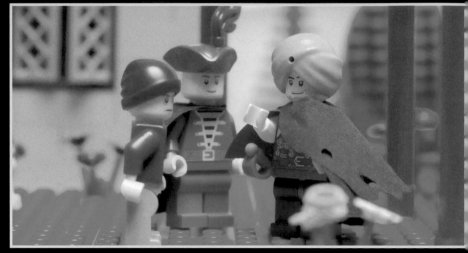

TRANIO
See not your bride in these unreverent robes:
Go to my chamber; put on clothes of mine.
PETRUCHIO
Not I, believe me: thus I'll visit her.

BAPTISTA
But thus, I trust, you will not marry her.

**PETRUCHIO**
Good sooth, even thus; therefore ha' done with words:
To me she's married, not unto my clothes:
Could I repair what she will wear in me,
As I can change these poor accoutrements,
'Twere well for Kate and better for myself.
But what a fool am I to chat with you,
When I should bid good morrow to my bride,
And seal the title with a lovely kiss!

**TRANIO**
He hath some meaning in his mad attire:
We will persuade him, be it possible,
To put on better ere he go to church.

**BAPTISTA**
I'll after him, and see the event of this.

**TRANIO**

But to her love concerneth us to add
Her father's liking: which to bring to pass,
As I before unparted to your worship,
I am to get a man,—whate'er he be,
It skills not much; we'll fit him to our turn,—
And he shall be Vincentio of Pisa;
And make assurance here in Padua
Of greater sums than I have promised.
So shall you quietly enjoy your hope,
And marry sweet Bianca with consent.

**LUCENTIO**

Were it not that my fellow school-master
Doth watch Bianca's steps so narrowly,
'Twere good, methinks, to steal our marriage;
Which once perform'd, let all the world say no,
I'll keep mine own, despite of all the world.

**TRANIO**

That by degrees we mean to look into,
And watch our vantage in this business:
We'll over-reach the greybeard, Gremio,
The narrow-prying father, Minola,
The quaint musician, amorous Licio;
All for my master's sake, Lucentio.

**TRANIO (cont.)**

Signior Gremio, came you from the church?

**GREMIO**

As willingly as e'er I came from school.

TRANIO

And is the bride and bridegroom coming home?

GREMIO

A bridegroom say you? 'tis a groom indeed,

A grumbling groom, and that the girl shall find.

TRANIO

Curster than she? why, 'tis impossible.

GREMIO

Why he's a devil, a devil, a very fiend.

TRANIO

Why, she's a devil, a devil, the devil's dam.

GREMIO

Tut, she's a lamb, a dove, a fool to him!

I'll tell you, Sir Lucentio: when the priest

Should ask, if Katharina should be his wife,

"Ay, by gogs-wouns," quoth he; and swore so loud,

That, all-amazed, the priest let fall the book;

**GREMIO (cont.)**
And, as he stoop'd again to take it up,
The mad-brain'd bridegroom took him such a cuff
That down fell priest and book and book and priest:
"Now take them up," quoth he, "if any list."

**TRANIO**
What said the wench when he rose again?

**GREMIO**
Trembled and shook; for why, he stamp'd and swore,
As if the vicar meant to cozen him.
But after many ceremonies done,
He calls for wine: "A health!" quoth he, as if
He had been aboard, carousing to his mates
After a storm; quaff'd off the muscadel
And threw the sops all in the sexton's face;
Having no other reason
But that his beard grew thin and hungerly
And seem'd to ask him sops as he was drinking.
This done, he took the bride about the neck
And kiss'd her lips with such a clamorous smack
That at the parting all the church did echo:
And I seeing this came thence for very shame;
And after me, I know, the rout is coming.
Such a mad marriage never was before:
Hark, hark! I hear the minstrels play.

**PETRUCHIO**

Gentlemen and friends, I thank you for your pains:
I know you think to dine with me to-day,
And have prepared great store of wedding cheer;
But so it is, my haste doth call me hence,
And therefore here I mean to take my leave.

**BAPTISTA**

Is't possible you will away to-night?

**PETRUCHIO**

I must away to-day, before night come:
Make it no wonder; if you knew my business,
You would entreat me rather go than stay.
And, honest company, I thank you all,
That have beheld me give away myself
To this most patient, sweet and virtuous wife:
Dine with my father, drink a health to me;
For I must hence; and farewell to you all.

**TRANIO**

Let us entreat you stay till after dinner.

**PETRUCHIO**

It may not be.

**GREMIO**

Let me entreat you.

**PETRUCHIO**

It cannot be.

**KATHARINA**

Let me entreat you.

**PETRUCHIO**

I am content.

**KATHARINA**

Are you content to stay?

PETRUCHIO

I am content you shall entreat me stay;
But yet not stay, entreat me how you can.

KATHARINA

Now, if you love me, stay.

PETRUCHIO

Grumio, my horse.

GRUMIO

Ay, sir, they be ready: the oats have eaten the horses.

KATHARINA

Nay, then,
Do what thou canst, I will not go to-day;
No, nor to-morrow, not till I please myself.
The door is open, sir; there lies your way;
You may be jogging whiles your boots are green;
For me, I'll not be gone till I please myself:
'Tis like you'll prove a jolly surly groom,
That take it on you at the first so roundly.

PETRUCHIO

O Kate, content thee; prithee, be not angry.

KATHARINA

I will be angry: what hast thou to do?
Father, be quiet; he shall stay my leisure.

GREMIO

Ay, marry, sir, now it begins to work.

KATHARINA

Gentlemen, forward to the bridal dinner:
I see a woman may be made a fool,
If she had not a spirit to resist.

**PETRUCHIO**
They shall go forward, Kate, at thy command.
Obey the bride, you that attend on her;
Go to the feast, revel and domineer,
Carouse full measure to her maidenhead,
Be mad and merry, or go hang yourselves:
But for my bonny Kate, she must with me.
Nay, look not big, nor stamp, nor stare, nor fret;
I will be master of what is mine own:
She is my goods, my chattels; she is my house,
My household stuff, my field, my barn,
My horse, my ox, my ass, my any thing;
And here she stands, touch her whoever dare;
I'll bring mine action on the proudest he
That stops my way in Padua. Grumio,
Draw forth thy weapon, we are beset with thieves;
Rescue thy mistress, if thou be a man.
Fear not, sweet wench, they shall not touch thee, Kate:
I'll buckler thee against a million.

**BAPTISTA**
Nay, let them go, a couple of quiet ones.
**GREMIO**
Went they not quickly, I should die with laughing.
**TRANIO**
Of all mad matches never was the like.

**LUCENTIO**
Mistress, what's your opinion of your sister?
**BIANCA**
That, being mad herself, she's madly mated.

**GREMIO**
I warrant him, Petruchio is Kated.
**BAPTISTA**
Neighbours and friends, though bride and
bridegroom wants
For to supply the places at the table,
You know there wants no junkets at the feast.
Lucentio, you shall supply the bridegroom's place:
And let Bianca take her sister's room.
**TRANIO**
Shall sweet Bianca practise how to bride it?
**BAPTISTA**
She shall, Lucentio. Come, gentlemen, let's go.

# ACT IV. Scene III (1–162).

T

S

*A*t the commencement of Act IV, Grumio enters Petruchio's house frigid and complaining of his most recent journey with his master and Katharina. Curtis stokes a fire for him, and Grumio tells the story of how Petruchio's horse fell, tossing Katharina into the mud. Instead of helping his bride who was stuck under the horse, Petruchio instead began beating Grumio. Grumio finishes his story as Petruchio rushes into the house, trailed by Katharina, and jumps into an onslaught of orders to the servants. Katharina urges him to be less difficult, and Petruchio ultimately steals her away without having eaten dinner, under the claim that it has not been cooked properly. The servants observe this behavior and rightly note that Petruchio is giving her a taste of her own medicine. Petruchio's plan to tame Katharina is slowly coming to fruition: as he becomes exceedingly more difficult, Katharina becomes more attentive and wifely.

As it becomes clear that Lucentio (disguised at Cambio) has successfully wooed Bianca, Hortensio decides that he can no longer love a woman who would fall for someone of such low stature. Tranio (disguised as Lucentio) convinces Hortensio that they should both quit vying for Bianca's affections and swear that they will find someone much better for themselves. Tranio steers Hortensio into a different direction, leaving Bianca free and clear for Lucentio to claim her in marriage. Hortensio recalls a wealthy widow who had appealed to him and resolves to marry her instead. Meanwhile, Biondello has found a merchant to pretend to be Vincentio, Lucentio's father, to give Baptista assurance of Lucentio's wealth.

**GRUMIO**
No, no, forsooth; I dare not for my life.
**KATHARINA**
The more my wrong, the more his spite appears:
What, did he marry me to famish me?
Beggars, that come unto my father's door,
Upon entreaty have a present alms;
If not, elsewhere they meet with charity:
But I, who never knew how to entreat,
Nor never needed that I should entreat,
Am starved for meat, giddy for lack of sleep,
With oath kept waking and with brawling fed:
And that which spites me more than all these wants,
He does it under name of perfect love;
As who should say, if I should sleep or eat,
'Twere deadly sickness or else present death.
I prithee go and get me some repast;
I care not what, so it be wholesome food.

**GRUMIO**
What say you to a neat's foot?
**KATHARINA**
'Tis passing good: I prithee let me have it.

**GRUMIO**
I fear it is too choleric a meat.
How say you to a fat tripe finely broil'd?
**KATHARINA**
I like it well: good Grumio, fetch it me.
**GRUMIO**
I cannot tell; I fear 'tis choleric.
What say you to a piece of beef and mustard?

KATHARINA

A dish that I do love to feed upon.

GRUMIO

Ay, but the mustard is too hot a little.

KATHARINA

Why then, the beef, and let the mustard rest.

GRUMIO

Nay then, I will not: you shall have the mustard,
Or else you get no beef of Grumio.

KATHARINA

Then both, or one, or any thing thou wilt.

GRUMIO

Why then, the mustard without the beef.

KATHARINA

Go, get thee gone, thou false deluding slave,

KATHARINA (cont.)

That feed'st me with the very name of meat:
Sorrow on thee and all the pack of you,
That triumph thus upon my misery!
Go, get thee gone, I say.

PETRUCHIO
How fares my Kate? What, sweeting, all amort?
HORTENSIO
Mistress, what cheer?
KATHARINA
Faith, as cold as can be.

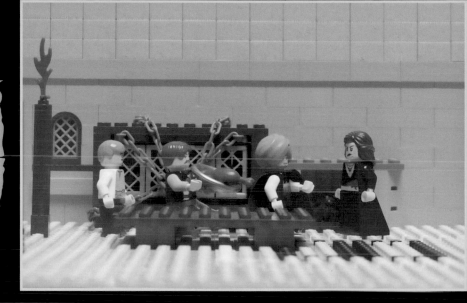

PETRUCHIO
Pluck up thy spirits; look cheerfully upon me.
Here love; thou see'st how diligent I am
To dress thy meat myself and bring it thee:
I am sure, sweet Kate, this kindness merits thanks.
What, not a word? Nay, then thou lovest it not;
And all my pains is sorted to no proof.
Here, take away this dish.

KATHARINA
I pray you, let it stand.
PETRUCHIO
The poorest service is repaid with thanks;
And so shall mine, before you touch the meat.

KATHARINA
I thank you, sir.

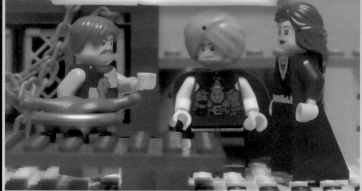

HORTENSIO
Signior Petruchio, fie! you are to blame.
Come, mistress Kate, I'll bear you company.

PETRUCHIO
Eat it up all, Hortensio, if thou lovest me.
Much good do it unto thy gentle heart!

PETRUCHIO (cont.)
Kate, eat apace: and now, my honey love,
Will we return unto thy father's house
And revel it as bravely as the best,
With silken coats and caps and golden rings,
With ruffs and cuffs and fardingales and things;
With scarfs and fans and double change of bravery,
With amber bracelets, beads and all this knavery.
What, hast thou dined? The tailor stays thy leisure,
To deck thy body with his ruffling treasure.

**PETRUCHIO (cont.)**
Come, tailor, let us see these ornaments;
Lay forth the gown.

**PETRUCHIO (cont.)**
What news with you, sir?
**HABERDASHER**
Here is the cap your worship did bespeak.
**PETRUCHIO**
Why, this was moulded on a porringer;
A velvet dish: fie, fie! 'tis lewd and filthy:
Why, 'tis a cockle or a walnut-shell,
A knack, a toy, a trick, a baby's cap:
Away with it! come, let me have a bigger.

**KATHARINA**
I'll have no bigger: this doth fit the time,
And gentlewomen wear such caps as these.
**PETRUCHIO**
When you are gentle, you shall have one too,
And not till then.

**HORTENSIO**
That will not be in haste.

**KATHARINA**
Why, sir, I trust I may have leave to speak;
And speak I will; I am no child, no babe:
Your betters have endured me say my mind,
And if you cannot, best you stop your ears.
My tongue will tell the anger of my heart,
Or else my heart concealing it will break,
And rather than it shall, I will be free
Even to the uttermost, as I please, in words.

**PETRUCHIO**
Why, thou say'st true; it is a paltry cap,
A custard-coffin, a bauble, a silken pie:
I love thee well, in that thou likest it not.

**KATHARINA**
Love me or love me not, I like the cap;
And it I will have, or I will have none.

**PETRUCHIO**
Thy gown? why, ay: come, tailor, let us see't.
O mercy, God! what masquing stuff is here?
What's this? a sleeve? 'tis like a demi-cannon:
What, up and down, carved like an apple-tart?
Here's snip and nip and cut and slish and slash,
Like to a censer in a barber's shop:
Why, what, i' devil's name, tailor, call'st thou this?

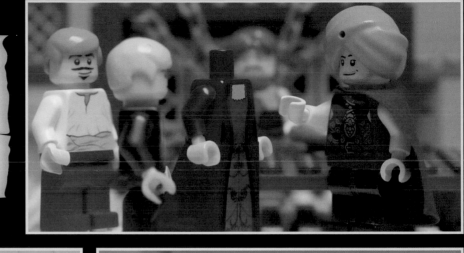

**HORTENSIO**
I see she's like to have neither cap nor gown.

**TAILOR**
You bid me make it orderly and well,
According to the fashion and the time.

**PETRUCHIO**
Marry, and did; but if you be remember'd,
I did not bid you mar it to the time.
Go, hop me over every kennel home,
For you shall hop without my custom, sir:
I'll none of it: hence! make your best of it.

**KATHARINA**
I never saw a better-fashion'd gown,
More quaint, more pleasing, nor more commendable:
Belike you mean to make a puppet of me.

**PETRUCHIO**
Why, true; he means to make a puppet of thee.

**TAILOR**
She says your worship means to make
a puppet of her.

**PETRUCHIO**
O monstrous arrogance! Thou liest, thou thread, thou thimble,
Thou yard, three-quarters, half-yard, quarter, nail!
Thou flea, thou nit, thou winter-cricket thou!
Braved in mine own house with a skein of thread?
Away, thou rag, thou quantity, thou remnant;
Or I shall so be-mete thee with thy yard
As thou shalt think on prating whilst thou livest!
I tell thee, I, that thou hast marr'd her gown.

TAILOR
Your worship is deceived; the gown is made
Just as my master had direction:
Grumio gave order how it should be done.
GRUMIO
I gave him no order; I gave him the stuff.

TAILOR
But did you not request to have it cut?
GRUMIO
Thou hast faced many things.
TAILOR
I have.
GRUMIO
Face not me: thou hast braved many men; brave not
me; I will neither be faced nor braved. I say unto
thee, I bid thy master cut out the gown; but I did
not bid him cut it to pieces: ergo, thou liest.

TAILOR
Why, here is the note of the fashion to testify.

PETRUCHIO
Read it.
GRUMIO
The note lies in's throat, if he say I said so.

PETRUCHIO
Proceed.
TAILOR
"With a small compassed cape:"

GRUMIO
I confess the cape.
TAILOR
"With a trunk sleeve:"
GRUMIO
I confess two sleeves.

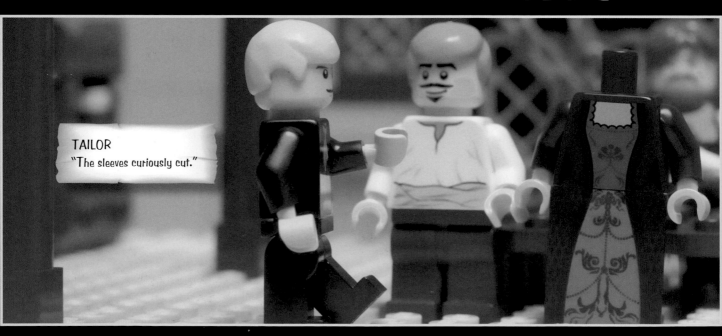

TAILOR
"The sleeves curiously cut."

PETRUCHIO
Ay, there's the villany.
GRUMIO
Error i' the bill, sir; error i' the bill.
I commanded the sleeves should be cut out and
sewed up again; and that I'll prove upon thee,
though thy little finger be armed in a thimble.
TAILOR
This is true that I say: an I had thee
in place where, thou shouldst know it.

GRUMIO
I am for thee straight: take thou the
bill, give me thy mete-yard, and spare not me.

HORTENSIO
God-a-mercy, Grumio! then he shall have no odds.
PETRUCHIO
Well, sir, in brief, the gown is not for me.
GRUMIO
You are i' the right, sir: 'tis for my mistress.
PETRUCHIO
Go, take it up unto thy master's use.
GRUMIO
Villain, not for thy life: take up my mistress'
gown for thy master's use!
PETRUCHIO
Why, sir, what's your conceit in that?
GRUMIO
O, sir, the conceit is deeper than you think for:
Take up my mistress' gown to his master's use!
O, fie, fie, fie!
PETRUCHIO
Hortensio, say thou wilt see the tailor paid.
Go take it hence; be gone, and say no more.

HORTENSIO
Tailor, I'll pay thee for thy gown tomorrow:
Take no unkindness of his hasty words:
Away! I say; commend me to thy master.

# ACT IV. Scene V (1–26).

T

S

*T*he tailor has gone and Katharina is without a fashionable gown. Petruchio tells her not to fret and that their honor will show even in the most humble attire. He adds that it is seven in the morning and that they will make it to Baptista's house just in time for lunch. When Katharina points out that is it already past 2 p.m., Petruchio declares that he will not go, until she can agree that, "it shall be what o'clock I say it is" (IV.iii.188).

The merchant arrives to Baptista's house and is instructed to play the part of Vincentio, Lucentio's father, so that Baptista will accept the terms of the marriage contract. At this point, Baptista believes Tranio to be Lucentio, Lucentio to be Cambio, and the merchant to be Vincentio. They agree to draw up the papers for Tranio (as Lucentio) to marry Bianca, and Baptista tells Lucentio (as Cambio) to inform Bianca of her future nuptials. As Baptista chats "with the deceiving father of a deceitful son" (IV.iv.80), Lucentio is free to find Bianca and elope with her, given that the contract is underway.

**PETRUCHIO**
Come on, i' God's name; once more toward our father's.
Good Lord, how bright and goodly shines the moon!
**KATHARINA**
The moon! the sun: it is not moonlight now.

**PETRUCHIO**
I say it is the moon that shines so bright.
**KATHARINA**
I know it is the sun that shines so bright.

**PETRUCHIO**
Now, by my mother's son, and that's myself,
It shall be moon, or star, or what I list,
Or ere I journey to your father's house.
Go on, and fetch our horses back again.
Evermore cross'd and cross'd; nothing but cross'd!

**HORTENSIO**
Say as he says, or we shall never go.

KATHARINA
Forward, I pray, since we have come so far,
And be it moon, or sun, or what you please:
An if you please to call it a rush-candle,
Henceforth I vow it shall be so for me.

PETRUCHIO
I say it is the moon.
KATHARINA
I know it is the moon.
PETRUCHIO
Nay, then you lie: It is the blessed sun.

**KATHARINA**
Then, God be bless'd, it is the blessed sun:
But sun it is not, when you say it is not;
And the moon changes even as your mind.
What you will have it named, even that it is;
And so it shall be so for Katharina.

**HORTENSIO**
Petruchio, go thy ways; the field is won.

**PETRUCHIO**
Well, forward, forward! thus the bowl should run,
And not unluckily against the bias.

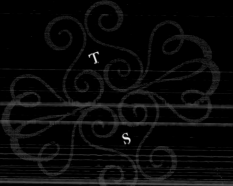

$\mathcal{K}$atharina is gradually bending to Petruchio's will. They continue on their journey and bump into Vincentio, the true father of Lucentio, who is also on his way to Baptista's house. To continue his trickery with Katharina, Petruchio greets Vincentio as a woman. Following his lead, Katharina addresses him as a "young budding virgin" (IV.v.38), only to be scolded by Petruchio for thinking a man a maiden. Petruchio explains to Vincentio that his son has married Bianca and they continue on their journey. Aside, Hortensio seems pleased with Petruchio's accomplishments with taming Katharina.

They arrive at Lucentio's house and Vincentio invites Petruchio and Katharina in for a drink. The merchant pretending to be Vincentio peers out the window and sees the true Vincentio. The two quarrel over whom is the true Vincentio, and the merchant imposter says that the real Vincentio should be arrested. Vincentio pleads for Biondello, Lucentio's servant, to assure everyone that he is the rightful person. Not wanting to ruin Lucentio's plan, Biondello refuses, and Vincentio beats him. Baptista enters and the men all quibble about who is who. Lucentio and Bianca arrive, having just eloped. The two clear up the confusion and explain about those who had traded places in order for Lucentio to win Bianca's heart. The two fathers, Baptista and Vincentio, are exhausted from the mayhem and decide to leave the room, contented that all is now well. Katharina, having just witnessed the madness, decides to follow the crowd and see what comes of everything. Petruchio famously pleads, "Kiss me, Kate" (V.i.122), and Katharina finally kisses him in public.

A banquet is prepared and Lucentio proposes a toast to the newly united families and friends. At the dinner, Katharina and the widow (Hortensio's new wife) bicker back and forth about their husbands. Amused, the men stir up a bet regarding Petruchio's ability to tame unruly women.

BAPTISTA
Now, in good sadness, son Petruchio,
I think thou hast the veriest shrew of all.

PETRUCHIO
Well, I say no: and therefore for assurance
Let's each one send unto his wife;
And he whose wife is most obedient
To come at first when he doth send for her,
Shall win the wager which we will propose.

HORTENSIO
Content. What is the wager?
LUCENTIO
Twenty crowns.
PETRUCHIO
Twenty crowns!
I'll venture so much of my hawk or hound,
But twenty times so much upon my wife.
LUCENTIO
A hundred then.
HORTENSIO
Content.
PETRUCHIO
A match! 'tis done.
HORTENSIO
Who shall begin?

LUCENTIO
That will I.
Go, Biondello, bid your mistress come to me.

BAPTISTA
Son, I'll be your half, Bianca comes.

PETRUCHIO

How! she is busy and she cannot come!

Is that an answer?

GREMIO

Ay, and a kind one too:

Pray God, sir, your wife send you not a worse.

PETRUCHIO

I hope better.

HORTENSIO

Sirrah Biondello, go and entreat my wife

To come to me forthwith.

PETRUCHIO

O, ho! entreat her!

Nay, then she must needs come.

HORTENSIO

I am afraid, sir,

Do what you can, yours will not be entreated.

HORTENSIO (cont.)
Now, where's my wife?

BIONDELLO
She says you have some goodly jest in hand:
She will not come: she bids you come to her.

PETRUCHIO
Worse and worse; she will not come! O vile,
Intolerable, not to be endured!
Sirrah Grumio, go to your mistress;
Say, I command her to come to me.

HORTENSIO
I know her answer.
PETRUCHIO
What?
HORTENSIO
She will not.
PETRUCHIO
The fouler fortune mine, and there an end.

BAPTISTA
Now, by my holidame, here comes Katharina!

KATHARINA
What is your will, sir, that you send for me?
PETRUCHIO
Where is your sister, and Hortensio's wife?

KATHARINA
They sit conferring by the parlor fire.

PETRUCHIO
Go fetch them hither: if they deny to come.
Swinge me them soundly forth unto their husbands:
Away, I say, and bring them hither straight.

**LUCENTIO**
Here is a wonder, if you talk of a wonder.
**HORTENSIO**
And so it is: I wonder what it bodes.

**PETRUCHIO**
Marry, peace it bodes, and love and quiet life,
And awful rule and right supremacy;
And, to be short, what not, that's sweet and happy?

**BAPTISTA**
Now, fair befal thee, good Petruchio!
The wager thou hast won; and I will add
Unto their losses twenty thousand crowns;
Another dowry to another daughter,
For she is changed, as she had never been.

**PETRUCHIO**
Nay, I will win my wager better yet
And show more sign of her obedience,
Her new-built virtue and obedience.
See where she comes and brings your froward wives
As prisoners to her womanly persuasion.

335

**PETRUCHIO** (cont.)
Katharina, that cap of yours becomes you not:
Off with that bauble, throw it under-foot.

**WIDOW**
Lord, let me never have a cause to sigh,
Till I be brought to such a silly pass!
**BIANCA**
Fie! what a foolish duty call you this?

**LUCENTIO**
I would your duty were as foolish too:
The wisdom of your duty, fair Bianca,
Hath cost me an hundred crowns since supper-time.

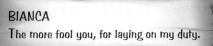

**BIANCA**
The more fool you, for laying on my duty.

**PETRUCHIO**
Katharina, I charge thee, tell these headstrong women
What duty they do owe their lords and husbands.

**WIDOW**
Come, come, you're mocking: we will have no telling.

**PETRUCHIO**
Come on, I say; and first begin with her.

**WIDOW**
She shall not.
**PETRUCHIO**
I say she shall: and first begin with her.

337

## KATHARINA

Fie, fie! unknit that threatening unkind brow,
And dart not scornful glances from those eyes,
To wound thy lord, thy king, thy governor:
It blots thy beauty as frosts do bite the meads,
Confounds thy fame as whirlwinds shake fair buds,
And in no sense is meet or amiable.
A woman moved is like a fountain troubled,
Muddy, ill-seeming, thick, bereft of beauty;
And while it is so, none so dry or thirsty
Will deign to sip or touch one drop of it.
Thy husband is thy lord, thy life, thy keeper,
Thy head, thy sovereign; one that cares for thee,
And for thy maintenance commits his body
To painful labour both by sea and land,
To watch the night in storms, the day in cold,
Whilst thou liest warm at home, secure and safe;
And craves no other tribute at thy hands
But love, fair looks and true obedience;
Too little payment for so great a debt.

## KATHARINA (cont.)

Such duty as the subject owes the prince
Even such a woman oweth to her husband;
And when she is froward, peevish, sullen, sour,
And not obedient to his honest will,
What is she but a foul contending rebel
And graceless traitor to her loving lord?
I am ashamed that women are so simple
To offer war where they should kneel for peace;
Or seek for rule, supremacy and sway,
When they are bound to serve, love and obey.
Why are our bodies soft and weak and smooth,
Unapt to toil and trouble in the world,
But that our soft conditions and our hearts
Should well agree with our external parts?
Come, come, you froward and unable worms!
My mind hath been as big as one of yours,
My heart as great, my reason haply more,
To bandy word for word and frown for frown;

**KATHARINA** (cont.)
But now I see our lances are but straws,
Our strength as weak, our weakness past compare,
That seeming to be most which we indeed least are.
Then vail your stomachs, for it is no boot,

**KATHARINA** (cont.)
And place your hands below your husband's foot:
In token of which duty, if he please,
My hand is ready; may it do him ease.

**PETRUCHIO**
Why, there's a wench! Come on, and kiss me, Kate.

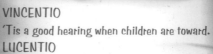

LUCENTIO
Well, go thy ways, old lad; for thou shalt ha't.

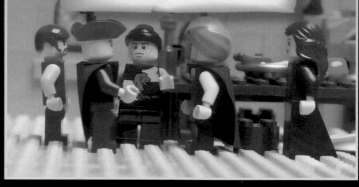

VINCENTIO
'Tis a good hearing when children are toward.
LUCENTIO
But a harsh hearing when women are froward.

PETRUCHIO
Come, Kate, we'll to bed.
We three are married, but you two are sped.

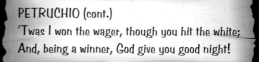

PETRUCHIO (cont.)
'Twas I won the wager, though you hit the white;
And, being a winner, God give you good night!

HORTENSIO
Now, go thy ways; thou hast tamed a curst shrew.

LUCENTIO
'Tis a wonder, by your leave, she will be tamed so.

*T*he play comes to a close, and Christopher Sly returns to view in dingy clothing outside of the tavern. Rousing from a drunken sleep, he asks the nearby tapster if he is indeed a Lord, citing a strange dream he had of fine clothing, wealth, and a play. The tapster tells him the bad news that he is not a Lord and suggests that Sly head home to his wife before she gets angry and beats him. Amused, Sly exclaims that he has had the best dream of his life and says, "I know now how to tame a shrew" and that he'll go to her soon "and tame her too" (Appendix.16, 20).

Members of the Hollan Publishing team, John McCann, Monica Sweeney, and Becky Thomas all collaborated to make *Brick Shakespeare* possible.

John McCann, Brick Engineer: John designed, constructed, and photographed the brick scenes. A New England native, John has over two decades of experience playing with LEGO bricks. He enjoys relaxing lakeside and can solve a Rubik's Cube in three days flat. John has a BS in biomedical engineering from the University of Hartford and is currently pursuing his masters. He is also the coauthor of *Brick Shakespeare: The Tragedies—Hamlet, Macbeth, Romeo and Juliet, and Julius Caesar, Loom Magic! 25 Awesome, Never-Before-Seen Designs for an Amazing Rainbow of Projects*, and *Loom Magic Xtreme!: 25 Spectacular, Never-Before-Seen Designs for Rainbows of Fun*.

Monica Sweeney, Shakespeare Wrangler: Monica selected and interpreted Shakespeare scenes for construction and wrote corresponding narrative. Monica loves all things related to Spain and Chaucer and has yet to say no to a mini powdered donut. She graduated with honors in English from the University of Massachusetts–Amherst. She is also the coauthor of *Brick Shakespeare: The Tragedies—Hamlet, Macbeth, Romeo and Juliet, and Julius Caesar and Loom Magic Xtreme!: 25 Spectacular, Never-Before-Seen Designs for Rainbows of Fun*.

Becky Thomas, Shakespeare Wrangler: Becky selected and interpreted Shakespeare scenes for construction and wrote corresponding narrative. In her spare time, Becky enjoys breaking the bindings of all books Jane Austen, playing video games, and trying out new recipes. She lives with her husband, Patrick, and her two cats, Leo and Leia. She graduated with honors in English from the University of Massuchesetts–Amherst, and she is also the coauthor of *Brick Shakespeare: The Tragedies—Hamlet, Macbeth, Romeo and Juliet, and Julius Caesar, Loom Magic! 25 Awesome, Never-Before-Seen Designs for an Amazing Rainbow of Projects*, and *Loom Magic Xtreme!: 25 Spectacular, Never-Before-Seen Designs for Rainbows of Fun*.

# ALSO AVAILABLE

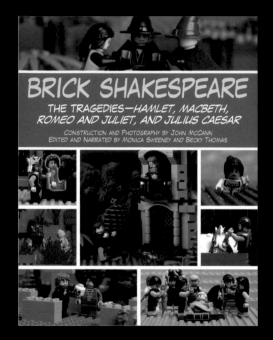

## Brick Shakespeare

The Tragedies—Hamlet, Macbeth, Romeo and Juliet, and Julius Caesar

Construction and Photography by John McCann
Edited and Narrated by Monica Sweeney and Becky Thomas

Enjoy four of Shakespeare's tragedies told with LEGO bricks. Here are *Hamlet*, *Macbeth*, *Romeo and Juliet*, and *Julius Caesar* enacted scene by scene, captioned by excerpts from the plays. Flip through one thousand color photographs as you enjoy Shakespeare's iconic poetry and marvel at what can be done with the world's most popular children's toy.

Watch brick Hamlet give his famous "To be or not to be" soliloquy, and feel brick Ophelia's grief as she meets her watery end. Lady Macbeth in brick form brings new terror to "Out, out, damn spot!" and brick Romeo and Juliet are no less star-crossed for being rectangular and plastic. The warm familiarity of bricks lends levity to Shakespeare's tragedies while remaining true to his original language.

The ideal book for Shakespeare enthusiasts, as well as a fun way to introduce children to Shakespeare's masterpieces, this book employs Shakespeare's original, characteristic language in abridged form. Though the language stays true to its origins, the unique format of these well-known tragedies will give readers a new way to enjoy one of the most popular playwrights in history.

$19.95 Paperback • ISBN 978-1-62636-303-8

# ALSO AVAILABLE

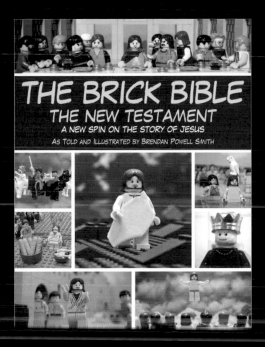

## The Brick Bible: The New Testament
A New Spin on the Story of Jesus
by Brendan Powell Smith

From the author of the highly praised and somewhat controversial *The Brick Bible: A New Spin on the Old Testament* comes the much-anticipated New Testament edition. For over a decade, Brendan Powell Smith, creator of popular website bricktestament.com, has been hard at work using LEGO to re-create scenes from the Bible. Now, in one volume, he has brought together over 1,000 "brick" photographs depicting the narrative story of the New Testament. From the life of Jesus—his birth, teachings, and parables—to the famous last supper scene and the crucifixion; from the fate of Judas to the life of Paul and his letters to the Ephesians; from the first book burning to the book of Revelations, this is the New Testament as you've never experienced it before.

Smith combines the actual text of the New Testament with his brick photographs to bring to life the teachings, miracles, and prophecies of the most popular book in the world. The graphic novel format makes these well-known Bible stories come to life in a fun and engaging way. And the beauty of *The Brick Bible: The New Testament* is that everyone, from the devout to nonbelievers, will find something breathtaking, fascinating, or entertaining within this impressive collection.

**$19.95 Paperback • ISBN 978-1-62087-1-720**

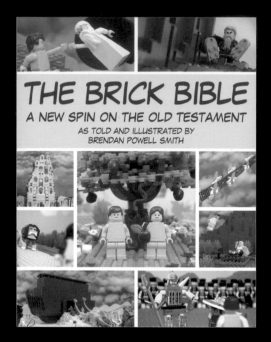

## The Brick Bible

A New Spin on the Old Testament

by Brendan Powell Smith

Brendan Powell Smith has spent the last decade creating nearly 5,000 scenes from the bible—with Legos. His wonderfully original sets are featured on his website, Bricktestament.com, but for the first time, 1,500 photographs of these creative designs—depicting the Old Testament from Earth's creation to the Books of Kings—are brought together in book format. The Holy Bible is complex; sometimes dark, and other times joyous, and Smith's masterful work is a far cry from what a small child might build. The beauty of *The Brick Bible* is that everyone, from the devout to nonbelievers, will find something breathtaking, fascinating, or entertaining within this collection. Smith's subtle touch brings out the nuances of each scene and makes you reconsider the way you look at LEGOs—it's something that needs to be seen to be believed.

**$19.95 Paperback · ISBN 978-1-61608-421-9**

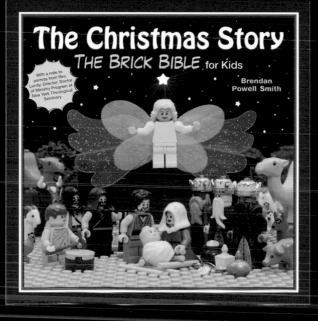

# The Christmas Story
The Brick Bible for Kids
by Brendan Powell Smith

Santa, sleigh bells, mistletoe, reindeer, and presents: these are the tell-tale signs of Christmas. But for Christians, December 25 is also the time to celebrate the birth of Jesus, and what better way to introduce your kids to the story of the Savior's birth than through LEGO!

Every year, children of all ages revisit the scene in Bethlehem with Joseph, Mary, the three wise men, the angels and shepherds, and the baby Jesus, swaddled and lying in a manger. Kids will love seeing the story of Christmas played out using their favorite toys. Brendan Powell Smith, author of The Brick Bible for Kids series—beginning with *Noah's Ark*—creates a magical "brick" world around the simplified text of the Immaculate Conception, the census, the guiding star high above Bethlehem, and the promise one little baby brings to the Christians of the world. This important Christmas story is sure to be the perfect holiday gift and a book for families to cherish for years to come.

**$12.95 Hardcover · ISBN 978-1-62087-173-7**

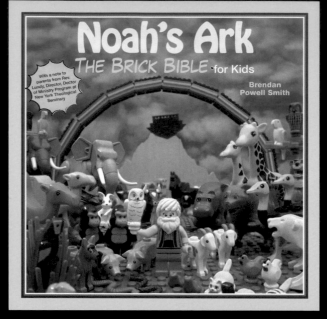

# Noah's Ark
The Brick Bible for Kids
by Brendan Powell Smith

The story of Noah and his ark full of two of every animal on Earth has been a favorite Bible story of children for years. And now, for the first time, *Noah's Ark* is brought to life through LEGOs!

Kids will love seeing the world's flood and God's subsequent covenant with Noah to never destroy mankind again played out using their favorite toys. Brendan Powell Smith, creator of bricktestament.com and author of *The Brick Bible*, creates a magical "brick" world around the simplified text of the story of Noah, the flood, a wooden ark full of animals, and the promise of a rainbow. A story with a powerful message of forgiveness and love, this is the perfect gift for children.

**$12.95 Hardcover · ISBN 978-1-61608-737-1**

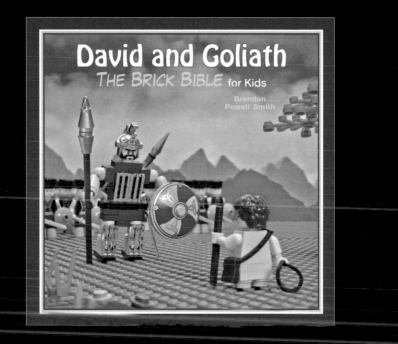

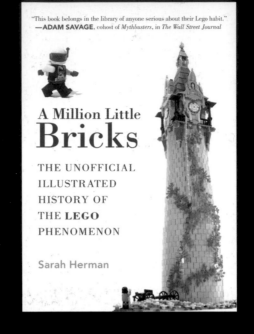

A Million Little
# Bricks

THE UNOFFICIAL
ILLUSTRATED
HISTORY OF
THE **LEGO**
PHENOMENON

Sarah Herman

# A Million Little Bricks

The Unofficial Illustrated History of the LEGO Phenomenon

by Sarah Herman

There aren't many titles that haven't been bestowed on LEGO toys, and it's not hard to see why. From its inception in the early 1930s right up until today, the LEGO Group's history is as colorful as the toys it makes. Few other playthings share the LEGO brand's creative spirit, educative benefits, resilience, quality, and universal appeal. The LEGO name is now synonymous with playtime, but it wasn't always so. This history charts the birth of the LEGO Group in the workshop of a Danish carpenter and its steady growth as a small, family-run toy manufacturer to its current position as a market-leading, award-winning brand. The company's ever-increasing catalog of products—including the earliest wooden toys, plastic bricks, play themes, and other building systems such as DUPLO, Technic, and MINDSTORMS—are chronicled in detail, alongside the manufacturing process, LEGOLAND parks, licensed toys, and computer and video games.

Learn all about how LEGO pulled itself out of an economic crisis and embraced technology to make building blocks relevant to twenty-first-century children, and discover the vibrant fan community of kids and adults whose conventions, websites, and artwork keep the LEGO spirit alive. As nostalgic as it is contemporary, *A Million Little Bricks* will have you reminiscing about old Classic Space sets, rummaging through the attic for forgotten Minifigure friends, and playing with whatever LEGO bricks you can get your hands on (even if it means sharing with your kids).

**$16.95 Paperback · ISBN 978-1-62636-118-8**

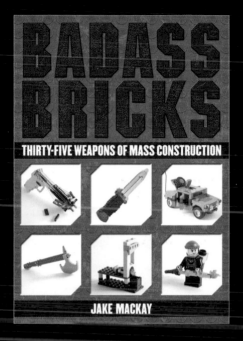